HARLOW STONE

HARLOW STONE

THE UGLY ROSES TRILOGY
FRAYED ROPE – BOOK ONE

Reviews

Harlow Stone is a bit of an emotional terrorist with her writing. She lures you in, lays the foundation of where you just know things will go and then BANG never saw it coming! —**Amazon Reviewer**

You are completely thrown, slammed and brutalized by Harlow. I'm not saying anything else. READ THIS SERIES and prepare yourself. — **Ramblings From Beneath The Sheets**

Five huge dark stars! I love my books dark and this book didn't disappoint! The characters were exciting and intriguing and the story was insane! —**Alpha Book Club**

I was completely blown away by this book. All the characters are great and it's full of twist and turns, many you don't see coming. A must read. —**Cat's Guilty Pleasure**

The connection and chemistry of these two characters is so strong I experienced it in every word they exchanged. I never read a male character with so much raw emotion. Ryder Callaghan has become one of my favorite book boyfriends'. — **JB's Book Obsession**

HARLOW STONE

Copyright

Frayed Rope
The Ugly Roses Trilogy #1
Copyright © Harlow Stone, 2015

ISBN: 978-0-9940376-0-2

©2015 Harlow Stone

Edited by Gregory Murphy

Cover: Adobestock image

Cover Design by Harlow Stone

A note from the author,

"Whether you think you can, or you can't —
You're right."
Henry Ford

That's how I started writing this book.
But I didn't just *think* I could,
I *knew* I could.
I knew it in my heart and I felt it in my bones.
Come hell or high water, I was writing a book.
One book turned into two, and then...
The Ugly Roses Trilogy was soon available, and the first book
made the top one hundred list on Amazon.

Bottom line:
What you think about, you bring about.
If you want something bad enough, you'll make it happen.
Good things don't come to those who wait, they come to
those who work their asses off to get what they want.

Keep working. Don't give up. Stay positive.

Much love,

Harlow

xx

HARLOW STONE

Prologue

Five months ago

"Why won't you scream?"

The warm liquid dripped down my spine and curved between my legs. I watched as it made its journey south, dripping off my big toe, slowly adding to the puddle of crimson on the concrete floor.

Blood.

It's the only warmth I've felt in this frigid tomb that this sick bastard calls a basement. Or perhaps it's the blood loss that's slowly adding to the chill seeping deep into my bones.

Whack!

I bite the inside of my cheek, grunting upon impact. He wielded what felt like a two-by-four, smashing it into the fresh wounds on my back. I suppose I should be thankful the wood absorbs some of the impact. If he'd chosen the steel piece of pipe on the other side of the room, surely I would've passed out or be dead by now.

"Scream you selfish bitch because I'm not stopping until you do! Tell me what a whore you've been when you were supposed to be a good girl with me!" His rage increases as he delivers another explosive blow to my ribs. I can feel them break against the heft of his weapon but its still nothing compared to the ache in my chest.

Pain means you're alive. Even if you don't care to be.

He works his way around to my front. His nostrils flare and his chest heaves like he'd just got back from an eight-mile run.

Perspiration dampens his shirt and the smell is beyond nauseating. If he would just leave, take a break or a shower, maybe I could work at getting out of this evil place.

This man has practically lived in this hell hole with me since I got here. I can smell the rank odor of piss coming from a bucket—my bucket. I can tell he's afraid to take his eyes off me. Afraid that if he can't see me, I'll be gone. He wanted me desperately and now that I'm here, he has no intention of letting me go.

SLAP!

"Look at me!" He snaps in my face. "When I speak you will look at me and show me the respect I deserve. The respect you should've shown me years ago when I was nothing but kind to you, when I tried to get you to see me*! Tried to look after you and make you mine! But you had to fuck that all up with that lowlife piece of shit you spread your legs for!" I watch as he heaves in a deep breath, seeming to come to a conclusion as he tells me, "You're nothing but a dirty whore."*

He slaps me again across my bruised cheekbone. Saliva flies from his mouth as he yells and screams at me for what an ungrateful bitch I am after all he tried to do for me.

The kicker to all this?

I still don't know his name.

He's what I'd call standard. Ordinary. Brown hair, brown eyes, medium skin tone, maybe five foot ten—not someone who stands out. Completely forgettable in his plain red polo shirt and Levi's. He's not someone you'd meet and remember long after the introduction.

Just fucking plain.

THE UGLY ROSES

The only thing I'll remember of him is the hate showing in his psychotic eyes. I consistently rack my brain but still have no recollection of ever meeting this man. All I can think of is that some kind of messed up karma is making me pay my dues for not being taken with the rest of my family that day.

Maybe this is it. Maybe he'll put me out of my misery. I've been down here for at least a day, maybe a day and a half. My shoulders ache from being hung on this beam for so long. The rope has rubbed my wrists raw and I'm almost certain my shoulder is dislocated.

The first beating he gave me when I got here was mostly a hail of blows to my ribs and face. I'm no doctor but feeling the pain in my lungs I'm certain my ribs must be broken. My left eye is mostly shut from the swelling and judging from the amount of blood on the floor I'm certain my back looks like Freddy himself came out to play.

If he kills me, it'll be over. The pain would be over. I don't mean the physical kind, but the tragedy that left me cold and numb a year and a half ago. The life-changing day that took my once vibrant self and shattered her into nothing but the broken shell I am today.

I prefer to keep myself there —numb. It's a place I inhabit and the population here is one.

I ignore everyone because I don't want to make small talk or fill the void in my chest that was once so full of love. I don't want to see faces filled with pity and I don't want hugs from people I don't know anymore. I felt like hanging a sign around my neck that said 'Don't touch me' but as the months went by it turned out the permanent miserable look on my face and my attitude made its own sign. I know I could've been nicer to people. I could've been more considerate and listened to the nonsense that came out of their mouths. Shit, maybe that's why I'm here now. I understand it wasn't anyone's fault my family was taken from me, but becoming a miserable bitch was out of my control.

When you lose what's most dear to you, it's hard to sit around and tell yourself the old 'think of the glass half-full, not half-empty,' and let's not get me started on the 'everything happens for a reason' bullshit. People drive me insane. No words will ever make my life better and they certainly won't bring back what I've lost.

If he'd just kill me, I could sail on through to the afterlife to be one again with those I've lost. Forget this hate, the fury and this fucked up asshole in front of me. Forget everything that happened and everyone I want to hold responsible. Forget the blackness in my head, the empty bottles of vodka and the overflowing ashtrays of stress.

Forget it all.

Then the psycho's voice pulls me out of my thoughts.

"You're still not listening! Maybe you'll remember after a little nap, you stupid bitch!"

I see the two-by-four in his hands swinging toward my face.

Then it's black.

Chapter One

"It's great to see you again, Ms. Green. Let's have a look at the progress you've made since last week."

Doctor Revere studies me as he takes a seat on his customary black leather swivel stool.

"So long as we don't see any excess swelling or signs of infection, we can get you on your way," he says.

From the moment I met him there was a connection of some sort. As if he could sense that what I was here to do needed to be done. Not just because I wanted it, because I *needed* it. He's been a big part of my life these past two months. Those kind grey eyes couldn't harm a soul. His slight build and thinning light hair streaked with grey spoke nothing of the magic that was his hands. The man's hands were as graceful as a dancer and kinder than a nun.

As kind as he is, I'm sure he still goes home at night to talk to his wife about what a troubled, miserable patient I am. For weeks I was distant and horrible to the good doctor and his staff. However, paying a pretty penny to rent one of the clinic's small townhouses, a personal shopper and their part-time nurse apparently grants you some sort of immunity to retaliation around here.

I've cursed a few staff members. They never curse back.

Money talks.

One would think after all the shit I've been through, I would've sought the kind of doctor that wields a pen like Doc Revere does a scalpel and covets notebooks like he does his million-dollar hands. (*If I were him, I would have those babies*

Insured. He probably does). Truth is I have no interest in
therapy. If I did, I would have to admit to myself and someone
else that something is wrong and that I'm broken enough to
need fixing.

That's not going to happen.

The day I let someone pick my brain will be shortly after
I've died and donated my remains to scientific research.
Therapist? Not happening. If a new shrink ends up anything
like the phony bitch I woke up to in the hospital after my
attack, I'll carve my eardrums out.

I don't need therapy, I don't need a hug and I don't want any
goddamn pity. What I needed was the incredibly talented
Doctor Carson Revere, a leader in facial reconstruction, skin
grafts and scar removal. He's been my slightly bluer sky on a
hurricane kind of day—or year; however, you want to look at
it.

I feel the bandages being pulled from my face. It's not
painful, just uncomfortable. Not once had I truly thought about
surgery prior to the hell that has become my life. My face was
okay before. High enough cheekbones, small nose, clear skin
and bluish green eyes that popped against my fair Irish skin.
I've never really been one to complain about looks. Not my
face anyway.

If you would've asked me a year ago why I would need a
cosmetic surgeon, my best guess would be to tame the stretch
marks I could never get rid of. Other than *that* road map on my
abdomen, I didn't complain. *Shake what your momma gave
ya!* That was my take on life.

Not anymore.
Sure, my slightly wider nose was never quite as sharp as
my mother's and my stomach has a little jiggle if I don't keep
up on my Pilates routine, but that's life.

I've always been the 'petite' girl. I didn't win any high jump competitions in school with my five-foot-five frame. Not a whole lot up top. However, my relatively small but still fleshy ass makes up for lacking in the tits department. Or so I tell myself. Either way, I never cared, and my jeans fit me well. I've hovered around 120 lbs for the better part of my adult life and I'm okay with that and the rest of my appearance.

Past tense—*was okay with that.*

Hopefully the good Doctor has granted my wishes. When I contacted him three months ago, he didn't seem eager to oblige me in my quest for a new face. The broken nose and excessive swelling from the facial fractures weren't pretty. As cliché as it sounds, desperate times call for desperate measures. I needed a new face and a new identity if I was going to survive for much longer.

After numerous phone conversations, two Skype calls and a week of silence, he agreed to perform the surgeries. Doctor Revere is an incredibly busy man, but I think seeing my banged-up face on Skype really helped him with his decision. Or maybe it was the fact I offered him double to get the job done that really got the ball rolling.

Now, three months later, I couldn't be happier this is the man I chose to help me build a new life (*Not that I'll show him my smile, it's been missing for years*). My once wide nose is still the same size but much sharper. The slight pudgy crooked chin that never seemed to match my high cheek bones has been re-shaped beautifully and my jaw line is much smoother looking. To top the whole look off, my once beautiful blonde locks had been dyed the week prior into one of the darkest shades of brown they had and I've been ironing it pin-straight ever since. Add in the past few months of Nevada sunshine and we're golden.

"Everything looks absolutely wonderful to me Ms. Green; I could not be more pleased with the results. You've healed beautifully. If you don't have any questions or complaints, we can get your paperwork finished and send you on your way."

He regards me with those kind eyes, always looking at me as if he's waiting for me to say something so he can carry a conversation. It's how everyone looks at me.

I hate it.

This miserable bitch I've become doesn't do small talk or platitudes unless it's absolutely necessary. That's not to say I've lost my manners. Most days the please and thank you's are still as ingrained in me as they used to be. I just have absolutely no desire for idle chit chat. If it's not important or doesn't need to be said, I keep my mouth shut. I really wish others would do the same.

Talking is overrated. In a way, that's always been my thought on the subject. Once upon a time, get a bottle of Grey Goose into me and the words would flow. It could be wine or a case of beer, I'm not picky. Consume some alcohol, throw on some music and add a few good friends. Now let the useless chatter begin.

That was then, this is now.

I regard the Doctor over the mirror as I look at the new woman I'm now supposed to be. Thirty looked pretty good, but not in an overly flashy way that would make me stand out. That's my new rule. *No flash*. No gaudy jewelry, no flashy hair-do, no bright colored or skimpy clothing. Not that any of this was really my life before, I just have to work extra hard at remaining as dark, drab and as un-interesting as I can be.

"You did an excellent job Doc. Other than the tenderness around my nose, I have no complaints."

The Doc shuffled some forms around for me to sign.

"I'm thrilled you think so."

Upon handing me the final few forms regarding payment plans he knows I don't need, I grab my bag from the table to retrieve his money. One of my deal breakers in this life is pretty much everything is cash only. If I can't pay cash or it can't be bought with a pre-paid credit card, then no deal. I'm thankful a lot of people here are used to large amounts of cash. I don't know if it's because we're less than four hours from Vegas or if the good Doctor is familiar with this routine, but either way I look forward to cashing out and hitting the road.

A few months in one place without my new identity is too long. My cash service with the Doc was under a fake name I'd used, *Ms. Harley Green.* The thing is there's no such Harley Green. Or if there is, it's certainly not me.

I'd come up with the name quickly while on the phone trying to see Doctor Revere. Stuttering when asked, the beginning of my real name naturally wanted to spill out from my lips. I thought fast to come up with a name that I could not only stomach but would remember.

My daddy loved his Harley and my Irish roots are green.

Thus I had created Ms. Harley Green from Nowhere Town who pays in cash, and pays extra not to ask for identification.
A few signatures later and my hobo bag quite a few thousand dollars lighter, I accept the demise of Ms. Harley Green and the birth of my next —hopefully for longer— alias.
"Hey, Doc?"

He looks stunned that I've spoken to him casually. Usually it's small nods or a wave over my shoulder as I leave his office. Other than the few curse matches with some of the staff, he doesn't hear me speak much. My voice is still raspy, mostly from lack of use. His eyes are wide with anticipation at what may come out of my foul mouth.

I relax my posture and look him directly in the eyes, committing this man to memory because I know it's the last time I'll ever see the Doctor that has helped change my life. I try for the sincerest tone I can deliver before parting.

"Thank you for your help. It's appreciated."

The gentle curve of his lips is the last thing I see before I round the corner en route to my new life.

* * *

I take one last look at what's become my home these past few months. The two-story cream-colored townhouse sits beyond a modest front yard made up of rock and cacti, reflecting a typical desert landscape. A small stone walkway leads to the rust colored front door.

It's a modest yet tiny abode that serves as a resting place for Doctor Revere's high paying clientele. I could've found my own place; I certainly have the money to do so. However, it wouldn't have come with the perks like an on-call nurse and a personal shopper close by. These things made my life easier while I was recuperating from surgery. The townhouse also lacked the sickening smell of disinfectant and antiseptic that I refused to fill my lungs with had I chosen the regular hospital stay.

Another plus to my temporary home was that it had eight-foot privacy fencing surrounded the narrow but long back yard. I took advantage of the fact that my dog Norma would have ample space to move around. I grew up in a rural area and I'll be damned if I would confine my innocent and large Pyrenees to a choker and chain.

The main level in the house boasted a living room-kitchen combo with a small island to separate the space. The open floor plan was perfect. Furnishings served a purpose in the home. No dust collectors or personal touches.

The bedroom had its own entry into the bathroom which held a large soaker tub and what I refer to as a 'handicapped' shower. Handles were mounted all over the dark tile and it was flush with the floor in case you needed to be wheeled into it. Ms. Faneuille was my on-call nurse and although she was professional I was thankful I got to hold onto a bit of my dignity and shower on my own.

All in all, I appreciated the small but airy home since I developed an aversion to close quarters and basements since the attack. The openness kept the panic attacks at bay, yet another new aspect of my life that I need to get used to.

Too many walls? I won't stay there.

Stairway leading to a basement?
Get the hell outta Dodge.

My time in Phoenix is done. It served its purpose and regardless of my shit attitude toward the people I encountered here, I will forever be grateful. Ms. Faneuille will return after my departure to clean out the fridge and get everything washed and ready for the next inhabitant. She was good to me. Maybe one day if I decide to speak more, I'll tell her so. Since that's not likely to happen I left her a wad of cash on my pillow.

The sun is hot on my back as I trudge to my car with the last suitcase. I didn't bring much when I came to this little townhouse in Phoenix. My clothing, my dog and my new miserable self is all I have. That's the thing I've learned about living and being alone. You don't need much, and the less you have the faster you can run without the worry of leaving something important behind.

HARLOW STONE

There's very little that's important to me anymore, but there were a few things I refused to leave behind after the loss of my loved ones. Mostly personal memorabilia, like photographs and home videos. They remind you of things you're bound to forget and that's something no matter how much I ache that I wasn't willing to part with.

The brain can only hold so much before little by little old memories get pushed out and new ones take root. I cannot let them go like I did every other sentimental little knickknack in the place I once called home. There are a million memories still in my mind but I know with time things fade. The memories I once remembered so clearly started to get hazy in my mind and lack the once vivid detail.

This thought is what has me punching the address into my GPS—directions to my high security storage unit in Denver that holds what's left of my old life in a box. That's it, that's all I have; one bag and a box in a five-by-ten storage room. When you're forced into a life on the run, you quickly learn what's important in life that you need to hang onto and what can easily be let go.

I could've fit what's left of my life into a large safety deposit box at the bank, but that involves questions I can't answer and identification I refuse to provide.

Chapter Two

Twelve hours to Denver.

I enjoy driving, always have. The new sights and smells, the wind rustling my hair and my favorite music blasting from the speakers calms my mind. Driving has always been an escape. My peaceful place. Something to clear my head, allowing me to focus on the road instead of the shit hand life has dealt me.

I would normally get the jaunt over and done with in a day, however I have to think of Norma sharing the back of the SUV with my suitcases, having just enough room to stand up but not quite enough to wander. Between the heat these past few months in Arizona and the stress of being in a car for so long, she'll enjoy a break. If I'm honest I probably will too after being cooped up for so long after surgery.

I plan to stop in Durango for the evening at a campground that rents little cabins near Huck Finn Pond off the Animas River.

It's early spring, but to me it still feels like the blazing heat of summer. Something I'm not used to after living in Canada for thirty years. The roads are clear, and the sun is bright through the windows of the SUV. The winding roads and desert like landscape is a sight to behold. I'm forty miles in and proud to say I can scratch 'seeing a tumbleweed float across the highway' off my bucket list.

The barren miles of sand and stone are breathtaking, but not enough so that I'd ever consider this area my home. The perfect backdrop for my future will hold much of the same scenery as my past; large and leafy trees shadowing green grass, and the scent of water nearby.

It feels good to be on the road, out of the house and enjoying some fresh air. I have a long road ahead of me, but I know this is one more step forward in getting there. The trip to the east coast will be a long one. It's a little more driving than I'd like but I'm happy I already have a place rented for when I get there.

I need to get in and out of Denver as quickly as possible and get to my new home. Some people feel safer when they're moving, I feel safer in a dwelling where I can assess my surroundings and lock my doors.

As I approach Durango, I instantly feel more at home here than I did in Phoenix. The old-style town with a mountainous backdrop embellishing an evergreen sea speaks to me in a way the cacti in Phoenix failed to do.

I drive toward the far side of town to find a small provision store where I can pick up a few supplies. We don't need much other than something quick to eat for dinner and something containing alcohol for my nightcap. I don't sleep much anymore, but a nightcap or two assures me a few solid hours of shuteye, hopefully nightmare-free.

I find a parking spot and hop out of the truck to stretch out the ache in my hips from sitting so long. Norma is eager to sniff her way around town, so I open up the hatch and walk her over to a grassy area beside the store. No leash for her. After everything that's happened in the past year, the dog will not leave my side.

After she does her business and gets a much-needed drink, I put Norm back in the vehicle and make my way into the store. It's quaint and clean with a friendly looking older man behind the counter who could easily pass as Mr. Rogers if you took away the suspenders and lumberjack coat hanging behind him. I make my way to the refrigerated section since food that comes in a box has never appealed to me.

I find some cured meat and a pre-made garden salad that will serve as my meal for tonight. Next to the cold aisle is an assortment of fruit. I grab a few apples and a bunch of bananas and make my way to cash out. The store is relatively quiet save for a few young boys counting change to see if they have enough for a pop after purchasing a bag of chips.

"Find everything you were lookin' for dear?" asks the older gentleman as he begins to load my groceries into a brown paper bag.

I simply nod my head and add a few bottles of vitamin water out of the cooler beside the check-out to my items on the counter. Mr. Rogers gives me a side look that shows he's unimpressed I didn't elaborate more.

He's a talker, I can tell.

He wants to chat me up about the weather and tell me all about his daughter Emmy who's giving him grandchild number seven next week, and that he couldn't be happier about another little whipper snapper entering the family fold.

He wants to ask me where I'm from, where I'm headed and what I'm going to do when I get there. He wants answers I'll never be able to give him. Answers to things I refuse to elaborate on. That's the thing with small towns; everyone seems to always need to know everyone else's business.

I'm not about to share mine, he'll catch on to that quickly.
"Ain't seen a beautiful girl like you around this place before. Mind ya, we got lots a beautiful girls in town. My daughter bein' one of 'em."

See, I knew Emmy would get a mention.

He continues, "She lives outside of town though, so I don't 'spect people see her as much since she only comes in to do her once weekly shoppin'. She's about your age. You stickin' around for a while dear or just passin' through. Not alotta food here if ya stickin' around."

Sweet Jesus, every time.

I can't be the psycho that flees the store with my purchases just to avoid speaking with someone. That raises suspicion, and the last thing I need is unwanted attention. I love small towns but this is why slightly bigger ones are safer. People don't ask questions.

"Just passing through."

I hand Mr. Rogers a twenty as I gather up my sac of goods and make for the door.

"Ms. don't forget your change," he reminds me. I just point to the jar for cancer collections on the counter and make my way outside.

Norm's head is between the seats of the truck staring out the window waiting for my return. She does this often. She's afraid I won't return—just like the rest of them.

She doesn't understand why we're alone now. Just sulks the days away and follows my every lead. There have been many days I'd love to give up, just say fuck it and be done with. But I feel like that's the coward's way out. One of us has to keep our shit together. I remind myself regardless of how much life hurts there are many people out there who are suffering a much harsher fate than mine. It doesn't do much to soothe me, but it reminds me I'm not alone in my suffering.

* * *

The cabin isn't far now. The tall trees have blocked out the sun and the air through here is cooler. I know I'm close, I can smell the water. Norm perks up from the backseat knowing this leg of our journey is about to come to an end. I spot the small home that serves as an office near the road and pull into the little gravel lot. I spoke with an older woman in the office here a few days before I left Phoenix and she assured me renting for one-night midweek wouldn't be an issue as it's not a busy season.

The small reception is not much bigger than a bathroom. It has one small desk and a little bench on the opposite wall. The door on the opposite wall I assume is what leads into the actual home and a small bell sits on the counter. 'Ring for Service' taped on the front of it.

I ring the bell and wait for the old gal I spoke with on the phone; she told me she'd be here any time after four o'clock today. I hear a small dog bark in the back room and shuffling footsteps heading my way. The door opens, and I get an eyeful of silver hair before a little old bird standing five-foot-nothing comes through the door.

"Heya deary, you must be the young lady I spoke to on the phone. One night at one of my cabins? That you dear?"

If I still laughed and smiled, I'd be doing both right now. But it's enough my lips are twitching. This woman could be Estelle Getty's sister. I'm not sure if I want to start singing the theme song to Golden Girls or muster up my man voice and say, *"Stop or my mom will shoot!"*

"Yes, ma'am that would be me."

She shuffles behind her desk; a large appointment book rests on top. No computer for Estelle, she likes to take appointments the old-fashioned way.

"Well dear let's get you registered then, my grandson made me that fancy page on the computer, but I don't know how to do the bookings on that damn thing and he's gone back overseas. So, it's just pictures for folks to look at for now. Did ya see one you liked?"

Most of the cabins all looked exactly the same but some boasted more than one bedroom. My only requirement was the furthest one from other people.

"Yes, I'd like number eight if it's available," I say kindly to the woman.

"Told ya on the phone deary, they're all available. Number eight it is."

"Thank you, ma'am."

She scribbles some Sanskrit down in her planner before addressing me again. "That'll be sixty dollars for the night dear. You mentioned you had a dog, and I won't charge ya extra seein' as it's off season." She gives me a stern look before continuing, "but, you mind my words Miss, if I find anything chewed or soiled on, you won't like what I have to say about it."

As tiny as she is, I could see her putting the fear of god into small children that didn't bother to wash their hands before supper, so I take her seriously. I don't for one second think she's joking. In fact, I'm pretty sure this little old woman probably has a gun in the pocket of her robe. I know I would if I were out here by myself answering the door to strangers wanting a room for the night.

"Norm's a good girl ma'am."

"Norm?"

"Short for Norma, my dog."

She eye's me through her bifocals as if predicting whether I was lying or not. Hell, she could probably predict what I would die from and who would get my kidneys after I become an organ donor.

After a perusal of my face and clothing, and a long gander out the office window to see Norma waiting in the truck, she nods her head and focuses on my eyes.

"I trust ya to be sayin' the truth. Now once we get you payin' your bill, I'll send ya on your way with the key".

I dug the money out of my bag and wondered if she was going to ask me for a credit card. Not that I'd know where she'd swipe it.

"Cash only around here," she says as if reading my mind. "I don't like them card machines and I don't trust them either. The good ol' paper kind is what works here and everywhere as far as I'm concerned. Can't use them damn cards if the power goes out now can ya?"

She answers for me. "No ya can't." She takes my money and grabs a key out of the desk drawer.

"Now once ya get back on the lane, you follow it down around the bend and you'll start to see my cabins. Yours is the last one on the right. Now I got an appointment for my wash and set in the mornin' so if you're gone before lunchtime you just leave the key in the box out there beside the door."

She hands me the large brass key attached to a little plastic fish key chain and stands up.

"Thank you, and I'll be sure to leave it in the box ma'am."

I leave the office and feel exhaustion setting in. Time to head up the lane to hopefully get a nightmare-free sleep.

* * *

The cabin is nothing to boast about. It has a simple square design, and the only closed off space is the bathroom. It has a bed, one night stand and a small card table with two chairs. There's a small counter supporting a microwave on top, with a mini-fridge stored underneath. Out the back door, there's a tiny porch and Adirondack chair looking out toward the water.

Norma flies toward the shore like a dog that's been stuck in the desert for too long. I suppose two months was a long time in the desert for a dog that prefers the cold and the mountains. She bounds through the water while I look around the property. Ample space between this cabin and the previous one, should anyone check into it. The trees provide lots of shade and a sense of privacy. It's perfect for a night's rest. I'll unload my small bag with toiletries and grab a change of clothes for the morning.

Hot shower, food and rest. Tomorrow I'll be in Denver where I can finally put most of the past behind me.

Chapter Three

It's been a long day having started driving shortly after the sun rose. I've never been a morning person, but when nightmares keep you awake at night, you might as well get moving since there's not a chance in hell of getting back to sleep.

I need to be on the south side of the city to hook up with my contact here and tie up some loose ends. After that I plan to hit the storage unit to pick up what's left of my previous life. Hopefully all goes smoothly, and I can be out of here in a day. Two tops.

I spot Blacktop, a dive bar, coming up on my left and note the number of bikes out front. I have no phone number for my contact, Tiny, just a meeting place. He always told me no matter what, I could find him here. If he wasn't sitting at his regular table, one of the boys would find him for me.

Norma and I spent a few weeks here a couple months ago, staying in one of the old dark and dingy rooms above the bar. The sheets were clean, and the people were friendly, so I tried not to complain about the sticky carpet and filthy toilet seat.

I wouldn't have known this place existed if it weren't for my good friend from home. Jimmy had told me about the motorcycle club that frequented this place, as well as the illegal yet crucial service they offer in making fake identification to help someone disappear. I remember our conversation vividly as I turn into the parking lot in front of Blacktop.

We were standing in Jimmy's paint shop, waiting for the last customer to come and pick up his ride. Jimmy kept going on about his most recent trip to Denver and the guys that he'd met there.

Jimmy travelled a lot, always looking for the next custom car or motorcycle he could paint. When he couldn't find metal to paint, he'd find skin to ink. He's artistically talented, though unfortunately he doesn't get near enough credit for the work he does.

"These guys in Denver hooked me up with two other clubs to do work on their bikes. Custom work. They set me up with a shop space too.

"I painted seven while I was there, Jay. To tell you the truth I didn't really want to come back home. The guys up here don't pay for shit. I barely make enough to keep the shop open. These guys pay cash and I need more of it".

Jimmy had been my good friend since high school. He's talented, kind and an all-around fun person to be around. We tried more than friends once and quickly realized we were more like brother and sister. I adore him, but he doesn't always have the best ideas, often getting involved with the wrong people because he trusts too easily. He's a gentle man with a big heart that a lot of people take advantage of.

"Do you know what these guys are into, Jimbo? I'm all for your success, I just don't want you to become a drug mule before the year's out. If you're in a jumpsuit, who's going to help me finish that mural in my garage?"

Jimmy laughed; we'd been working on a mural about once a week for a month now.

"I have no intentions of ending up in the big house Jay, and as far as I know, they don't run drugs. A lot of protection detail in the south end of Denver. They own this bar called Blacktop, and recently purchased a few strip joints around town. Mav told me they bought out the previous owners after a few *women were found in bad shape at the club, one of them was only seventeen and raped by some big wig drug smuggler tryin' to run his shit through the club." He shakes his head in disgust. "After that, some of the girls were looking to change their names and get outta town. This guy Tiny helped them and turned the strip club around to make it a decent place for the rest of the girls to work.*

"I can only say I respect them a lot more for cleaning that mess up. Apparently, they haven't had any more rough shit happen to the women since they took over. Good guys in my book. Legit business owners too. Not like the last crew I met at Sturgis two years ago."

Sturgis was a flop for Jimmy. He went to meet new people and market his work but ended up with a few broken ribs after refusing to mule a drug shipment back to Canada, regardless of the money he would've made.

Meeting a crew that supports women the way he said would win Jimmy's heart, mainly because he grew up with a Dad that beat the shit out of his mother on a daily basis.

"I can't disagree with you on that, and you know I wouldn't Jimmy. I just wanted to make sure you're not getting yourself into any trouble." I smirk at him.

"Who are you Jay, my fuckin' sister?" he asked me, laughing. "Don't worry, No trouble for me, woman. I just need work. You've helped bring a lot in with your Dad's construction business, but it's not enough. I don't want to go back to working construction and painting walls, Jay. I'm thirty-five, and this has always been what I wanted to do, you know that. If I have to move down to Denver to do it, I will."

I couldn't have been more grateful for the fact that I actually listened to what Jimmy was saying that day. Not long after the attack, my memory of that conversation solidified my plan to head to Denver. Hoping to meet a biker named Tiny with a soft heart toward women, and the ability to help them disappear.

Blacktop is not a place to write home about. It's also not the place you'd necessarily wander into on your own to have a cold one after work. It's very much a biker bar, complete with scantily clad women and countertops so sticky you're afraid it didn't come from booze. The rough and tough men at Blacktop don't mistreat or disrespect women, but the women who hang out here aren't exactly the type you take home to meet your mother. The bikers enjoy their women like they do their bikes, which is rode hard and often.

I remember the first time I walked in here almost three months ago. My face was still that ugly greenish blue from the bruises and my left arm still hung in a sling with a cast on my wrist. My eyes were still red and bloodshot, and I wondered how much longer it would take until it fully faded back to white. No one here knew about the marks that were still bandaged on my back. That might've given too much away. I still needed to be discreet and no way in hell was anyone going to find out my real name regardless of how much I trusted them.

Trust could get me killed.

Now I'm back, months later and hoping that Tiny is in so I don't have to hang around this place longer than I have too. The men here never made me feel uncomfortable at all.
The motto around here is if you're dressed like a two-dollar hooker, it's open season. I learned quickly that jeans and a loose long sleeve top don't scream 'this pussy's open for business.' The men here gave me respect, and I appreciate that.

I let Norma out of the truck and make my way to the heavy front door. She lived in this dive with me, and the men used to enjoy having her around. If I'm honest with myself I think I'm bringing her in with me for fear that I won't be recognized. I'm a far cry from the bruised up, pale skinned blonde I was the last time I walked through these doors. I was a broken shell of what once used to be an incredibly strong woman. Now I've returned looking more put together and with steel armor coating my skin.

Nothing can break me anymore.

That damage has already been done.

Head held high and with eyes straight ahead, I enter the bar. The first thing that hits me is the smell. I'd like to say it just smells like a dirty old dive bar but in truth it's more like stale cigarettes and sex. I'm sure this place has never seen a bottle of bleach, but that would probably take away some of its character.

I believe the rule of this establishment is if it ain't broke, don't fuckin' touch it. It looks exactly the same as it did the last time I was here. The long bar stretches across the back wall in front of me. An array of beer taps and liquor laden shelves embellishes the bar, adding to its dingy character. To the far right sits a jukebox and a few pool tables. Closer to the middle is what one would use as a dance floor. To the left are a series of round tables and booths along the wall.

The whole bar is encased in the finest of eighties wood paneling. The floor is sticky as I take the first few steps in, and I can tell from the way Norma is walking that there will be white furry spots stuck to the floor wherever her paws stick.

There's about twenty-five people in here, give or take. A small group of younger men are playing pool and a few women that wouldn't be allowed in a supermarket due to a lack of clothing are lingering around the bar.

No shoes, no shirt, no service and all that.

Scattered around the array of tables is a mixture of the people I came to see. I recognize the older man with long grey hair and paunchy stomach. He's older than dirt and although slightly hunched over with age he still stands six-feet tall.

Tiny.

He was the first man to spot me many months ago and the first to offer help. He told me he had three daughters and that nothing hurt his heart more than to see marks on a woman at the hands of a man.

Tiny is looking at me from his seat at the table like a bird that might fly away. He sits still and quiet, afraid to make the first move. I thought maybe he didn't recognize me but when his old eyes drift down to Norma and back up again I can see when the recognition takes place.

The conversation at the table has slowly ground to a halt as I stand silent by the door waiting for the old man to make the first move. Tiny places his hands on the table and begins to rise from his chair.

"Who's the pretty woman boss, and where ya been hidin' her?"

Tiny cuts a sharp gaze to the young male in his early twenties, effectively shutting his mouth. I have an odd sense of déjà vu as the old man slowly makes his way toward me. I can remember what he said at this exact moment three months ago.

"Not a man on this green earth is gonna lay a hand on you again sweetheart."

He's lost a little weight since I saw him last, and his white hair is a little longer, tied in a ponytail at the base of his neck.

"Wasn't sure when I'd see you again, sweetheart."

He has a cane in one hand that wasn't there the last time I was here, either. I look up to make eye contact because of a deep respect I have for this man. I'd never disrespect him by staring at the floor.

"I told you I would be back, didn't I?" I smartly say.

His mouth tips up a bit at the corners before he replies. "That you did girl. That you did."

He knows not to hug me or offer any kind of sympathetic gesture. He learned the first time I was here what not to expect from me. I suppose when you're something like one hundred and two you get good at reading people.

"I brought your truck back old man." I tell him.

A small look of surprise flashes across his face. I think he half wondered if he'd ever see it again. After all, he still doesn't know my real name and when I left, I lied, of course, and told him I was headed to Tennessee to tie up some loose ends. He shakes his head in disbelief.

"That's good, girl. Have to say I missed the old Ford. Missed havin' a clean toilet upstairs too," he jokes, knowing the only time that toilet ever got clean was when I stayed here, soaking the seat in Lysol every day before I let my ass touch the surface.

"I suppose we should sit down and go over a few things, so you can get gone again." Tiny. Straight down to business, just as I like it. I'm sure he could sit and tell me stories for days and enjoy doing it. Part of me would love to hear them, but he knows I'm pressed for time. I just need to finish this and get outta Dodge. Or I suppose in this case, Denver.

I take a seat at one of the empty tables he picked, and Norm sidles up beside him. She sensed his good nature the first time we were here and now has her head in his lap just like last before, soaking up the affection.

"My boy Danny has been looking after your identification. The name and birthdate you chose to use, along with a social security number, have been established. Everything's a go once we get your picture for a driver's license."

That's exactly what I needed to hear.

We couldn't take my photo last time I was here due to the welts and bruises, and definitely not before I had the surgery. One photograph and this will be over, so I can be on my merry way.

"I appreciate that Tiny. When and where for the photograph?" I'm not trying to be rude, but short and sweet is how he met me and I'm not about to change now.

"Here and now, if you're good with your appearance sweetheart. Danny's got a room upstairs where he can take it." He lowers his eyes in thought, sadness takes over his features. "You know, I sure do miss that pretty blonde hair, girl."

I miss my blonde locks too, but I'm a different person now.

"Blonde hair could get me killed, Tiny."

He looks at me with his sad but kind grey eyes and nods his head. We both know he meant nothing by it, but that doesn't mean we're not mourning the loss.

"Alright girl, let's get you set up with Danny."

* * *

I punch the number into the panel beside my storage unit. No cheap lock and key business here. I paid a pretty penny for this space with a full-time front desk guard, a passcode to get into the lot and another to enter your unit.

8675309.

THE UGLY ROSES

Clever, I know.

When you're leaving an old life and trying to start a new one, from scratch I might add, your memory tends to get a little bogged down with all the new info you're supposed to retain. 8675309 is easy and so annoying it's unforgettable.

The locks disengage, and I slide the door open. I'm greeted by one big empty shell that contains an old military issue ruck sack I picked up at a flea market and a lone box sitting on the back wall.

Not just any box mind you, it's the box that holds my past life, the box that contains flash drives of my family memories, a good sum of cash and numerous notes and information from my attack. Much of the information went through one ear and out the other with the authorities, but I'm determined to sit down and sift through every shred of evidence to show them I'm not crazy. I know I'll prove them wrong, but today's not that day.

Today I need to get back to Blacktop and hook up with Tiny, so I can pick up my new wheels before the dealer closes.

Tiny is standing on the front stoop of the bar when I roll in. He's not one to waste time, much like I'm not one to waste his seeing as he probably doesn't have much of it left. I roll down the passenger window when I come to a stop. "I'm ready when you are old man."

Tiny ambles down the steps and into my truck. Well, his truck I suppose. Last time I was here I paid him cash for a year's advance on the insurance and use of the vehicle. I got wheels without needing to use my name, and he got a significant tip that I'm sure has funded his upcoming funeral.

"Have a look at these before we head out girl. Danny does good work and I think they look plenty fine. But we're not leavin' here until you're happy with 'em."

He hands me an envelope containing my new I.D. First up is my new social security card.

Elle Davidson.

I've been preparing for this; we'd chosen my name months ago. I suppose it's just going to take some getting used to on paper. The driver's license shows me from yesterday. Grey long sleeve top and hair pin straight around my face. I wore little makeup and put in my fake colored contacts to mute the bright green in my eyes. My birth year is the same, but I'd chosen a different month and day.

"These turned out great old man."

I can't say much more than that because my mouth is dry.

This is it; I can start my new life.

"Like I said before girl, I ain't got a passport for ya. So long as you don't plan on leavin' the country, the stuff in that envelope should get you by. Social security check would show you worked as a waitress and bartender most of your life. It ain't much but it covers your ass if you need it."

He knows as well as I do that I've no intentions of working any day soon. I have enough to get me by for quite a while. A good chunk is in my rucksack waiting to be handed over for the smell of leather and shiny new paint.

Tiny knows the owner of the dealership where I'm picking up my new BMW, a sleek black SUV with plenty of room and a great safety rating. After a few hushed words and a stack of cash later, it's time to part ways.

I've loaded up the truck with my gear and folded the seats down to make room for Norm. It'll take us a few days to get to North Carolina at the pace we've been travelling. I give one last look to the old man. Without him a lot of this wouldn't be possible; I'd still be struggling with fake names and no identification to get around with.

"You take care of yourself out there sweetheart. Don't forget, you ever need anything, anything at all, you know where to find me."

I reach my hand out and rest it on his chest on top of his worn leather vest. Other than a handshake, it's the first time I've really *touched* anyone since the attack. I reach up on my toes to plant a chaste kiss on the old man's cheek. His eyes are closed and I'm pretty sure that small sentiment of gratitude means more than all the money I've given him these past few months. In fact, I know it does.

"I won't forget old man."

I pat him on the chest then climb into my SUV and turn over the ignition. I could've said thank you, but this moment was the perfect parting for both of us. He knows what I just said with my actions will mean more than any words that could've come out of my mouth. I put on my sunglasses, give one last nod, and make my way out of the lot.

Elle Davidson.

I can breathe again.

Chapter Four

His hands squeeze tighter around my throat. My eyes roll back into my head. My lungs are on fire.

"Say it you cunt, say that you'll be better! Tell me how sorry you are!"

I open my swollen eyes as much as I can manage and look him in the eye before speaking,

"Fuck you," I hiss, blood pouring out of my mouth.

He slams my head back against the wall and starts pacing like the madman he is. I can feel blood running down my neck from the uneven cinderblock that my head just made contact with.

I take in the shrine on the far wall that's been mocking me for days. Photos of me getting out of my pickup truck. Photos of me at the local waterhole with a beer in my hand and older photos of me having dinner with an old flame. How didn't I notice this psychopath following me? It's a small town for Christ's sake.

I don't show him my fear at how well he knows my life, how much he's documented me. Sick bastards like this feed on fear.

I'll leave him starved.

His pacing begins to slow which means he's got something to say to me. Or, he wants to torture me again.

Both are hell.

THE UGLY ROSES

The beatings usually happen when I'm hanging from the beam across the ceiling. He lowered me this time to use to the washroom, which is nothing but a piss bucket in the corner. I know there's a real bathroom outside this room. I've heard the toilet flush and the constant drip from the tap.

Maybe he wants me to feel humiliated.

If he let me use it, he'd have to undo the ropes that are still wrapped around my wrists, a rope leading to a giant ring bolted to the floor.

I'm led around this room like a dog, only dogs have the pleasure of seeing the sun rise and set. This windowless tomb gives me nothing. He begins to gather up the slack which means it's time to stand up. I hate to give him the satisfaction when I help. Days without food and very little water hasn't helped much in terms of my energy level.

He yanks on the rope and I drag my bloody feet across the cold concrete floor. I make my way toward the middle of the room where I am to hang like mistletoe on Christmas, but he surprises me by moving around so he's facing my back. This is new, I'm not hung up yet; the eye bolt in the floor to my right is where he's been tying the rope off, where he pulls the slack through to hoist me off the ground.

Not today.

Quick as lightning he wraps a loop of the rope around my neck and begins to pull it tight. I've barely recovered from his hands around my throat and now I'm struggling against the harsh abrasiveness of the frayed rope.

"Tell me you're sorry. Tell me you're sorry. Tell me you're sorry. Tell me you're SORRY!" He chants, over and over again into my ear.

I can't breathe!

My vision is going blurry. My lungs are burning from a lack of oxygen. The mural of my life mocks me as I fight for one last mouthful of air.

I give up. Fuck it, I give up.

* * *

I wake with a start and I'm gasping for breath, my hands clasping my throat. I hear whimpering from Norm beside the bed. "I'm alright, Norm."

She's used to these, my nightmares and the screaming. I pat her on the head and climb out of the sweat-soaked sheets, stripping off my clothes on the way to the bathroom for a shower. It's one of the few things that clear my head after the evil invades my sleep. A glance at the clock tells me that it's only five in the morning.

This is what I like to call a good night. I went to bed around eleven so the fact that I got six hours of solid sleep that wasn't alcohol induced is a small miracle.

We've been in our new home for over a month now, and things here are starting to look better. I rented the house from an older man named Tom Morgan who used to live here with his wife until she passed last year. After that, he took up living on his large fishing boat in Singer Harbor.

"This place is not much of a home without her," he'd said about my new abode.

So now it's mine to do with as I wish for meager rent that was so cheap, I paid a year in advance. I might not be here that long, but I don't like the idea of being kicked out for another renter either. Tom was more than happy to rent it to me long term since the few weekly rentals he had become more of an inconvenience to him.

I asked him if I could upgrade a few things while I'm here since the cabin was very outdated and the appliances made horrible noises in the night. He said, *"don't care what you do, so long as when you leave, it's still rentable."* The decor was old, and the upgrades keep me busy.

Wooden steps lead up to the home that's built up off the ground. A small porch with a bench welcomes you before you open the squeaky screen door; I never lubed the hinges since I consider it a security feature.

The home interior has slowly transformed to my liking. The original dark wood floors are a nice contrast to the tan colored L-shaped sofa I bought last week. I had a more modern fireplace installed underneath the television on the wall in front of the sofa. The kitchen and living room are one open space but there's a long island that separates the two rooms, much like my rental in Phoenix, but this one is home to four deep red leather bar stools that I picked up in Jacksonville last week.

I know I don't *need* four, I have no friends to eat with and I don't plan to invite anyone for dinner anytime soon, but they suit the space and only buying one stool would've aggravated my mild case of OCD. I kept the old solid wood table that Tom left here and use it as a desk for my laptop.

The left side of the house boasts one large bedroom with a walk-in closet and an ensuite bath. The door on the right in the hallway leads into the laundry room, and from there you can continue on into my closet. Beyond the closet is my bedroom. The bathroom also has two doors, one access from the hallway and one access from my bedroom. Full circle is what I like to call it. I can walk into my bathroom, through my bedroom then into my closet and out the laundry room door. If anyone tried to break in or someone found me it's highly unlikely they'd assume all the exit points from one of those rooms. It's a relatively small abode but it's more than enough space for me, perfect for a close couple or single woman with a dog. I couldn't have found a better spot to stay.

* * *

I make my way to the kitchen after my shower to start the coffee. Tightening the sash on my robe, I look out the window at the calm water while I wait for my brew. As much as I hate the mornings, this view always brightens my day. The colors on the water when the sun starts to rise are spectacular. It's the bright orange mixed with a deep red you normally only see at Christmas. It's quite spectacular. I'm grateful that the temperature is just warm enough to enjoy my coffee on the deck.

I grab a throw from the back of the couch and stuff my cigarettes into the pocket of my robe. I've cut back on smoking significantly since we moved here. I'm by no means close to quitting, but the amount I indulge in has cut in half.

Baby steps.

I work my way out the screen door off the kitchen to the back porch. The double-wide lounger I bought for out here is phenomenal. The back porch facing the water has an extended roof, so I don't need to worry about bringing the double-wide cushion in every time it rains. I set my coffee down on the small side table and curl up in my new favorite resting place.

The porch is about ten feet wide by twenty-five feet long. The lounger is to the left out the door, and the barbecue sits adjacent to a small table to the right of the door. A wide set of steps lead down the middle of the porch and another off the far end near the barbecue. I have gates on both of them, so Norma can enter the fenced portion of the side yard at night. I don't want to have to look for her in the woods at night, not because I'm afraid of the dark itself, it's what could be in the dark that terrifies me. Through the day she's full speed ahead where the grass meets sand then fades into water.

There are a lot of trees to the left of my home and close to the water. I've seen a few people making a loop to walk around the shore. Homes and cottages are sparse at this end of the lake. The opposite side is mostly marsh so there aren't any there. There are only a few to the right of mine. Well, I can see one from my porch and another that's a bit further down. I don't explore much since I've been too busy trying to settle in and get a handle on my surroundings.

Tom told me it stays pretty quiet here and the man who owns the place closest to me is away more than he's home. It's a military town and most of the people here come and go frequently, so my unknown neighbor's absence doesn't worry me. I put great thought into moving here. The first thing that drew my attention was the beautifully scenery, the second was knowing there would be people living near, most of whom fight for a living. I consider that group of people honorable and admirable.

There are many cowards in the world, but not many inhabit this town. That solidified my decision after remembering the man I encountered the night I was taken. He was in the parking lot the night of my abduction, and he refused to help me. I was completely helpless and screaming, being dragged toward a van.

The man just watched, stunned.

Useless.

I wasn't sure if he was going to piss himself or run. Or maybe put his hands in his pockets and grab a bucket of popcorn to watch as I was taken against my will.

I'd like to think if something similar were to happen here, that a man who sacrifices his life for his country and the people in it certainly wouldn't be such a pussy and come to my aid— unlike the useless prick that stood by in a washed-up suit with his mouth hanging open, nothing coming out.

Perhaps its wishful thinking, and it's not often that lightning strikes the same spot twice, but I'd like to think my odds of having help are greater around those who are so selfless.

I found out shortly after my attack that the useless man did call the police. Only it was two days later.

After I was reported missing.

The authorities informed me that he was at the bar that night to meet up with his mistress. Calling the cops right away might have caused him a divorce, which apparently happened anyway.

If he just would've said something, called for help, followed the vehicle I was taken in. I remind myself that what ifs will get me nowhere, and simply pray that the new people I've moved among have more morals than the idiot who thought saving his marriage was more important than saving a life.

I suppose if my new neighbor is never home, hoping that someone will come to help is a bit of a long shot. Or no shot at all if someone were to attack me at home without anyone around to hear my cries for help.

I try not to dwell on that too much by keeping myself busy around the house.

Other than some paint and new furniture, the house is pretty much complete. I painted the bedroom a deep golden color that looks nice behind the nearly black furniture. I also spent a fortune on a killer mattress with a low bed frame and leather headboard. The cream-colored Egyptian sheets and abstract fluffy duvet bring it all together.

Other than that, I don't plan on making any larger purchases. There could come a day when I have to leave at the drop of a hat, and I'm prepared for that. I keep my spare truck key locked inside the vehicle and my rucksack is packed with the essentials, ready to grab and go.

Danny from Denver was kind enough to hook me up with two small handguns. They make me feel safer at night. I always have one close by and they too are ready to go when I am. I'd like to say the guns are enough, but I couldn't stop there, I needed more protection. Or at least the illusion of safety that weapons provide.

Something I've learned about living in the USofA is that pretty much every town has a store related to hunting and fishing. Thus my latest form of protection is the two knives that sheath into the lining of my boots.

Easy, accessible and they could possibly save my life. One can never be too careful. After what I've been through, I assert the true meaning of preparedness.

I also made a getaway bag that stays stashed in my SUV. Under the floor covering in the back and above the spare tire is a bag containing five thousand in cash, a change of clothes with cheap flip flops and a prepaid credit card. Enough essentials to get me back to Denver if I ever need to flee.

I opened up a safe deposit box at the bank two towns over to stash some money. The rest I put into a small bank account to give me access to a debit card. I still mostly pay in cash wherever I go but putting down six thousand in cash on furniture at the small store in town may have raised some questions. For instances like these I use the debit card.

Now that my coffee is finished, and the sun is up, I decide to head into town to pick up some groceries. Minus the essentials, my fridge has been pretty bare since I moved here. I love to cook so it's time to stock up on spices and fresh food so I can get back to eating regular meals and living a more *normal* life.

Chapter Five

I choose to shop in Jacksonville since I have a long list of things I'd like to pick up and need bigger stores. I throw on my typical going out attire which today is a sensible loose dark grey top that hangs slightly over my shoulders paired with dark skinny jeans tucked inside knee high brown boots. I make sure my knives are concealed in place, throw on a light scarf to hide the minor scarring that's still on my neck and put on wide leather cuff bracelets to hide the dark marks still covering my wrists.

I lock the front of the house and bid Norma farewell. She doesn't like not being able to come with me but it's getting warmer outside and it will be too long of a wait for her in the truck.

When I pull out of my driveway, I take in my surroundings for any notable changes. This too is the norm for me now. On the other side of the lane leading to my new home are mostly trees and small hills. It would be tough to notice any changes there, but I still look for dangers every time I leave the house.

I drive closer to the neighbor's home and note the emptiness of the place. Someone comes to tend to the lawn and I'm sure I saw a woman walking out with what looked like cleaning supplies one day. But other than that, it's pretty silent.

A truck was there last night but it's gone this morning. I'm constantly assessing my surroundings, so I know the truck is not one I've seen before. I also know it's a newer model Ford, black in color. I scan the area once again, memorizing the landscape.

Quiet.

No people.

No threat.

The home is bigger than mine with newer renovations. The board and batten-style home is a graphite color and if the chunky outdoor furniture and grill are any indication, I assume he lives alone. The dark home with its lack of foliage strictly screams 'man'.

I'm assuming he too must be like most of the families around here that have dedicated themselves to serving this Country because the home is way too nice to be left empty for any other reason. A little landscaping and a few potted plants is really all that's lacking around the clean lines of the home.

Mind out of the architectural gutter, Elle. Time to shop.

* * *

Jacksonville is the closest city, and by that I mean it has more than two stoplights. I grew up in a small rural town of a few thousand people and though the bigger towns and cities are a necessity for most, I choose not to live directly in the middle of one.

Too many unknown variables.

Too many risks.

I could've handled it all a few years ago. Hell, I could've handled anything, but not anymore. This chapter in my life is all about risk assessment and planning ahead. Two things I didn't even blink at before.

My old life was one of spontaneity and taking risks. I didn't strategically plan where to stay on vacation or what I was going to do when I got there.

THE UGLY ROSES

I didn't assess each person on the street or in the store like they could be hiding a Ka-Bar behind their back ready to stab me to death.

I also spoke, made jokes and made the odd idle friendly chit chat with strangers. Not often, but it happened depending on my mood.

Lost in thought I miss my turn for the clothing chain I wanted to hit, so I make my way through suburbia to get myself turned around. I'll hit the food stores last so it's not rotting in the truck while I debate skinny or boot cut jeans.

My windows are down; the weather is mild, Avenged Sevenfold pounds through my speakers as a cigarette burns between my fingers. It's truly the simple things that give me happiness these days, if only a little. I could almost smile if it didn't make me feel so goddamn guilty for doing so.

Most people would say you should smile as often as you can, *you're alive*.

Most people would also say life is a gift.

I most days, however, see it as a punishment.

I wait at a stop sign for an old granny across from me to pass through the intersection. It's a four way stop, and she stopped first. However, I think she decided to take a nap because the old bat hasn't moved an inch since she stopped— an hour before me.

"What the hell grandma, move your ass!" I shout through the windshield. Patience is not a virtue I possess.

Still no movement on her behalf.

To go or not to go?

I don't need an accident written up on my driving record; even if it would be her fault for t-boning me in the middle of the street.

Lay low; don't attract any unwanted attention to yourself.

I chant the ol' man Tiny's words to myself and notice she's staring in her side mirror, assessing what's behind her. I lean over my steering wheel to look down the street and see a group of shirtless sweat-ridden men heading our way.

"Huh. Maybe granny didn't need a nap after all," I say to myself.

Dirty old bird.

I'd like to say I'm not affected since my need for men has significantly dwindled since the attack. Don't get me wrong, I'm still a hot-blooded female, I just haven't wanted the attention. I'm also reluctant to bare my scars and stripes.

The questions *that* would bring could blow my cover in this small town, so it's not worth it. I should also accept the fact it sure as shit isn't pretty to look at either.

Men with scars are badass—for women, not so much.
Maybe one day, in the dark, if he has his hands tied behind his back so they can't make their way up mine to feel the ridges and flaws. Maybe then, under those circumstances, I could be intimate with someone again.

Until that day, I suppose there's no harm in looking.

Or in this case, eye fucking.

Five of them are jogging. From a distance they look relatively similar. All around the six-foot mark, most with tattoos along their arms or neck. I'm guessing most are mid-thirties. The only thing that truly sets them apart at this distance is hair length and color.

The man closest to granny's side of the street captures the most attention as they edge closer. Well, should I say my attention? Beautifully tanned skin, longer inky dark hair that brushes the back of his neck and what looks like tribal fire in black burning up his left arm. His face is stuck on a scowl most likely from the exertion if I judge by the amount of sweat pouring off his body. Light scruff coats his jaw and for the first time in what feels like a century I wonder what it would feel like between my legs.

Jesus Elle get your shit together.

Most of the men have sunglasses on so eye color is a miss at this point. I haven't really taken in any other predominant features from the rest of the group because I can't take my eyes off Mr. Broody leading the pack.

One of the men bringing up the rear breaks off and heads to granny's car. Two more follow, it's apparent they must know each other. Either that or this golden girl has more game than I do when it comes to picking up men. Mind you she could be their grandmother. The silver lining here is she seems occupied enough that I begin to carry on through the intersection to get started on my shopping.

I reach over to dump my smoke in the half-empty water bottle in the cup holder and hear a bang on the hood of my vehicle. I slam on my breaks and note the pack leader leaning on the hood of my truck, the scowl still on his face.

I know for a fact I didn't hit the broody prick, he was still on the sidewalk when I edged through the intersection!

"What?" I scream over the music at the smug-looking bastard.

51

He walks toward the passenger window and leans his forearms on the door.

"That shit'll kill you one day. Or perhaps it'll kill the innocent man about to jog through the intersection while you were too preoccupied trying to put out that smoke."

I'm slack jawed at a voice that could melt the panties off a nun, but the racing of my heart from shock is enough to make me remain pissed off.

I'm debating putting my foot back on the accelerator and flooring it so I can wipe that smug look off his face but I don't want to be charged for careless driving and I'm positive that from where he stands assessing me he's already clocked my size, weight, zodiac symbol and has memorized the tags on the vehicle. I gather up all the calm I can before I reply.

"Thank you for your concern, surgeon general, however last time I checked anyone old enough to buy a pack is entitled to abuse them as often as they wish. And unless you ran out into the street prior to looking in both directions which, may I add is knowledge ingrained into even the *smallest* of children's minds, then it's due to your own stupidity that you almost dented my vehicle. Now, if you'll kindly take your hands off of my truck, I've got shit to do."

What started out as my sweet voice turned bitter the moment I heard myself. My voice is still so goddamn raspy from being strangled half to death. I was told it may never return to normal. It's not so much that it's a bad voice, it's just not the one I'm used to hearing due to lack of use. My innocent rant turned heated, now I just want to get the hell out of here.

The stunned look on his face even though I can't see his eyes is almost enough to make me want to apologize.

Almost.

To hell with it, I put my truck back into drive as he backs up, so I can continue on my way.

"Fuck!" I bang my hands on the steering wheel and speed toward the shopping center. What started out as a good day is quickly going down the shitter.

I know the only reason I'm pissed is because I'm out of my comfort zone and attracted to him. Deep down I know he's someone the old me would've flirted with and soon took home. But when your voice and looks and attitude are nothing like they used to be, whether for the better or worse, it still makes a woman feel like a fraud. Add in a new name to boot and it's full on actress. I don't know if I could play that game, being a different person with a man?

Who am I kidding; I'm different regardless of the voice, the new name and face. I changed a long time ago and there's no turning back now.

* * *

Four stops and many stores later, I'm heading back home. It's almost supper time now and I have a pile of shit to get into the house before it gets dark. When I turn the corner onto my lane I notice the black Ford truck from last night backed in the drive in front of my neighbor's house.

The front door is propped open and whatever is in the back is being unloaded into the house. Maybe my neighbor has returned home and is restocking his pantry much like I'm about to do. Or maybe he's not unloading but loading and moving out.

I pull around the bend into my driveway and park the truck as close as I can get to the door. Norma is barking in the house and I'm sure it's at the neighbor since she should be used to the sound of my vehicle by now. This is one of the reasons I don't mind leaving her at home. Any dog owner can tell whether it's a frantic you're in danger bark or a '*hurry and let me the heck out, gotta pee*' kind of bark. It's another security feature for me, much like the squeaky hinges on the front door.

She waddles outside while I prop open the door. I don't mind shopping but carrying a hundred bags in makes me want to consider delivery next time. I'm on my last load of canned goods when the damn bag rips open and sends soup and spaghetti sauce rolling in every direction from the porch to the house. A heavy soup can hits my kneecap on the way down.

"For shit sakes." I mumble. I could cry right now.

I'm exhausted. I've been up since before dawn and I just want to stuff my face and down a bottle of wine before I crash into bed. Norm won't stop barking and it takes me a moment to realize it's not the friendliest kind.

"Do you always have a filthy mouth, or is it only when I'm around?"

I know that voice, and after this morning I hoped I'd never have to hear it again.

Okay, maybe that's a lie, but definitely not so soon.

I whirl around to face the broody bastard as Norm comes barreling up the steps. I give her a settle down motion with my hands and address the stranger while reaching my hand inside the hobo bag that holds my gun. I'm sure I won't need it. He doesn't look threatening, actually he looks pretty damn good in worn out jeans and a long sleeve Henley.

"What the fuck are you doing at my house?" I'm not sure whether I want to weep or shoot him because I haven't had any visitors here, and although it gets lonely, I haven't come to terms with the fact I may need to have a friend again one day.

Definitely not today though. Wisely he takes a few steps back, not because he's afraid of the dog that he's looking at with adoration but obviously he's noted the confused and pissed off expression on my face. He holds up his hands in a placating gesture.

"I saw the dog outside; I also saw what looked like somebody moving in. Wasn't sure if Tom finally moved back and got a dog or rented the place out."

He's looking over my head into the home, which is much different from Tom's older decor.

"It's rented."
"So it is," he says, giving me a skeptical look.

"What?"

He sighs, "The *what* is, I'm glad Tom finally moved on. And I guess I'm here now to introduce myself to my new neighbor," he says with a shit eatin' grin on his face.

I scowl. "I don't have any neighbors, now if you'll excuse me I've got-" He cuts me off. "Yeah, yeah, shit to do, so you said this morning. Well, I live next door. Just thought I'd give you a heads up."

"Neighbors?"

"That's what I said, woman." He looks way more pleased than I am.

"You're fucking kidding me?"

"Afraid not," he replies.

The smug grin returns.

I back into the house and begin to close the door. What are my odds? *Apparently not too damn good.* I should be more afraid of this morning's stranger showing up on my porch, but the mention of Tom moving on and the truck next door brings it all together. Of course, he'd live in the nearly black box next door. I don't know him from Adam, but the dark and broody house suits him, I can admit that much.

I really have nothing left to say so I bend down to pick up the soup can that's blocking the door while he begins to collect the few that are left on the porch.

"I can get it," I say more forcefully than intended.

"Already done." He frowns, hands me the rest and backs away from the door. I can't handle the attention, or him looking at me like he's trying to figure me out. I give him a nod and close the door behind me. From what Tom mentioned he's not home often so I shouldn't be running into him every day.

I can't decide whether that pleases me or not.

Chapter Six

I wake up with a pounding headache to something that sounds as loud as a chainsaw.

Gah, shoot me now.

I take stock of my surroundings when the room starts to settle. It still baffles me waking up somewhere new, but I'm slowly getting used to it.

No nightmares last night, or at least not the kind that woke me up. Perhaps it was the two and a half bottles of wine I drank before bed that kept me comatose throughout the night. *They may keep me handicapped for the better part of the morning as well.*

I peer toward the window. It looks like it's going to rain soon, judging by the lack of sunshine. I hate days like this, they remind me of the loss. I used to embrace cloudy cool days, curl up on the sofa and read some mystery smut in front of the fire with a good bottle of wine. Now I'd just prefer to sleep the day away or forgo the smut and head straight to the wine.

Nature calls and I have no choice but to drag my sorry ass out of bed. I finish my business and get to brushing my teeth. One look in the mirror reminds me how I feel. The bags under my eyes reflect my constant lack of rest; my hair is a giant mass of bed head curls because I didn't iron it after my shower last night.

I'm always pale after I drink which makes the marks stand out more around my neck. I could've gotten the scars fixed at Doctor Reveres, but he wouldn't do everything at the same time and I refuse to be there longer than I had to. I can hide what's left on my body with clothing and jewelry.

A handful of Ibuprofen later and coffee in hand, I make my way to the back deck. The noise has stopped thank god so it should be my typical quiet morning staring at the water. Norm takes off like she usually does to make her morning rounds as I curl up in a light blanket on the lounge.

If this were the past, I'd have my cell phone stuck in my hand right now checking Facebook updates and planning a dinner with friends and their kids.

Now my morning routine consists of coffee and blank stares in the distance. I hoped to contact my best friend from home when I finally got settled under a new name. But either I haven't found the time, or I'm still too afraid to potentially put her life in danger.

Most likely the latter.

I have one prepaid burner phone in my bag. I've only used it twice in the past month to confirm deliveries to the house. That's it.

I've survived on practically a few sentences, with a handful of strangers for the past six months. I wonder if I'll ever be able to go home again and be at least partially the woman I once was. Then I wonder, do I even want to go home again?

My old passport and identification is in the safe deposit box with some money. I don't know if I'll ever need it again, but it's there none the less. I used it to enter the United States the day I ran from home. The day I left the only sister I'll ever have, hopefully not only to ensure her safety, but mine as well.

The visit to my home from the useless Detective Braumer cemented it all for me that day, solidified the fact I couldn't stay in my old town any longer. I was still recuperating from my attack, hell bent on proving to the Detective that another man was out there to get me. He blew the theory out of the water and dismissed me like shit off his shoe.

Detective Braumer sat across from me on the black leather chair. Smug as always, seeming to do his job well as oppose to pushing early retirement.

"Ms. O'Connor, we've gone over this a dozen times. At this point there's nothing more we can do."

I hate this man.

"Detective Braumer, I've woken up at this house every day with a single rose lying on my doorstep. The same rose that was left on my doorstep every damn day up until the night I was taken. How is there nothing more you can do?"

I'm trying to keep my calm but for fuck's sake a girl can only handle so much shit before she loses her mind.

"A kind neighbor perhaps, Ms. O'Connor. Maybe an old friend?"

The bastard.

"You know I've been in touch with everyone I know, I've also had people ask around town. Nobody knows who it is, and this isn't questionable to you? You're not even going to look into it?"

He moves to stand and straightens his jacket.

"As I said, nothing can be done. Until a threat is made, it's a dead end."

"Have you called flower shops? Anything? Wouldn't that help? I told you there were two people in on my attack! And the flowers prove it!"

I can tell by the look on his face he's about to shut me down again. This man is useless and Detective Miller is gone to some family function on the east coast so he's not able to help me. If he were here, he would help. I know he would.

"You know what" I heave, "Forget it. Get the fuck out of my house and I hope the door knocks you on your ass on the way out!"

Norm breaks me out of my funk and I realize I have tears streaming down my face and my coffee is cold. I could probably count on one hand the number of times I've cried and it's usually when I'm extremely angry. Maybe that's what these are—angry tears— because sometimes I just don't know what the hell to do with myself.

The sound of someone clearing their throat brings my head up. My neighbor is standing at the base of my stairs, I never heard him approach. The damn dog never even warned me. I give her a death stare for being disloyal and he obviously catches it.

"She was over at my house, staring at the burgers I was grilling for lunch. I suppose you could say we came to a truce."

This means he obviously fed her.

I'm too afraid to speak yet while trying to discretely dry the wetness off my face so I just nod.
"She's a nice dog. Nothing other than the bandana around her neck though, so I don't know what to call her."
His approach is gentle, he senses my unease and he's doing his best to tread lightly. Much like his feet when he snuck up on me.

I take a deep breath and look at his face. No sunglasses today due to the dark sky. His eyes are so dark they're almost black. For some reason I figured he would fill the tall dark and broody cliché, sporting those cerulean blues everyone talks about but rarely sees.

Nope.

They're blacker than night with a ring of grey around the outside. I clear my throat before responding to his question.

"Norma."

His lips twitch like he wants to smile, and he pats his leg to get her attention. She waddles over, tail wagging and scrubs up against his thigh. Next to me she looks like a horse, next to him she might as well be a Pomeranian.

"It was nice to meet you Norma, thanks for joining me for lunch."

He looks up at me in question, waiting or ready to ask me something. "We may have got off on the wrong foot yesterday. My name's Ryder. Ryder Callaghan."

Of course his name is Ryder. Why wouldn't he have a kickass name? I don't know why he's gracing me with his whiskey voice when I was nothing but a bitch to him yesterday. Now he's being kind and I'm honestly not sure if I'm ready for that yet. I'm not sure how to handle it.
Maybe it was the tears that got to him?

Civil. Civil I can do. Being too friendly implies having friends and I'm not ready for that to happen yet either.

I keep my response short and sweet.

"Elle. Thanks for feeding my dog."

That's as much as I can manage at this point. He'll pick up eventually that I'm not much of a talker. I stand up to make my way into the house to hibernate for the rest of the day when he speaks again.

"Elle," he says, slightly shaking his head in a contemplative way.

I give him my signature nod and head into the house.

* * *

The sand stirs up behind me as I pound my way back toward home. It's been a long time since I jogged outdoors, and I realize just how dull burning miles on the treadmill back in Phoenix was. I missed the wind in my face and the smell of the outdoors.

I've really pushed it today. Sweat is pouring down my temples and my calf muscles have begun to burn. I'm coming up on the neighbor's house, *Ryder's house,* and notice Norma sitting on his back deck. She's too lazy to come jogging with me, so I assumed she'd be waiting at home like she normally does.

Traitor.

I give a quick whistle and she waddles toward me. I notice the lone figure on a deck chair as he gives a small wave. I don't plan on stopping to chat; I didn't wrap a scarf around my neck to cover the marks, since it would look fucking ridiculous with my running gear, so I continue home.

I haul my sweaty self up the steps and make my way inside. It's the first sighting of Ryder since I met him four days ago. He seems to keep to himself and that's perfectly fine with me.

I don't have many plans for today. It's Friday. Not that that matters. Every day is Friday in my life. Or whatever day of the week I want to call it. I decide on a shower and a nap due to my once again lack of sleep last night. Then maybe I'll cook myself a steak and open a nice bottle of wine. My new shipment of books arrived at the post office yesterday, so maybe I'll settle in after dinner for a night of smut.

I peel off my sweaty running gear and turn on the shower. One thing people take for granted is a good hot shower. I came to this conclusion twice in my life, once when I was bloody and beaten in a cool, damp basement with a psychopath. The other when I'd been mummified at the hands of Doc Revere and had to endure sponge baths and dry shampoo for a week. Thus, I've become what you might call a hot water whore.

After both these incidents I spent ample time under the hot running liquid. What were once five-minute trips in and out turned into me standing under the spray until the water ran cold.

After my shower, I wrap up in my robe and a blanket and curl up on the couch. Sometimes running gives me an extra boost of energy, sometimes it takes me straight to bed.

"What time are you going to get here hunny?" Asks my mom. They're all packed and ready to go while I'm still stuck in traffic due to a broken-down train forty minutes from home.

"I haven't a damn clue mom. I've been sitting here for almost an hour. I'm blocked by traffic in front and behind I can't even get turned around to try a different route."

Why I didn't cancel this useless checkup at the doctor's office today is beyond me. I'm healthy; I should've stayed the home. Now I'm stuck in traffic while the rest of them are ready to head to the airport. Shit!

"Temper, temper. It won't help you right now. The traffic will clear eventually, until then it doesn't sound like there's much you can do."

My poor mother, I know she hates traveling at night and if I don't get there soon, she will be.

New plan.

"Mom, head to the hotel. If I have to pay more parking for the extra vehicle it's not a big deal. I'm not going to miss the six-a.m. flight tomorrow, that's for sure, but for all I know I could be here until the sun goes down."

"I don't want to leave without you Jayne, but if we don't get moving soon Lilly's going to be one crabby child for the early flight tomorrow."

The family trip to Florida is already heading down the shitter. I planned and paid for this trip six months ago. I can't disappoint Lil', I'll just drive through the night on my own.

"Go without me mom. I'll figure this shit show out and meet you there later tonight or early morning. Leave my suitcase behind though; I'd like to change before I get back on the road."
I can't stand the scent of antiseptic and sick people stuck on me from the Doc's office.

"Alright honey, I think it's our best option, at this point we're already two hours behind schedule. Your Dad is going nuts. Well, not more nuts than when we were ten minutes late, but you know what he's like. Call me when you leave the house to let me know you're on your way."

God bless my mother. My father has probably been in the truck for two hours waiting for me to show up. He's a planner, very on schedule. Mom has kept him balanced with her sharp attitude and fly by the seat of your pants lifestyle. It's what's kept them together for over thirty years.

"I will mom, and thanks. Give Lil' some love for me. I'll meet you all at the hotel."

"Alright, drive safe."

"You too, Mom."

I'm woken up by the sounds of deep male laughter in the distance. I sit up on the couch and stretch the aches out of my body. I might need a soak in the tub later to ease my muscles after this morning's jog.

I slowly make my way to the kitchen and look out the side window toward Ryder's home, noticing a few extra trucks in the driveway. A quick scan of the property shows Ryder and three other men out on his back deck, standing around a smoking barbecue with beers in their hand. My rumbling stomach reminds me of the steak I planned to cook, so I head to my room to get dressed before starting dinner.

I take the steak out of the fridge and season it, leaving it on the counter to get to room temperature while I wash up some new potatoes and asparagus. I layer the vegetables separately in tin foil with sea salt and pepper before carrying it all out to the barbecue. I don't always cook dinner; I usually eat a late big lunch and finger foods later in the evening. Tonight, however calls for a hearty meal.

After successfully grilling my dinner, I choose to eat on the deck and listen to the men next door. There's at least an acre separating our properties, with some random trees in between but it doesn't stop the sounds of hearty male voices making it to my porch. I have a sense of longing listening to their laughter, which most likely comes after some good natured ribbing and inside jokes.

It's been well over a year since I experienced something similar. Mostly due to my own selfish reasons but the later part of the year was to ensure other peoples' safety. Doing what's right doesn't always make you happy. But sometimes it's a necessity to protect those you love, regardless of how much you want to stay close to them.

I miss my weekly dinners with close friends. I stare out at the water and recall the last meal I got to experience with them.

"Hey hooker, what do you want Brad and I to bring tonight?"

This is from Laura; her mouth is almost as filthy as mine. She's been my rock for the past thirteen years, ever since we met in high school.
"You've been into the tequila, already haven't you?"

She's snickering and I can only guess it's because Brad can't keep his hands off her. She met him last year. Single mom with two six-year-old twins and Brad took them all on, while treating them like the true treasures they are. I couldn't be happier my best friend has such a great man in her life to support her and her children.

"Why yes, my beautiful bitch, I have. The kids have been with their Grandma since noon so I figured I'd get an early start!"

This is no surprise to me only because I'd probably do the exact same thing, minus the Brad in my life. That man is a keeper, but I have not quite found where the rest of the 'Brads' of the world are hiding. That's the downside to small town living. Either someone has already found them, or they've slept with someone you know.

"Of course you did. However, if you hadn't started your protest to prohibition so early you'd recall telling me you were bringing the buns."

Shit, she's forgetful. She's lucky I love her.

"I already had me some buns today sister, and they were nice and firm!"

THE UGLY ROSES

She's still laughing. I hear Brad holler in the background regarding what he'll be sticking between her buns later tonight, and since I need to finish prepping for dinner I speed this along.

"Alright, you're in charge of nothing but yourself. Not because I don't think you can manage something so simple, but more because I'm concerned of whether or not you've washed your hands after all that 'bun' business you had going on today."

She's still cackling so I tell her I'll see her soon and finish with getting things ready.

This is normal, weekly dinners with friends. Sometimes it happens on a Tuesday, sometimes we manage it on the weekend. But no matter what, we always make time for each other—and wine.

I pull myself out of memory lane and clean up my dinner mess. The sun's beginning to set and I decide it's a good time to soak in the tub. I grab the half-drunk bottle of wine from the counter and plug my iPod into the stereo. I bring up my playlist which is a mix of the blues and bands like CCR.

My bath time tunes.

I pin my brown locks on top of my head; I don't flat iron my hair when it's just me at home. When I go out I stick to the pin straight look that's so far off from my appearance before that nobody should ever recognize me. My usual is what I like to call an untamed riot. It sticks in every which direction and I always make sure to keep a hair tie in my pocket.

I settle myself down into the coconut scented water. I always add coconut oil to my skin in hopes it'll tone down the appearance of my scars. A little in the tub adds a great fragrance to the room as well.

My favorite scent used to be anything with the scent of lily in it. Then the smell became too much, and the word *lily* became unbearable to hear.

Enter coconut. The good Doc recommended it for the marks on my skin. The scent has stuck without triggering the memories from my past that lily does.

Creedence begins singing about the rain when I hear a knock at my back door. Since I spend the majority of my time on the waterside of the house, my front door is always shut and the lights at that end of the house are usually off. I hear Norm scratching at the door to get out as I wrap my robe around myself and head for the door. As per usual my gun is not far so I grab it off the bathroom counter and put in the pocket of my robe.

I holler from the hallway before I round the corner.

"Who is it?"

The whiskey voice from next door greets me.

"Ryder."

The porch light illuminates him, like a halo on his body. He's wearing dark jeans with a black t-shirt and flip-flops on his feet. His chest looks about three feet wide and he practically fills out the door with his hands resting on the frame, arms spread wide. I'm sure he could plow through with little effort.

He doesn't scare me, *not really*. His size is intimidating, but in a good way that makes me feel like he could toss me over his shoulder and carry me to safety if need be.

Jesus Elle, focus.

"What are you doing here?" I finally manage to ask after some well-deserved ogling.

His black eyes stare back at me through the screen as I wait for his answer. I stand stupidly with a birds nest piled on top of my head, my black and red silk kimono doing little for his imagination.

He clears his throat before speaking.

"Me and some of the guys from work are having a barbecue. You're new, not sure if you've met anyone around here yet but you're more than welcome to join us."

I have to give him credit; his eyes have remained mostly on mine throughout the conversation. *Mostly.*

He's not making this easy on me. I'm a thirty-year-old woman for shit's sake and I feel like a damn teenager when he's around. Time to get my shit together. I cross my arms over my chest and lean my hip against the wall.

"Thanks, but I noticed the smoke earlier so I think I'll pass."

A deep rumbling laugh greets my ears and I can't believe how warm it makes me feel. The wind from the water blows his scent through my door. Damn he smells good, too.

Jesus, now I sound like a romantic.

Following his laughter he shakes his head. "Not what you're thinking. I hadn't used it in a while and there was a bee's nest built under the grill lid. Apparently it was flammable."

He gives me a half-grin while his eyes wander down to my legs.

"Well thank you for the offer, but I cooked a steak earlier and I planned on staying in tonight."

His eyes are still glued to my legs before they slowly make their way back up.

I begin ogling the tattoos on his arms; I consider the tribal art on his body beautiful. The lines are clean, the detail in them are exceptional from what I can see at five feet away. I'd love to read what's written among the beautiful designs but I'm not willing to get that close to him yet.

The silence has grown long so I glance up to his face and notice him staring at my chest.

Typical man!

Or maybe it's my neck. *Shit.*

I grab the top of my robe and pull it tighter around me before I speak. "Maybe some other time. Thanks though."

My voice is weak. Ryder seeing marks on my body makes me feel a kind of vulnerability I don't like and completely unfamiliar with.

I reach over to close the main door, since he can see all of me through the screen one. Norma tries to push it open to head out to the porch.

"Norm, inside. Now."

He holds the door for her while she mopes back into the house and I resume closing up.

"Sure, Elle. Maybe some other time," he says with an edge to his tone.

Either he's genuinely upset I said no, or he did get a good look at the marks on my body. Either way I breathe out a sigh of relief once I get the door shut.

Chapter Seven

"SHIT!"

I fall to the sand on my hands and knees and roll over onto my ass, grasping my leg. I've pushed myself too hard this morning and now I'm paying for it.

I haven't gotten much sleep the past few days. Ryder's bonfire the other night seemed to turn into a whole weekend booze fest. Judging by the man hugs I witnessed from afar the next day, I'd say his friends are happy he's home.

The happiest of all would most likely be the trio of whores that showed up yesterday with their tits overflowing out of their halter-tops, ass cheeks on display for all to see. It must've been a warm welcome home for him.

The silver lining for me was that most of the women seemed to be permanently attached to a few of the other men hanging around, and other than a ginger haired looking hooker who followed him around like a lost puppy, I didn't witness any dry humping or naked body parts.

Not that I should care.

I tell myself that this must be some kind of attraction by proximity. That's the only thing I can think to call it. Ryder is the first man that has entered my life in the past year that I've been attracted to and now he's got some kind of hold on me.

I hate to admit it intrigues me because my libido has been virtually nonexistent for what feels like a century. It also frightens me because all I can think is 'why him?'

Perhaps it's because not only is he attractive, but he also seems kind and incredibly intelligent. It's not often a woman finds all those qualities in the same man.

I assess my left leg and note the tenderness from knee to ankle. This is what you get when you're sexually frustrated, therefore you try to burn off your pent-up energy by pushing yourself too hard. Combine that with a lack of sleep and it's a recipe for disaster.

I ease up from the ground so I can walk the rest of the way to the house. I barely make it into a standing position before I give up.

"Aaaarrrgghhhh, fuck!"

I wail as the pain shoots through my leg. I sit my ass back down to rest for a minute. I'm not far. I can see Ryder's house from where I'm sitting. I'll rest for a little while and then crawl my ass back if I have to.

I lie back on the sand and close my eyes, taking in a few deep breaths while stretching out my leg. It feels like if I push it out all the way, a rubber band will snap. I stare up at the sky for a while, watching the dark clouds slowly move toward my location on the beach before I hear footsteps. Then a familiar shadow looms overhead.

"You alright?"

Ryder's deep voice washes over me. Shit. It's eight in the morning on a quiet Sunday. He's not in jogging gear so that means he probably heard me wail when I tried to stand up.

"Just peachy, neighbor," I say in my most sarcastic voice.

Surely he notices the expression of pain on my face, and my arms around my leg. He moves in front of me and bends down to a squat.

He begins reaching out for my bum leg. I'm going to boot him with my good one if he touches it.

"What are you doing?"

"I spent some time in the service as a medic."

Of course he fucking did.

My pissy mood assumes he also fixes random broken-down cars on the freeway, rescues wildlife on the weekends and probably volunteers his spare time at his Nan's nursing home.

Bastard.

"I won't tell you I'm a doctor, that was a long time ago. But let me see if I can help you out."

He goes to remove my shoe. I wonder why until I notice the cankle that's developed. My leg is swelling so fast I now have proof as to why my ankle sock feels so tight.

Strong looking hands remove my shoe and move toward my ankle.

"Neighbor, you touch that foot you're going to know what the other one feels like planted up your ass." I hiss through clenched teeth.

It hurts. Not a lot hurts me anymore but Jesus Christ this doesn't tickle. He removes his hat and scrubs a hand down his face before settling those angry blacks on me.

"Tell you what, *Elle.* You have two options. Fuckin' sit here, or let me help you back to your house. It's going to storm soon and I'm looking forward to spending the day on my couch, in peace after all the company that came here over the weekend. So, you want to sit here in a storm? Or do you want me to get you home?"

He already knows the answer, so do I. I'm a grown woman and, pride set aside, crawling home proves nothing right now other than the fact it would make me look like an idiot.

I give him the go ahead with a nod and notice him staring at my neck again. It's not hideous anymore, but purplish colored marks still mar the side of it.

I always figured if anyone asked, I could say it was from a seat belt in a car accident, but in light of what happened to my family, that would make me feel like an ungrateful lying asshole. I don't bother to explain, and Ryder doesn't bother to ask.

He moves to my side and puts one arm around my back and one under my legs before lifting me up. An ugly grunt sounds through my gritted teeth at the shock of pain that runs through my leg. I wasn't expecting the bridal carry, but damn if I can walk on one leg and use him as a human crutch.

"Sorry," he says as he stands up.

His morning scruff is in front of my face. He smells freshly showered so I'm assuming he chose to bypass the shaving part. Not that I mind. It suits him. He takes a deep breath that I assume is from exertion, but I quickly realize he's inhaling my hair that's in its usual untamed bird's nest atop my head with wisps flying in every which direction.

I reach my hand up to smooth my hair back from blowing in his face.

"Coconut," he says.

I don't answer or play dumb because I know what he's referring to. I simply hold onto his arms and try to stare at the water instead of his handsome face. It's times like this when I miss my old self.

The old me.

Jayne.

She wouldn't think twice about kissing him right now, flirting back or making the first move.

She'd dive in head first, going after what she wanted, not looking back.

Unfortunately, Elle Davidson has too many telling marks on her body, so she needs to stay under the radar for as long as possible instead of shedding her clothes with the good-looking man next door.

We reach my deck and he carries me up the steps. Norm is wagging her tail with lips curled up in that sweet smile only dogs can do.

"Hold on," his whiskey voice says from above me.

I reach my arms around his wide shoulders and do as he says.

He moves his arm away from my back. I reach up to put my arms around his neck so I don't fall. He uses his free hand to pull the screen door open and carries me into the house. I loosen my arms as he squeezes me tighter, leaning down to put me on the sofa.

He lingers for a moment but not in a creepy way. More so in a way that if I were more open he would no doubt be following me down on said couch right now. Reluctantly he slowly releases his arms from their hold and stands.
"I'll get you some ice."

He turns away from me and heads toward the kitchen.

"Any zip lock bags?"

THE UGLY ROSES

Those black eyes staring back at me from the other side of the island are wreaking havoc on my womanhood.

"To your right, second drawer from the top."

He busies himself in the freezer and comes back with the ice-filled bag wrapped in a dishtowel. His hands move toward my foot to remove my shoe again. The marks left on my ankles aren't nearly as bad as my wrists. They're barely noticeable, and with the grey sky and lack of lights on in the house I doubt he'll notice.

My shoe comes off, followed by my sock. I'd object to his help but the thought of leaning forward to ice my own ankle and calf, let alone getting the damn shoe off, is painful to even think about.

"I'd suggest seeing a Doctor to get it x-rayed and wrapped, but I have a feeling you'd decline."

He draws his eyes up from my foot to look at me.
I regard him with what I hope is a sincerity before I reply. "We both know nothing's broken. And aside from pain medication that I would refuse to take, I'm sure it's nothing a few days of rest won't cure."

He nods, "Your probably right Elle, but it should still be wrapped up so you don't strain the muscles any more than you need to. I have some at my house I can grab for you."

I cut him off before he can leave. If he leaves, I don't know if I'll let him back in the house.

"I have some in the closet in my bathroom, no worries. I need a shower anyway so it hits two birds with one stone."

His eyes turn dark and I now realize he may have taken that the wrong way.

"Thank you for the help," I say, quickly cutting off his wayward thoughts.

"Woman, you can't walk, how do you suppose you're going to make it to the bathroom?"

He has a good point, although I'm not about to let him bathe me—as tempting as that sounds.

"Tell you what, I'll carry you to the bathroom and you can see how well you make out from there. Not that I'm declining any offer to help you."

Damn, do I want him to.

He lifts me back up with ease and heads toward the hallway.

"First door on the left please," I start to say, but he's already reaching for the handle.

"May was like a second mother to me, so I've been in the bathroom here before."

He answers my unasked question. It's the first mention of Tom's late wife. I can relate to the sense of longing in his voice in regard to losing someone close to you. His deep voice brings me out of my head.

"Although I have to say, it didn't look like this when she lived here. I guess you could say she preferred the brighter colors."

He's referring to the new slate grey walls and dark vanity I installed. It's more modern, not that I needed it but if I don't keep busy my mind takes over.

"Yes, I guess I spruced it up a little. Or drabbed it down, however you want to look at it."

His deep chuckle vibrates through my body as he sets me down on the edge of the tub. His face is less than a foot from mine as he reaches down to remove my other shoe.

My black painted toenails stand out against the white tiled floor as he sets my foot down. He lifts his head to look into my eyes and the heat in them does not go unnoticed. He truly is one of the most beautiful men I've ever seen.

This close to him I can make out a few faint small scars around his hairline, and one on the lower portion of his jaw. A warm hand squeezes my thigh before he breaks the silence.

"I'll be back in twenty. I have some salve for muscle aches that should numb up your leg for a while."

He gives me one last look before he stands and leaves the bathroom. I say nothing as he closes the door. The attraction spoke for itself and I'm nowhere near ready to acknowledge it.

Chapter Eight

Showering was a circus act. My balancing on one leg limited what got washed, so aside from conditioning the bird's nest and only soaping what my hands could reach without bending over was the extent of the task.

After I've dried off, unsuccessfully, I throw on my robe and use the doorframe for balance so I can cross the hall to the laundry room. I know there's a clean pair of loose yoga pants and a few tanks in the dryer.

"Hold on, Elle."

I shriek at the sound of his voice, since I'm pretty damn certain it hasn't been twenty minutes.

"Cocksucker, you startled me!"

I take a deep breath while balancing in the hallway.

"I told you I'd be back. Maybe I should've brought some soap for that filthy mouth of yours?"

He doesn't say it like he's offended. No, he says it in a deep bedroom voice that suggests he'd really like to know what else I can do with said mouth.

A lot, I think to myself.

"Just caught me off guard," I say, a little more breathy than intended.

His long legs move toward me as he wraps an arm under my shoulder to help support my weight.
"Laundry room?"

He starts leading me that way after I nod. He's changed into a long sleeve Henley most likely because I'd soiled his other shirt with sand and sweat when he carried me home.

"Thanks," I manage to say as I close the door behind me, resting my forehead against it.

I hate this. I've never been the shy girl. Hell, I'm still not. A year ago, he would've been in the shower with me, and I wouldn't be searching the dryer for clothes twenty minutes later. Or at least I hope not. I think he can handle more than twenty minutes. Hell, he can probably handle hours judging by the build of his muscular body.

I throw on a white tank and my yoga pants, all the while trying not to whimper too loudly at the strain from trying to get my legs through them. There are no bras in here so I tie my robe back on over top and open the door to head back toward the living room.

He's standing in the hall waiting for me and once again leans down to lift me up. He carries me back to the sofa where he deposits me before doubling back toward the hallway.

"Where are you going?" I can't help but ask.

Before I get my answer, he's coming my way with a pillow from my bedroom and a towel from the bathroom. I guess he likes to help himself. He gently lifts my leg and places the pillow underneath it with the towel on top.

"You need to keep it elevated. And I'm pretty sure you don't want any of the muscle salve on your pillow."
Attractive and thoughtful. Also, two qualities you rarely find in the same man. Shit, he's going to be the end of me.

His fingers lightly run down my ankle and off my foot. It's insane to think that that simple a touch is practically my undoing. But when you haven't had physical contact with another human being for over a year, apparently it doesn't take much.

He lifts the pillow along with my leg and settles it on his lap. Salve in hand, he opens the lid and fingers a good portion of it before setting it down beside him and moving his hands toward my leg.

I hiss at the first contact of his fingers with my ankle. He smoothes it out using a gentle rhythmic pattern with his hands. I'm tempted to close my eyes and revel in the feel of him touching me, but I don't want to relax myself that much around him yet. I'm still wary around people, especially those of the opposite sex.

I didn't do much in terms of relationships after my family was taken from me, but I did have the odd random hook up for casual sex. Nothing meaningful—nothing memorable. Nothing that came close to how I feel right now this close to him on the couch.

I'm not sure how much time has elapsed before he speaks again. "You're different, Elle."

Wow, not sure where he's going with that one but way to break the ice with a woman.

"Gee, that a compliment neighbor?"

He looks up at my face and studies my expression before continuing. "A major part of the jobs throughout my life Elle have been studying people, learning what makes them who they are, sometimes before they know themselves. Understanding what they do, and what moves their going to make before they take the first step."

I can understand what he's saying. If he was a soldier, or whatever the hell it is he does, that would be one of the main attributes of the job, knowing the people around you, knowing your enemy better than you know your friends. I'm sure it's what keeps the men in this town alive overseas, able to come home to their families.

Sometimes I wish I could've been that observant of the people in my life and my surroundings.

If so, it may have saved me many days in hell.

It may have even saved my family.

"You don't like new people. Actually, I take that back. You don't like unknown people, especially not in groups because there's too many to try and read at one time. It makes you uncomfortable not knowing who they are and who you can trust."

He resumes his ministrations and moves toward my knee, keeping his eyes on mine.

"It takes a lot of time for you to trust someone, I get that. I can even understand it. You don't know me Elle but give it time and I promise I won't let you regret it."

I don't know where he's going with this but damn if he didn't hit the nail on the head with that one. As much as I'd love to have a come to Jesus with this intoxicating man, I need to remember why I'm here.

"Is there a point to this story, soldier?"

His hands stop their journey north and he turns his head back to face me.

"I'm not a soldier anymore, smartass." He says with more force in his tone than is necessary. "You would know that by now if you weren't trying to push me out your door as quick as I came in. I moved on from that part of my life a long time ago. I do security work now, and occasionally help train on base."

This is news to me, not that I thought I knew him at all. But seeing him jogging that day in Jacksonville near the base I put two and two together. Or so I thought.

"A long time ago. How old are you Mr. Callaghan?"

"Thirty-seven. Spent twelve years with the Marine Corps out of high school and the rest building my security business in Jacksonville. What about you Elle?"

The tone in his voice suggests his pride toward his company and he seems genuinely interested in my answer. Unfortunately there's not much I can tell him.

"You mean how old am I or what do I do?"

"How about both?" he sincerely asks.

Christ, if it were only so simple. However, the thought of saying I was a waitress (as per my social security info from Tiny) seems incredibly dull compared to my old life. Nothing against waitressing, it was my first job in high school and it kept my gas tank full. But it's a far cry from what I used to do.

"Thirty." That should do it, and perhaps we can bypass the rest.

Ryder nods his head. I think he understands he's not going to get much more than that.

"Fair enough, beautiful. Maybe one day you'll realize I'm not someone to be afraid of and you'll tell me the rest."

His genuine interest is heartbreaking. How long has it been since someone seemed genuinely interested in me, not just because they wanted to know my business. However, the beautiful comment puts my guard back up. I'm a miserable bitch most of the time. I'd say I'm ugly from my scars but I believe it's my heart that's the ugliest at this point. And if he's referring to my face as the beautiful part, I'm not sure I can take it as a compliment since it's a purchased and altered version of my former self.

"We'll see."

It's the best response I can give him. He has yet to break eye contact and resumes his massage of my calf muscles as I close my eyes.

"You want to throw the TV on?" he asks, most likely understanding we're not going to sit here and make small talk about our lives.

"I don't usually watch it, but Tom won't quit paying for it."

"Well, as much as you may find your dog's snore soothing, I'd prefer listening to the news."

He reaches over my legs for the remote on the coffee table.

"Don't you have your own TV to watch?"

I can hear the smile in his whiskey rough voice when he responds but I don't dare open my eyes. "The company is better over here. And before you assume that I'm giving you a compliment, which I'm certain you'd reject, I was talking about the dog."

The first genuine feel of a smile touching my face is the last thing I remember before falling asleep.

Attractive, thoughtful, and funny to boot.

I'm fucked.

* * *

I look out the window and see the sky is not quite dark yet. It's early evening and I'm feeling a nice little buzz after my dinner and drinks at Frank's.

Frank's is one of the few small dives to get a beer and a burger in this town and it's only about a ten-minute walk from home which is a bonus. I'm alone tonight which is normal. Once a week for as long as I can remember I indulge solo and entertain Frank with my wit. In turn he feeds me and makes sure my beer stays full. I quit coming in for a while after the accident that took my family, but soon realized a little bit of my old routine might do me some good.

Frank's was my first paying job as a teenager. He and his wife Megs were good to me, and we've remained close. The older couple acts as surrogate parents to just about everyone in this town. Not afraid to dish out advice whether you want it or not, and not afraid to call your spouse to come and haul your ass home when you've had too much to drink.

They're good people, and their little hole in the wall bar serves the best homemade burgers you've ever eaten.

"I'm outta here Frank, I'll see you next week."

He looks up from where he's polishing the bar.

"Don't remind me darlin'," he jokes, shaking his head.

"You love me old man, don't forget it. Give Megs a hug for me when you get home tonight."

I wave as I make my way out the door. My wit isn't accompanied with my usual bright smile, but I'm slowly getting there.

THE UGLY ROSES

Walking home alone in this town is not something to fear. I can't say everyone knows everyone here but it's pretty damn close. I guess you could say every fifth car you pass on the street is an acquaintance. I get a few waves as I make my way around the back of the establishment toward home.

I've walked this route a hundred times, from when I was a child until now. I used to live east of Frank's when I was a kid until I moved away to University. Now, and for the past eight years I've lived northwest in my own little two-bedroom bungalow on Peters Road.

I make my way through the parked cars out back, not rushing, just enjoying the calm summer night air when a hand reaches in front of me. I go to turn right and see who the arm belongs to, but his other hand grabs hold of my hair. I panic and swing my arm in front to brace myself on a lamp post and then bring the other back to elbow him in the ribs.

I hear a grunt but it doesn't slow the attacker down. I stomp on his instep and attempt to hit him again when his left arm wraps around my neck and the other one goes for my mouth.

I thrash and kick, do whatever I can to get loose from this person. His hand and arm squeeze tighter and I start looking around the parking lot for help. I see a man to my left in a cheap wrinkled suit staring at me with a look of shock on his face. Help me you stupid bastard! FUCKING HELP ME! I try to scream around the soaked cloth that's now smothering my mouth.

The stranger sees me struggling but makes no move to help, just watches with his car keys in hand, seeming to debate what the best course of action would be, but never actually moving from his spot on the pavement.

My vision begins to blur and my breathing shallows as my head lolls to the other side. I look at the van in front of me and see my attacker's reflection in the window, and then I see two of them as my vision doubles before it all goes black.

My shoulders are shaking and I feel dampness on my face.

"Elle!"

I'm afraid to open my eyes, afraid to see the reflection of his face in the window again. Afraid that it might not be a reflection this time, but the real thing and I'm back in that damn basement again, hanging and helpless with my arms tied above my head.

"Goddamnit woman wake up!"

Strong hands grip my shoulders tight, shaking me.

I jolt forward which causes me to face plant into a hard chest. I cry out at the pain that runs through my leg from the quick movement. My breathing is heavy and the wetness I feel on my cheeks confirm the tears that have run down my face. His arms surround me and I pull my hands up between us to push away from his chest.

"Don't move, Elle."

Ryder squeezes me tighter and begins running his hands up and down my back in a soothing motion. I lie to myself that the tears still coming down my face are from the nightmare, and not from how good his affection feels. This is the first hug I've experienced since the attack, the first warm set of arms to embrace me in almost a year. I take deep breaths and attempt to calm my racing heart.

We sit like this for a while, in no hurry to move and afraid to let go. He smells like fresh laundry and man. I turn my head into his neck and breathe in the subtle scent of his cologne. My thoughts are changing course. I want so bad to lick him, and I'm pretty close to doing so which forces me to put gentle pressure on his chest once again so I can distance myself from what would most likely be a huge mistake.

He slowly releases some pressure in the bands that are his arms around my back and looks down upon me. I see his mouth coming and close my eyes in rejection before I feel his lips on my forehead. I hear his own intake of breath, feeling his nose buried in my hair before he gently pulls back.

"Not sure what that was all about Elle, but if you want to talk about it I'll listen. I'll also help if you need it. Just ask."

Dammit he's kind. I've no idea why he's not married with four children yet, surely someone should've snatched this man up by now. I can hear Laura's opinion of him in the back of my mind while I sit here trying to figure him out. I know exactly what she'd say.

"Lacks in the sack, sister! No man is ever kind, good looking AND single. Especially at our age, unless he's gay. That's the only exception to men like him."

If he's gay, maybe we could be better friends if I didn't have to worry about him coming onto me or seeing me in my birthday suit. But after the heated looks in the bathroom and what I am certain is the so called 'chemistry' women talk about but never often experience, I'm left in a grey area.

I don't for one second think he 'lacks in the sack', but it wouldn't be the first time I spread my legs for a good looking, linebacker size of a man and was left unsatisfied.

You take them home expecting a nice English cucumber, but regrettably end up with a pickle.

Laura and I had a name for this, or I should say we had a label for them.

Gherkins.

That one, itty bitty small word was enough to sum up the morning after talk, which usually ended the talk because the description said it all.

"You haven't eaten anything in a while, I'll make some food. Maybe you can find something more interesting on television than the infomercials."

It's said as a request and I don't have the energy after my nightmare to protest. I'm also trying hard not to laugh, as I was just thinking about a certain food product.

Shit, an 'almost laugh'

I'm making progress.

I look at the clock in the kitchen and notice I was asleep for three hours. Did he stay here the entire time?

"What did you do while I was asleep?" I ask to his retreating back as he heads into the kitchen.

He looks over his shoulder and I'm certain I can see his lips twitch as he replies.

"Watched infomercials."

Lying bastard.

Chapter Nine

It's been a few weeks since Ryder witnessed my nightmare. He's tried to come around a lot more and I only reject him about half the time. I'm trying so hard not to let him get close but I'd be lying if I said I didn't enjoy the company. Other than helping my handicapped self to and fro he hasn't bothered to touch me much, which I can respect as much as I hate.

I know he wants to touch me, I can see it in his eyes when I catch him staring at me. I suppose I don't exactly put off that 'come touch me' vibe that most women do, or certainly most women in the presence of Ryder Callaghan.

That man could make a nun shed her habit. I've reiterated the friend vibe through my actions rather well and surprisingly he's followed suit. I respect him even more for that.

I see him through my kitchen window leaving his house. He's dressed in a dark black button-down shirt with the sleeves rolled up, dark jeans and black boots on his feet. I have no idea what his schedule is with work, he seems to be home more often than he is away lately. Perhaps owning your own security business allows you the pleasure to make your own hours. I've never asked and he's never supplied the information, simply says 'gotta get to work'. Part of my not making small talk leaves me in the unknown more often than not.

As much as the talk remains small, or void, I can say that life has felt a little lighter with him around. I haven't left the house much and for the first week he brought me groceries and spent some time on my couch in a comfortable silence while watching TV.

HARLOW STONE

He hasn't asked me any personal questions or mentioned the scars on my neck or wrists. Being who he is and what he does for a living, I'm pretty sure he has a good idea and knows the topic is sensitive or would be sensitive for most women. I'm not sensitive at all about it. More like I'm a hardened bitch when it comes to talking about it, which I won't because I don't want him to know who I am.

I watch as he pulls out of the drive and heads for town. I finish up my tidying and make to do the same. I've spent a little more time on my feet today than I should have; making up for lost time spent on the couch these past few weeks. When I push it my leg starts to hurt again, so I've embraced being a couch potato and spent a lot of time reading.

Now that the overdue cleaning and laundry is caught up, I decide to treat myself to surf and turf dinner in town. Well, take out surf and turf dinner I should say. I don't mind eating alone in public at all, but I know Saturday night and one of the town's only decent restaurants will be busier than I can handle. The loud crowds and half-drunk patrons leave me too many variables to assess.

I jump in the truck with Norma in tow. It's a nice night and even though my ankle is still tender I plan on taking advantage of the boardwalk to the restaurant with my dog. It's a nice place to walk and watch the sun set behind the large array of fishing and sail boats.

* * *

I park in the beach lot which isn't too far from the restaurant. I grab my bag and open the back door for Norma to jump out. The sun is setting and the wind is a little cooler. I've dressed in black tights, a flowing black tunic that cinches on the side of my waist, paired with my customary wrist cuffs and scarf.

My feet are covered in my knee-high black boots, once again with my knife stashed inside. Daytime footwear probably would have involved sandals of some sort, but being out later I feel more comfortable in what I like to refer to as my armor.

Don't draw unwanted attention to yourself. Blend in and be prepared at all times.

I replay Tiny's words of wisdom as I make my way toward the boardwalk, scanning my surroundings. Nothing makes the hairs on my neck stand up and I don't see many people about, just a younger couple and their children, and an old man out with his dog.

Making our way toward the restaurant, Norm sniffs her way through the sand while I walk on the old wooden planks. Snapper's, known for their steak and seafood, has a front entrance off the street and a large rear patio with an entrance next to the boardwalk.

This little harbor really is beautiful. Different sailboats and small fishing ships line the docks. It's big and busy enough that not everybody knows each other, but it still has that small town feel where you're not rushed and bussed from one place to the next without so much as a friendly smile.

I climb the small set of wood steps to the restaurant and ask the waitress for a menu, declining the offer for a table. I was right; the place is filling up rather quickly. I order the eight-ounce tenderloin with a lobster tail and mixed green salad to go. The waitress quickly enters my order while I take a seat on the bench to rest my leg, and watch Norm chase something in the water.

The sun is casting beautiful orange hues across the calm water and for a moment, I feel at peace. Water does that to me. Since I was a kid, being near the water was always something that would make me feel calm.

My peaceful moment doesn't last as long as I'd hoped when I notice my dog taking off at a run toward the opposite side of the restaurant.

"Norma, stay!" I yell in the deepest *I mean business* voice I can manage.

She never takes off, especially when we're in public. She slows down and wags her tail, still staring straight ahead. I go to remove my ass from the bench to bring her back when I see Ryder round the corner. He bends down to pet her while searching left and right, almost nervously. That is if a thirty-seven-year-old man who's probably killed people for a living has the ability to look nervous. That's the only way I can explain the expression on his face, unless it's confusion, not nervousness.

Maybe he's thinking, *what the hell is my hermit neighbor doing out of her house, in public no less?*

His eyes eventually land on mine and I give him a small tip up of my lips and chin, until I see a woman round the corner behind him. The same look is still plastered on his face until Ginger loops an arm through his and begins her trek toward the restaurant.

I recognize her from the bonfire Ryder had almost a month ago and she's dressed much the same as last time. If her heels were clear, someone could easily assume to stick a one-dollar bill in the side of her underwear- which are currently doubling as shorts at the moment.

They get closer and his eyes don't leave mine. I hear her mutter something about the smell of a wet dog, but I'm not paying attention to her. I'm too busy staring at him in his button-down shirt and jeans that are probably complimenting that beautiful behind of his.

The woman whips her ginger mop over her shoulder and prances toward the restaurant entrance, slightly wobbling on her fuck-me heels that weren't meant for the uneven boardwalk. She grabs a hold of his arm for support.

"This is why I suggested using the front entrance Ryder, I'm going to ruin my shoes or break my damn ankle." She whines, but he's not paying any attention to her.

His eyes are still glued on mine and I refuse to be the first one to look away. Not that I believe I have any sort of claim on him, I absolutely do not. I won't deny it stings a little to see him out with another woman, but I'm not naive enough to think that a man such as himself goes to bed alone every night. I certainly haven't invited him into mine, so he's bound to find what he needs elsewhere.

He comes to a halt at the bottom of the steps. I tip my chin toward him while Norm sits her ass beside his feet, waiting for more attention.

"Why is that dog following us everywhere?" She complains while grabbing onto the railing, trotting up the steps without him. Her focus settles on me and then back behind her to see why her date hasn't caught up with her quick enough, only to find his eyes glued to mine.

Ryder assesses me with a long look before speaking. He almost looks guilty even though we both know he has no reason to. His date has a body to kill for. So long as she doesn't speak when they get in bed tonight I'm sure he'll go to sleep with a smile on his face.

Our friendship has been purely platonic regardless of the sexual tension that always invades our space. I refuse to feel ill or act rude toward him in this moment. At the end of the day he's been nothing but kind to me, even if he is a bit of a bossy bastard sometimes.

"Elle." He finally tips his head toward me in greeting. Norm gives up on him and comes to sit next to me on the deck. I make a motion for her to stay as I stand to head toward the hostess station.

"Ryder."

I feel like I should say more, but I'm not sure exactly what. I turn toward the hostess who has my dinner ready to go and hand over enough money for the food and a tip. His date begins to whine that her feet are killing her and how long are they going to have to wait for a table. The hostess clears that up for her.

"I'm sorry ma'am but it's the dinnertime rush, if you'll give me a few more minutes I'll have a table ready for you. If you'd like to have a seat at the bar while you wait, I'll come get you when it's ready."

She huffs in annoyance and turns toward Ryder. "See, this is why I said you should have made a reservation."

She pouts out her ridiculous lips and places her hot pink fingers on her hip in annoyance. She eyes me from top to bottom before edging closer to Ryder to stake her claim.

I'm not threatened by her, I've never been the type to feel inferior regardless of whether the woman in question is more attractive or not. It's a petty game women play and I take no part in it.

Ginger eyes me with complete disdain before staking her territory. She wraps those arms tighter around his and settles her fake tits against his body.

"Who are you?" She asks with bite in her tone, lips soured in distaste.

Obviously she's upset she hasn't gotten one hundred percent of Ryder's attention since she walked up the steps.

I've always despised this category of women. I can eye them from a mile away. Call it judgmental if you want but seldom am I wrong about her type.

She's among the kind that will most likely fake a pregnancy to keep a man, or completely alter their personality to fit a certain man's likes. Then once they have moved in all of their hair care products and convinced you to add them to your benefits plan at work, the true personality really comes out. At that point it's more than a chore for the men to get out of it, since they've already moved them in.

This is why I always kept my own house, and always kept my benefits up to date. I also never moved more than a toothbrush and a change of clothes into another man's house.

I hate when things get complicated, and honestly I think people move way too quickly these days. Best to stand on your own two feet in case things go down the shitter.

I've seen awful things like this happen to many of my close male friends over the years, and a few good women as well. However, I'm certain Ryder is more intuitive and not throwing a rock on her finger anytime soon. I also don't picture him letting a woman crowd his space, therefore so long as he keeps it wrapped up he should be fine.

He's not out with this woman tonight to meet mom and dad for dinner. I have a level of respect for Ryder, and I know if he had good parents, he would respect them immensely. Knowing this I can say for certain this woman who cares more about her footwear than the beautiful view of this harbor is not someone Ryder, or much less any man, takes home to meet the parents.

This also means she's only good for one thing.

She's not incredibly intelligent, this much I know for sure. She's probably one of those women that sell weight loss products that never work, or skin cream that promises smooth skin but never really stops the wrinkles from forming and ends up giving you a rash.

I take in her looks closely. I'm guessing she's around my age, but the obvious overuse of tanning beds has made her skin look that of a forty-year-old. It doesn't suit her colored hair which I'm now assuming must be fake since she lacks the pale skin color to compliment it.

I'm not typically a judgmental bitch, but when I encounter a woman who's half-filled with plastic and wears that 'I'm better than you' attitude, I can't help but want to one up them in honor of the wholesome women in the world.

I can feel my old self bubbling to the surface, the sass along with a bit of the wit. Harley Green would have walked away by now, not looking for any form of confrontation or attention. Jayne O'Connor would have ignored her. She'd have grabbed her food and hit the boardwalk, never looking back because bitches like this weren't worth her breath.

But I'm not Jayne anymore, am I?

Nor am I Harley Green.

I'm Elle frigging Davidson, and I feel the need to introduce her.

'Who am I,' she asks.

She's about to find out.

I force my bright greens onto her dark blues, and plaster on a smile before I reply. "Who am I?"

I shake my head and let out a small, very fake little chuckle before continuing. "Sweetheart don't beat around the bush. You don't want to know who I am, or what my name is. What you're really dying to know and trying to figure out is if I've sucked his dick or fucked him yet? "

The shock slowly registers on her face and I don't let her respond before I continue. Nor do I acknowledge Ryder's sharp intake of breath.

"The answer is no. Now if you'll excuse me my dinner's getting cold."

I'm sure she'll still spend the evening wondering if I'm her competition, and I'll sleep well knowing it felt damn good to put the hooker in her place.

I look over my shoulder as I retreat toward the parking lot. "Enjoy your evening!" I say with a genuine smile on my face. Her shock is priceless and if I'm not mistaken Ryder looks like he's trying very hard to keep the laughter in, but his shaking shoulders give it away.

"How could you let that witch speak to me like that Ryder?" she whines.

I don't hear his answer because I'm halfway down the boardwalk with a dopey smile stuck on my face.

I smiled.

Maybe there's hope for me yet.

Chapter Ten

I'm curled up in the lounge on my deck and just opened my second bottle of wine. The first went down with my delicious dinner and now the dog is making do with the leftover lobster tail treat. She begins to wag her tail and look in the direction of Ryder's house. I heard his truck pull in a few moments ago and wonder if his date got cut short, or maybe he brought her back to his house.

I've noticed he stays out late sometimes and because of this I assume he goes to their house since I have yet to witness him bring a woman home for the evening. Not that I sit here and monitor his home but it's pretty hard not to notice since he's practically my only neighbor.

If the dog's tail doesn't wag when I hear footsteps, I would reach under my blanket for the gun I keep there. But the moment I hear the sound of earth crunching underneath heavy boots I know who it is.

His face holds a bit of humor as he makes his way onto my porch and leans against the railing, crossing his arms across his chest. He hasn't changed his clothing and he still looks fantastic. Not that I'm going to tell him that. I can smell his cologne being brought in with the breeze off the river, but this time it's mixed with a certain *eau de hooker* that almost takes my breath away, it's that repulsive.

It's like that cheap overpowering perfume mixed with roses the old birds used to sell out of magazines.

I hate roses after seeing them on my porch every day.

"You ruined my date," he says fighting a smile. I'm now fighting my own too.

"Handsome, you and I both know that hooker would have sucked your dick in the parking lot with, or without the dinner. So if your date was ruined, it was by your lack of attempt to console the girl after I did nothing other than state the fact we haven't shared a bed together."

He cocks his head to the side contemplating his next words.

"So, since my bed is now cold for the night are you offering to keep it warm?" he asks, a smirk ever present on his face.

"You had a warm and willing body at the restaurant Ryder, you should have kept it. However, the scent of her cheap perfume coming off your clothing is enough to make even *me* want to shower, so I would suggest if you warm a bed with that woman, let it be hers so you don't need to replace your sheets and air out your household after she leaves. I have disinfectant in my cupboard that smells more pleasing than that."

He's quick to come back at me. "I wasn't with her for the perfume, but I'll keep that in mind."

His black eyes bore into mine, he's trying to see if this conversation will make me jealous, but it's not. If anything I feel more empowered that Ginger didn't get invited back to his house for the night. Then again, I have yet to see him bring a woman home for the night but he has spent a few out late.

I've begun to know him better since we started hanging out, not that I really *know* him. But I know enough to turn the tables around after he pegged my demeanor that day weeks ago on my couch about my inability to trust people.

"You don't bring them back to your house though, do you Ryder? You like your space, you like your privacy, and as much as you enjoy a night of mindless fucking, you're not willing to be the bad guy that kicks them out of your bed at night. You'd rather be the one to leave, less trouble that way."

I know I'm right, and I half expect him to deny it. To my surprise he doesn't.

"You're right. But the only reason you're right is because you see in me a part of yourself, which tells me you do the exact same thing. Don't you Elle?"

He asks it like a question but he already knows the answer. I suppose we're on a roll with this conversation so fuck it, I'll indulge.

"I've never been booted from a bed and I've never been left. I do the leaving, Ryder, and I also do the choosing. However, I never shit where I eat. That helps me avoid situations like what happened at the restaurant tonight. I don't do the catty bitch routine, and as you noticed I don't fight over men. So, I suggest in the future you take my advice and find your pussy in the next town over, otherwise poor Ginger might get the wrong idea when you run into your neighbors."

I shoot him a wink.

My tone is playful, as is his when he speaks again.

"That's where your wrong, vixen. The 'Gingers' of the world don't give a fuck where I've been or who I've been with. Until it's their turn, all they care about is that I'm there one hundred percent until they get what I can give them and then get the hell out. I don't cuddle, and I don't stick around to whisper sweet nothings in their ear or drink their coffee in the morning. I make that clear from the get-go. But I'm not a total prick and a man's gotta eat, hence the trip to the restaurant beforehand."

Wow.

I'd like to say I believe him but his attentive behavior toward me and my bum leg this week proves otherwise. The man has a kind heart; he just chooses who he shares it with.

Although I'm not going to mention that to him right now, I'll table it and analyze the way he behaves differently with me as oppose to other women much later.

In private.

Maybe with a vibrator.

"I never pegged you for prince charming, handsome, but if you think a woman like her is going to let it go you're sadly mistaken. I'm betting at least twice on the drive to her home she showed some sort of remorse for her tone earlier in the evening and still asked you to come in for after dinner drinks."

I see the shock in his eyes before it quickly disappears. I know I'm right. I know how those bitches work. She can ramble all day about how it's just a quick screw, but that doesn't mean when she's alone she's not wishing for more and wondering what their offspring would look like.

"Just because she asked me in for a drink doesn't mean she wants more from me than fucking. Elle, as I said I'm clear with them from the get-go," he says with a firm tone.

"Are you trying to convince me, or yourself Ryder? You know what, don't answer that," I say on a sigh.

We're getting too involved in this conversation and I feel like I've reached my weekly quota for speaking. I'll blame it on the wine. He's silent for a few moments and the only sound is the low blues music coming from inside my house.

He slowly moves off his perch at the railing and makes his way toward the back door.

"What are you doing?"

I ask as he opens my screen door to head into the house. He turns around and points a finger at me while speaking.

"My night was cut short, and as much as I would rather have my dick buried down the back of someone's throat right now, which I'm sure you're not volunteering to do, I'm going to raid your fridge of beer since I still believe that it's mostly your fault," he says, turning around to head inside.

"What the hell neighbor?" I screech from the lounge. He breezes back out the door as quickly as he went in and with more than one beer in his hand. He moves around to the other side of the lounge, takes a seat and removes his boots before reclining back beside me and bringing an opened beer to his mouth.

"I don't recall inviting you for drinks, and there's a perfectly good table over there for you to park your ass at," I tell him with less bite in my tone than I hoped for.

This double-wide lounge always seemed huge to me. Now that he's sprawled out on it less than a foot from me it seems very small. I'm thankful I left the back in a sitting position and not reclined down like I do when I take my naps out here.

"You know, as much as you can be a bitch Elle, I'm not afraid to admit that your company is more refreshing than Tina's."

I'm taken aback by his compliment but focus on something else. "Who the hell is Tina?" I ask. Not in a jealous way, but in a way to remind him that I don't know anyone here.

He chuckles deeply, vibrating the lounge we're resting on.

"Tina is 'Ginger', vixen," he says around a smile.

"HA! Of course her name is Tina. And my company is more refreshing because I'm not falling all over your dick to make up for my lack of brain cells or inability to carry on a decent conversation."

I shake my head in disgust. Brainless women ruin it for the smarter ones such as myself. Mind you, if they have a mouth like a vacuum cleaner, I suppose IQ doesn't really matter. He confirms this on his reply.

"She has other talents," he tries to say in a serious tone.

"Yup, and I'm sure Hoover is contacting her about said talents in regard to their next prototype."

This earns me a full belly laugh and it's so goddamn beautiful I can't help but stare at him and fuse this moment to memory. It's a snapshot moment I not only find myself taking a mental picture of, but I'm also analyzing the irregular palpitation that just zapped through my stone-cold heart.

The lounge is shaking and his eyes are shining from unshed tears. I don't know when he stops laughing but he's staring at me now, probably wondering why I've been staring at him so long. He looks like he wants to ask me something important and I rack my brain to try and find something to say that will make light of the situation.

He beats me to it.

"Can I have a smoke?"

It won't be the first time I've seen him indulge but it's not often.

"I don't know, I remember a certain surgeon general warning me of the side effects from smoking, most importantly death. You sure about that?"

He leans over and reaches across me to the pack on the table. Not breaking eye contact. His arm brushes my chest when his hand reaches for a smoke on the table and he begins to pull back. Eyes still on mine, he's so close I can smell the beer on his breath. I can also smell Ginger's perfume and it's about to make me gag.

"Help yourself to the smokes. But if you're staying you need to take off the shirt."

Heat blooms in his eyes and I cut him off before he can lose himself to that train of thought.

"It stinks, like cheap perfume. If you want to stay here and drink with me you lose the button down. Or I may just lose my stomach contents onto it."

Black eyes study me before he lights up his smoke. He sits up and begins unbuttoning his shirt to reveal a white t-shirt underneath. I don't watch, or at least I pretend I don't. His beautiful long fingers make quick work of the buttons. His hair is messy in a just fucked sort of way, but obviously he hasn't been so he must have run his hands through it or drove here with all the windows in his truck down.

Dammit, I need to stop.

"I'm going to grab another bottle of wine."

I say as I throw off the blanket and move to get off the lounger. I weave a bit realizing I've drank almost two bottles but then come to my regular conclusion which is I don't give a shit what other people think of me.

I hit the ladies room then choose my favorite Pinot Grigio and head back out to the porch. Ryder is leaning back, relaxed, smoke in one hand—and my gun in the other.

Fuck.

He holds it up in question as I make my way onto the lounge. I don't turn to face him, I refill my glass and reach over to remove the gun from his hand. He doesn't let go right away so I look at him. His eyes are roaming over my face and I know he's trying to form the proper words to ask me why I sit alone on my lounge at night with a gun hidden under the blanket.

"It's not my business," he says.

I cut him off.

"No, it's not your business Ryder. I own a gun, two actually. And it helps me sleep at night. That's all you need to know."

I say all this looking directly into his eyes and not backing down.

"Elle, you have half a mind to what I do and what I've done for a living. I have no problem; in fact, I'm glad you look after yourself. I'm not judging you, beautiful."

He's so relaxed, legs out and crossed at the ankle, white shirt stretching across his beautiful tan skin. Beer in one hand, smoke now in the other. He just looks so at...home? But he still seems somewhat sad, or maybe disappointed.

"Then why the long face soldier?"

I tip my head to the side, studying him.

He calmly replies with a look of concern, his eyes never leaving mine.

"The long face, beautiful, is because the numbers are ground off. It's one thing to own a gun, keep it locked in a box in a closet somewhere like most women or stupid people do, a place where they can never get to it in time. But when it's beside you at night, while you're peacefully sitting on your deck enjoying a glass of wine? It means you're worried someone is coming to hurt you. That's why I have the long face."

His kind words said with so much sincerity forces me to remove my gaze from his. I reach for my smokes and light one up to occupy my hands. Half of me wants to bolt in the house and slam the door, but I know that will just raise more questions. The other half wants to fling myself into his warm body that now lacks the horrid scent of Tina's perfume and let him hold me until the sun comes up.

I blow out the smoke and think hard before I reply, hopefully in a tone that suggests I'm just your average overly-prepared American citizen. Not a Canadian on the run from someone who wants her dead.

"I think it's smart to be prepared for the unknown, Ryder. Bad things happen every day and I'd be stupid not to be prepared, single woman living alone and all," I nonchalantly say, hoping he buys it enough to drop the subject.

I also know he's not stupid, and even if he does drop it the wheels will still be turning in his head.

"Like I said before Elle, one day you'll realize that I'm someone you can trust. I just hoped it wouldn't take so long," he says, defeated.

I look him in the eye to gauge his mood. He takes a long swig of his beer then stares out at the water. My tone is as soft as my raspy voice will allow when I reply.

"You're a good man, I know that. But I don't fully trust anyone, Ryder. The sooner you realize that, the quicker you'll be able to drop the effort. I'm not someone to waste your time on. What you see is what you get. You need to accept that or move on."

I've downed another half of the bottle by now and my speech is becoming a little slurred. I don't know what else to say to him, he wants something I'm not able to give. Does he deserve the truth? Absolutely. He's a good man; I know this down to my bones. But just because I crave him desperately at this point, doesn't mean it would be a smart decision to bare my all. I will not put someone in danger because of my past ever again.

He spins to face me and I know I'm not going to like what's coming. The flare in his eyes and his deep intake of breath are the only notice I get before he drops the proverbial bomb on me.

"I'm not asking you to marry me, woman. I was asking for some fuckin' truth! And if you need my help, I'm here. That's the point I'm trying to get across. Spin it however you want to Elle, but something scares you enough at night that you feel the need to protect yourself 24/7. By that I mean it hasn't escaped my knowledge that you pack a knife in your boots when most women are wearing flip flops. You wear a scarf in public to hide marks on your neck, which are obviously caused by something painful you refuse to talk about; otherwise you wouldn't feel the need to hide them."

He takes a deep cleansing breath before continuing, eyes a little softer now.

"There's not a single personal item in that cottage that suggests who you are or what you like. You stay in the shadows, Elle. Only a person with something to hide does that. You're either hiding from someone or hiding from yourself. Which is it Elle?"

I can feel the angry tears building behind my eyelids. I want to scream, I want to run, and I want to hit something so bloody hard the pain in my knuckles will take away the pain piercing through my cold heart right now.

I go to stand up and he grabs me by my arm. Not enough to hurt, but enough to make a point. I turn my steely eyes on him and say in the deepest voice I have.

"Let. Me. Go."

The tears break through. They fall past my cheeks and run down my face. He grabs me by my other arm and pulls me across the lounge until his face is inches from mine.

"No. Answer the question, Elle. Fuckin' tell me, please. Play the tough bitch all you want, I'm sure it works with a lot of people but not with me."

He's shaking me now, his breath heavy on my face.

"How many times have I been here? It's been almost a month! How many times have I startled you and watched your hand fly up under the pillow on the couch? You think I'm stupid?" He shakes his head, "I knew what you had hiding under there, saw it when I was watching you sleep instead of watching fucking infomercials, Elle! Confirmed it a long time ago when you got up to hit the washroom. So, tell me, how many more times were you gonna let me startle you before I startled you so fuckin' bad one day that you pull that gun out from under your pillow in the middle of a goddamn nightmare and shoot me? Answer the goddamn question Elle!"

"I don't know, all right! I don't know. You afraid of me hurting you?" I yell back in his face. "Then don't come around anymore! Problem. Fucking. Solved!"

I wrench out of his grip and jump up off the lounger. The wine and my anger toward him cause me to hurl my empty wine bottle into a tree at the end of the porch. I hate losing my shit, hate it. But he's pushed me too goddamn far.

Tears are streaming down my face as I swing the screen door open and head into the house. I reach out to slam the main door behind me but it stops dead because his solid body is blocking its path.

"Get the hell out of my house Ryder."

I'm still heaving, not from exertion, from anger. I'm not yelling anymore. I'm above that, I rarely ever yell. It takes a lot of shit coming at me to do so.

"Not happening, Elle."

He gets in my space and I'm backed against the wall. "I don't have two words left to say to you. *My life* is not your business Ryder Callaghan. Get that through your thick fucking head!"

He leans down low and puts his face inches from mine, arms braced against the wall on either side of my head.

"I will make your life my goddamn business Elle. I will be in your face, every minute of every goddamn day until you understand that I'm not someone you should be afraid of, but someone you can trust. I'll keep saying it until your fuckin' ears bleed. Mark my words woman. When I set my mind to something, I don't fucking quit. And my neighbor— *my friend*— harboring so much fear that she has to sleep with a gun under her pillow at night is something that I'm setting my fucking mind to."

He sort of lost me at friend. That was incredibly sweet and almost melts my heart, but I choose to hold onto my anger and push forward like the stubborn cold bitch I am.

"Ryder riding in on his white horse to save the little 'ol neighbor? Fuck you! I never asked for your help and I don't want it! My life is just fine the way it is. I've been on my own for a long time Ryder, and goddamn it I can look after myself!"

He reaches forward and yanks the scarf off my neck, I grab at his hands but he's too fast. As soon as it's gone my hands instinctively fly to my throat. He takes the opportunity to grab my wrists and yanks off my bracelets.

I swing my leg up to connect with his groin, not wanting to hurt him, but not wanting him to see anymore. He's too fast and forces his body into my own against the wall. He grabs hold of both wrists and brings them up between our bodies.

"Is this protecting yourself, Elle?" His hands hold firm, forcing my wrists in front of my face. I know what they look like, he doesn't have to show me.

Struggling is futile; I couldn't pull my arms out of his grasp if I tried. His eyes are boring into mine and he lets one wrist go but grabs hold of them both with his right hand and pulls them tight to his chest.

His left hand reaches out and he runs his fingers gently from the base of my neck down to my collarbone. The harsh light of the kitchen doing nothing to hide the purple marks there. His breathing is ragged, and he takes a deep breath before continuing.

"Are these you protecting yourself too, Elle?" He asks in a softer tone. Kind hands touch me, but angry eyes bounce back between the marks and my face. Nobody aside from Doctor Revere has touched them. The Doc didn't know exactly what happened, and the old man's hands were much different from the hunk of testosterone currently pinning me to the wall.

"You're a strong woman Elle, I know that. But however these happened, whatever bastard did this, I know as well as you that he was strong enough to overpower you and make this happen. And that, beautiful, is why I'm asking you to trust me. Why I'm asking you to let me help you."

He cups my cheek and rests his forehead on mine. I close my eyes and savor the feeling of someone so close to me. Someone I want to trust, but fear to.

I lean into his palm and let his thumb wipe the tears from under my eyes. I want to let him comfort me but needing to feel that makes me feel weak.

"There's nothing left to help, Ryder." I admit softly in defeat. At this point I feel the only thing he could do would be to warm my bed. But that could mean his untimely death if I'm found again. If he starts digging into who I am.

He slams his hand against the wall in frustration.

"You're wrong Elle, so wrong." He puts his hand around my throat and lifts my chin up. I don't get a chance to protest before his wet mouth is on mine. He moves his hand around the back of my head into my hair and pulls me closer.

I'm stunned; it's been a long time since I've been intimate with someone, over a year to be exact. I don't feel like an active participant in the kiss and truth be told I'm afraid to open my mouth and let him in.

His hand that was holding my wrists lets go and moves down my ribs, over my hip and squeezes. It's enough to make me gasp and he uses the opportunity to plunge his tongue into my mouth.

I can't hold back anymore, I reach my arms up around his neck and climb my legs up his body. His hips hold me securely to the wall while we devour each other's mouths. Tongues searching, his light stubble scratches my cheek. I push my fingers into his long hair and pull the roots tight while my tongue explores every inch of his delicious mouth.

His hands move underneath my ass and he gently squeezes and massages through the threadbare yoga pants. I moan into his mouth which encourages him further and he pushes his groin into mine, plastering me to the wall.

I can't hold back the whimper that slips from my mouth, or the rush of dampness that seeps into my panties. I move my arms down his chest as his start to creep up under the back of my shirt, it's enough to bring me back to reality and I pull my mouth from his and push my back hard into the wall to halt the movement of his hands.

"Stop."

I hate to say that word. I'm panting and I can feel the sweat coating my brow. I'm afraid to open my eyes and see the rejection on his face at my command. I feel his forehead touch mine and he speaks before I push him further away.

"I'll stop, Elle. Anytime you ask me to, I'll stop," he says in a deep raspy voice.

I open my green eyes and peer into his blacks, thinking he's way too good for someone with my baggage. Baggage I won't let him help me carry, or anyone else for that matter.

"But let it be known, this is happening Elle. You feel it just as much as I do. It may not happen tonight, or tomorrow. Mark my words woman it will. And I promise you won't regret it."

He seals his mouth to mine once more before untangling my legs from around his body, setting me gently on the floor. His eyes roam my face before he kisses me tenderly on the forehead and heads out the door.

I'm stunned. My head resting back against the wall, I close my eyes and take a deep breath into my lungs, wondering how the hell that all just happened. I hear the porch door and open my eyes, turning my head that way.

Ryder walks back into my kitchen and places the empty bottles on the counter. He stalks over to me and looks down on my face tenderly as he takes my hand. I feel the weight of the gun settle into my palm and close my eyes. His lips touch mine lightly once again before he silently heads out the door.

For the first time in a long time, I dread the thought of sleeping alone.

Chapter Eleven

I wake with a mild ache in my head and roll over to look at the clock. It reads ten. I believe I tossed and turned until four a.m. which means I roughly got six hours of sleep. In my books it's a good start to the day.

I make my way to the kitchen to start the coffee after my bathroom routine. I turn on the old rock station that I like and peer out the window while the coffee brews.

It's mild, partly sunny and if my ankle wasn't still slightly buggered I'd consider a jog. It's been three days since my fiasco with Ryder and I haven't seen his truck home since then, I don't take it personally. Actually, I was glad for the reprieve instead of being bombarded with questions the next morning. Last night's beer bash—party of one—helped drown that night from my mind.

I take my java out to the deck and get ready to settle in before I screech in mild shock.

"What the hell, Callaghan! Were you expecting that bullet of mine to pierce through your skin sooner rather than later? Jesus!" I gasp with a hand to my chest.

He's successfully startled the shit out of me. And I may just think about shooting him, if he weren't shirtless and carrying a ladder.

"Morning, sunshine. I knocked, but no answer. Been here for an hour, and when I checked to make sure you were alive since you went to sleep with the door unlocked, you were still out. The gutters on the house need to be cleaned out," he nonchalantly says like it's no big deal he's over here to do work, or the fact he felt he could just barge into my house, door locked or not.

"Yeah, okay, tell you what. You leave the ladder, I'll finish my coffee and then when I get the energy after cup number two, I'll haul my ass up there and clean them. When I'm done you can come back and get the ladder."

He shakes his head in exasperation.

"And my dog never barked, so I knew there wasn't an evil intruder, smartass," I say to make me seem like less of an idiot for sleeping with the doors unlocked while living next to some sort of security specialist.

"I'm here Elle and I have nothing else to do today. It's not a big deal."

If I didn't find foot stomping childish, I'd do it right now.

"It is a big deal Ryder. Just because I let you stick your tongue down my throat does not give you the right to get all domesticated on me and clean my gutters! Trust me. I'm capable enough to do it myself."

I park my ass at the table with my coffee and smokes, and silently fume while I wait for him to leave.

He doesn't.

He storms his beautiful body up my steps. He has a hat on today which is rare, it's holding his hair back from his eyes and he has a pair of work gloves shoved in the back pocket of his jeans. His chest is mildly scattered with a light brush of hair and I realize I finally get to see where his sleeve of tattoos ends.

The tribal fire runs up his arm, over his shoulder and onto his left pectoral. The other sleeve ends at the top of his shoulder. There look to be quite a few words and some shapes of private meaning maybe scattered throughout. But without a close inspection I can't be sure.

I'm thanking my usual hangover morning attire of sunglasses, so he doesn't know how much I'm ogling his body right now. I notice he has something that looks like Sanskrit running down his ribs through a complex design I can't see the rest of because his pants are on.

Dammit!

He cuts me from my filthy thoughts of removing his pants, and any other clothing that would restrict me from viewing his linebacker body.

"I've been cleaning the gutters on this house since I was old enough to climb a ladder. So whether you can do it or just want to do it doesn't matter. I've helped Tom on this place for decades, and when I'm not around to do it I make sure to find someone who can."

He's leaning down on the table in front of me, hands flat against the top. Face close to mine. I'm trying incredibly hard to keep a calm facade, but I know I'm going to fail miserably since I haven't had my coffee yet, so I speed this along.

"Well soldier, I guess you're cleaning the gutters while I enjoy my java. Don't let me hold you up."

I wave him off and his lips quirk at the side, his two-day growth does nothing to hide it. I'm still ogling him behind my sunglasses but my head is turned to the side so he won't notice.

He straightens himself from the table and comes around to my side. Bending down, he puts his fingers under my chin and brings his face close before sealing his lips over mine.

117

Hard.

He pulls away just as quickly and leaves the porch to resume setting up his ladder.

I have nothing to say, apparently he doesn't either. So I resume my morning routine of coffee and cigarettes with a little more to stare at than just the water this time.

When he makes his way to the other side of the house, I decide to use the opportunity to make some lunch. I don't often eat breakfast but after a few hours of being awake and a night of drinking, I'm starting to get hungry.

I check the fridge and decide to make homemade burgers and a salad. After mixing up the meat and throwing together a quick salad I take it all out to the deck on a tray and fire up the grill.

The burgers are almost done, and the fresh buns that I've brushed with seasoned butter are almost toasted when Ryder comes walking up the steps.

"The downspout needs to be replaced on the east corner and a few brackets as well, but other than that I got all the shit the squirrels put in there cleaned out."

I look at him over my shoulder. His skin is glistening with sweat. He produces a shirt from somewhere to wipe his face off. I realize I don't have my sunglasses on and move my eyes back to the barbecue before I speak to him.

"Lunch is almost ready. If you want I'll go pick up what you need from town afterward," I say as I pull the buns and meat off the barbecue.

I feel heat but it has nothing to do with the barbecue. His lips settle on the top of my head, his chest presses against my back.

"How about you feed me, then I'll go pick up the parts since I need a few things at the hardware store for my place anyway," he says playfully.

I feel him breathe in the scent of my hair, which reminds me I have yet to shower today having just washed my face and brushed my teeth.

"Alright, well grab whatever you want to drink out of the fridge while I finish up here."

He gives my waist a gentle squeeze, before entering the house.

I have the plates made up and many condiments set out since I have no idea what he likes on his burger. He comes out with two beers and places one in front of me before sitting down at my little square table.

"Smells awesome, Elle. I'm starved."

He loads his burger up with mayo, mustard and tomatoes before digging in.

I cut my burger in half, adding the same mayo mustard and tomatoes to one side before cutting the other half up on a separate plate. I set it down on the deck for Norma who waddles over to enjoy lunch as well.

"Damn beautiful, this is good. I can also see why your dog waddles." He adds with a smirk. I look down at my healthy girl, who's content with the meal she just inhaled, curling up by Ryder's feet.

All one hundred and twenty pounds of her.

"She's healthy. And it's easier cooking for two than just one, so she eats well." I give a small smile her way as I dig into my food.

"Yeah, I can see that. How old?" he asks around a swallow of meat.

"Seven this summer," I muse, thinking most large breed dogs like her don't live much longer than ten.

We eat in companionable silence for a while before Ryder speaks. "Thanks for lunch beautiful. I'm going to head into town, so I can finish fixing the eaves before the rain hits. It's supposed to storm for the next few days."

He moves to stand, and to my surprise takes his plate and empty bottle with him. I follow behind with the tray and my dishes to find him putting his in the dishwasher.

"Thanks," I say stunned, as I put the tray on the counter.

His arms come around me and settle on either side of the counter with his chest close to my back. His heat feels good and his smell takes over my senses.

"Don't thank me. If someone cooks for you, it's common knowledge as far as I'm concerned to help clean up," he says with his lips on top of my head. Maybe they always end up there because I'm much shorter than he is.

"I'll be back in a bit."

He places a chaste kiss in my hair and heads for the door. I don't say bye, I'm still floored that in my thirty years this is the first man I've ever cooked for who has put his dishes away. Jesus.

* * *

I've showered and dressed in my typical home attire, which usually consists of yoga pants or a long peasant style skirt.

Today, it's going to be the skirt since it's still sunny and he's yet to mention the ankle marks.

I have on one of my trademark tanks, nondescript, black and with built-in shelf bra. Out of habit I put on my wrist cuffs and decorative scarf around my neck. I leave my hair in its natural chaos. Large loose dark brown curls flow down my back as I apply my usual light layer of makeup—eyeliner, mascara, lip gloss and a bit of bronzer.

I hear Ryder working on the house again and decide to finish folding all the laundry I washed yesterday.

My head is in the dryer when suddenly I feel a warm hand near my ass. I jump in shock, banging my head on the dryer door.

"Shit!" I shout while pulling my hand to the top of my head.

"Fuck! I'm sorry I wasn't thinking about your head!" I can hear the humor in his tone.

"No shit? You're a man! You see an ass and the rest of your brain cells go dormant!" I hiss at him, holding the goose egg that is quickly forming on my skull.

"I'm sorry," he says, fighting a smile I want to smack off his face. "How about since you cooked me lunch, you let me cook you dinner. My way of apologizing."

He brushes the hair out of my face and moves his hand over the lump on my head, grimacing slightly. He can feel it already. His thoughtfulness is overwhelming, and I need to step back for a minute.

"It depends what you're cooking. And if I come, you need to keep some distance Ryder because honestly, I don't know if I can handle this thing between us right now, and I don't know if I'm ready for it," I say with conviction because as much as I want what he has to offer it's still the truth.

He studies my face, looking for truth in my words before he nods his head. "I plan on steak, since you don't seem to be the typical bird eater that will only touch a salad. I assume that's good with you?"

"If you only would have offered me a salad I wouldn't have come." I say, deadpan.

He smiles and it's beautiful, like my cold heart does that ridiculous palpitation thing that makes me think I might have a heart-attack-at- thirty-kind-of-beautiful.

Hands still holding my head, he replies.

"I can give you space Elle, but if space means not seeing you and not being near you then that's not fuckin' likely to happen unless I'm away for work. I won't push you, ever. If I make you uncomfortable, you let me know. But until you tell me it's too much and my hands on your body don't feel right anymore, then I think the pace we have going right now is perfectly fine."

He leans down and presses his lips to my forehead before leaving the laundry room.

"Be over by seven, Elle."

I'm left speechless, the man certainly has a way with words.

Chapter Twelve

I make my way over to Ryder's with Norma and a bottle of wine. She leads the way since she's been here before and prances up the deck before letting out a low bark at the back door. I make my way up the steps onto his deck, which is way cooler than mine might I add.

His dark grey deck is complimented by a large sectional, deep red in color. The ottomans with matching cushions all push together to make it a bed.

Convenient, I think to myself.

His graphite colored home has wrought iron designs here and there under the extended roof which covers half of the deck. The other half is open to the elements and boasts a few loungers with a hot tub and small propane fired centerpiece. The true fire pit is in the sand near the water. The kind you roast marshmallows on and get out the folding chairs to sit around.

I hear the screen door open and turn my head to watch Norma prance into his house like she owns the damn place. "You don't need to let her in your house, she sheds a lot this time of year," I say to him.

He doesn't reply, simply grabs my hand and pulls me into the house.

His large stainless and black kitchen is the first thing I see and it's stunning. Dark granite countertops and sleek glass backsplash, large propane grill and double oven.

"Jesus Ryder, did you marry a chef, or do you just really love to cook in your spare time?"

I ask while taking everything in. He hasn't answered and seems lost in thought, so I don't push him. Then I remember him telling me that he doesn't bring his one-night stands home so maybe he's never had a woman complimenting him on his decor?

He turns slowly, looking like he still doesn't have an answer and shrugs his shoulders. I have a feeling I may have hit a nerve although I'm not sure which one and I'm also not one to pussy foot around something.

"What's with the long face again, soldier? It's a beautiful kitchen. I was giving you a compliment, but you look like I kicked your dog."

He shakes his head in exasperation, thinking before he speaks.

"I thought I'd share this place with someone once. It didn't work out that way. It was a long time ago; I've done some upgrading since then, as you can see."

He looks lost down memory lane. I don't need him to elaborate since that would make me a hypocrite, so I try to lighten the subject.

"Well handsome, feel free to blow me away with your culinary skills in your master chef kitchen. I'm starving."

It seems to have done the trick and he moves toward the fridge. The steaks are already resting on the counter and I take the opportunity to assess the rest of my surroundings while he works.

He has a large vaulted ceiling and a loft walkway, leading to bedrooms I assume up top. The whole space downstairs is open which I can handle, and I take in the large sectional in front of a stone fireplace with a huge man-sized television above it.

On one side of the room is a staircase leading up—not down, thank fuck. And on the other side is a small hallway leading to what I assume would be the bathroom and laundry room. I'm positive there's no basement here since most of the homes here were originally built on stilts but I have to ask.

"Your place is much bigger than mine. Do you have a basement too?"

I cringe just saying the word; my voice broke a little which I hope he doesn't notice. He looks up at me from where he's chopping up some broccoli and replies.

"No basement. I added the loft about ten years ago."

I nod thoughtfully and thank the heavens that I don't need to bail on dinner. I finally put the wine on the counter and he turns around to get me a glass from the cupboard.

"Thank you. Do you want some?" I ask as I open it.

He places two glasses in front of me, so I take that as a yes and pour us each a good portion.

"Do you want me to help with anything?" I ask.

His answer comes in the form of his hands around my waist as he hoists me up onto the counter near his workspace.

"Nope. Just keep me company."

He hasn't kissed me or made any grand touching gestures since I got here so I guess he listened to my little rant about space earlier. I glance around and notice Norma curled up on a dog bed near the bottom of the stairs.

"Did you have a dog?" I ask, seeing mine sound asleep and perfectly at home.

125

"Nope," he replies shortly, making me wonder where he got the dog bed.

"So you just pulled that old dog bed out of the attic when she started coming around?" I ask sarcastically.

He stops chopping and wipes his hands on a towel. He moves in front of me and I take in his clothing; dark grey t-shirt, dark jeans and bare feet. My eyes make it back up to his face before he cages me in with his hands on my thighs.

"She comes here every morning after her run in the bush and I let her in. She'd lie in five different places on the wood floor before finding a comfortable spot on a rug somewhere and passing out. I bought her a dog bed since she seems to take her morning naps here. Now, she doesn't move around five times, just goes to the bed and stays there without tracking sand all through the house. That okay with you beautiful?"

His thoughtfulness is astounding so I nod my head and tell him so.

"Thank you, I'm sure she appreciates that since she knows she's not allowed on the furniture, and her hips ache after she runs," I tell him.

Dark blacks' zone in on my greens before he responds.

"I noticed that. And you're welcome."

He looks like he wants to kiss me, but instead squeezes my thighs and gets back to work.

* * *

"How do you want your steak?"

Ryder asks from the kickass, built-in grill station on his deck.

"The only way a person should eat it. Medium-rare," I reply from my spot on the crimson colored patio furniture, watching his back muscles flex through his shirt every time he moves around.

Jesus, you know it's been a while when your studying a man's back.

"So if I told you I eat mine well done?" He questions me, and I don't hold back on my honest answer.

"Then you don't deserve to eat the good cut of meat in front of you, and I'll be going home so I don't have to watch you murder that dinner by cooking all the flavor out of it."

I see the turn of his lips and know he's ready to laugh at me. "I'm glad we agree on the cooking process of beef, then."

Flashing pearly whites at me, his smile is so big I force myself to remember I can't get used to this.

"It's ready, beautiful. If you want to grab the other bottle of wine from in the house, we'll eat on the deck."
He carries a platter full of food to the table by the grill and I head for the vino.

I'm good at that, finding the vino. I could probably sniff the stuff out with a blindfold on and still find it faster than someone with the ability of sight.

Even with the cork still in.

"To new neighbors," Ryder says as he clinks his glass with mine.

"To nosy neighbors," I counter.

A deep chuckle greets me before we both dig into our meal of steak, broccoli, and prawns.

We only eat for a few moments before Ryder breaks the comfortable silence.

"You're not hard to read Elle, but you're definitely not personable. I know you like big dogs, dark colors, and the blues. Ah, and wine. I'm not asking for anything personal, but maybe there's something else you can tell me about yourself while we eat. Anything Elle, even if it's something as mundane as favorite foods or movies you like."

While Ryder has gotten more words out of me than anyone else in the past year I still balk at the thought of carrying on a normal conversation. I'm getting better at it with him, but those walls of mine remain firmly in place. I feel like a teenager, thinking about discussing things such as movies and foods I like. I suppose it's a part of getting to know someone and I understand it's not enough to give away my identity, so I decide to tell him.

"I love movies, grew up with them mostly because we never had cable where I lived. If you wanted to watch something at six o'clock other than the news you went to the video store and rented something. I can't tell you exactly which ones are my favorite, however I can tell you that I rented The Karate Kid enough that I could have bought it fifteen times, and I thought Melanie Griffith's character in 'Working Girl' was the shit, including the giant hair. The only thing I would have changed would be a swift kick to the behind following the 'bony ass' comment she made toward Sigourney Weaver's character at the elevator before introducing the Trask company to radio broadcasting."

He chuckles, "Damn, I forgot about that movie. Harrison Ford and big haired women." He says, shaking his head smiling, obviously remembering the glorious work of film that was *Working Girl*. "Thanks for sharing that with me beautiful,

I was expecting you to say something typical like 'Dirty Dancing'."

I solemnly reply, "Excuse me Mr. Callaghan, but *nobody, puts baby in the corner.*"

I'm greeted with a deep rumble of laughter once again. "You got me babe." he says on a smile.

"Your turn, handsome."

Ryder's deep in thought for a moment before he answers, "They've changed many times over the years, but John McClane comes to mind."

He says this like I won't know the answer. I raise my glass in toast before I reply. "Well then, yippy ki yay—*neighbor.*" I clink my glass with his, and down the rest of my wine.

"Shit babe, I really didn't think you'd get that one."

"Well handsome, when you grow up without much for television, you spend a lot of time with movies."

"Yeah, sounds like it. Can't say I've watched a lot in the past ten years or more, I've been too busy with work or being overseas. The eighties and nineties I guess you could say were my movie years."

I nod in approval. "Nothing wrong with that, they were some of the best," I muse, thinking that they honestly truly were, despite how young I was in the eighties; I still got to grow up with those gems in film.

And the crazy big hair.

Ryder seems to be feeling okay on the wine, as do I, before his whiskey voice hits me with a line he thinks I won't know. "Live for nothing or die for something. You're call."

I know exactly where that came from, and I plan to tell him so. "Well said, John Rambo. Well said."

A giant grin greets me once again as beautiful as the last one, maybe even more so now that I've gotten to know him better.

"Dinner was delicious Ryder, thank you."

I'm absolutely stuffed and happy he didn't turn out to be one of those guys who invites you to dinner and thinks his cooking is fantastic, but you end up faking a stomach ache and hit a drive through on the way home.

"Glad you enjoyed it."

I begin gathering up the dishes when he moves to grab my cuff covered wrist.

"What are you doing, beautiful?"

I'm still not sure how to take that since I'm not one hundred percent comfortable with my purchased face, but I tell him. "I'm cleaning up. And if you object to me helping with that then I won't eat with you again. Ever," I say, deadpan.

"Well then, I would love the help," he says, standing and collecting the rubbish to take into the house.

I grab the wine glasses and the almost empty second bottle and follow him in. I begin to set stuff on the counter when his arms come around me from behind.

"Thank you for coming, Elle. I honestly didn't think that you would, but I'm really glad you did."

He turns me around in his arms and I have little strength left in me to push him away. He's been absolutely perfect. The fact that he fed me was just icing on the cake.

"I'd say I'm the one who should be thanking you for feeding me, but I already did that," I say, looking up into his beautiful black eyes.

He's held back all night and I know it's been hard for him. Hell, it's hard for me too. I can feel the wetness gathering between my thighs just from being in his presence.

"I'm going to kiss you now babe and you can push me away if you want to, but I hope you don't."

I can't hold back much more than he can so I press myself up onto my toes and meet him halfway. We're both still barefoot and I'm much smaller than he is. His mouth meets mine with a slow, wet kiss that only lasts for a moment before my mouth opens and it turns frantic.

He pushes one hand into my hair and another around my lower back, spinning me so my back is to the wall. My hands fly up into his hair and I hold on tight as he rocks his hips into mine. I feel his hardness on my stomach. I can't hold back the moan that escapes my lips before he pulls my legs up around his waist grinding into me harder.

"Fuck, Elle," he says between breaths before skimming his hand down my thigh and running it up under my long skirt that has gathered around my thighs.

His warm callused hand raises goose bumps on my flesh as it moves around my leg toward my center. It brushes the side of my panties, as if he's asking for permission. At this point I can't deny him, or my own need for him to touch me. His fingers slip past the lace and his fingers skim along lips.

"Christ, you're soaked," he growls into my mouth before his fingers dive between my folds.

I push harder against him, wanting more friction and he takes the hint and pushes two fingers inside. I gasp at the pressure; it's been so long since anyone has been there.

"So fucking tight, beautiful," he rasps.

My head falls back as he begins attacking my neck with open mouth kisses. I can feel the wetness running down my leg as he abruptly pulls his hand away and my feet fall to the floor. I whine out in protest.

"What the hell, Ryder?" I yell, but he's already on his knees in front of me bunching my skirt up around my waist.

"Hold your skirt before I rip it off of you." He thrusts the fabric into my hands, and just as quickly he's yanking my panties down my legs.

"I have to taste you," is the last thing I hear before my head pounds back against the wall and his tongue is inside me.

He throws my left leg up over his shoulder and shoves two fingers back inside as he feasts and bites on my clit like we didn't just finish a huge dinner.

"Ryder!" I moan while riding his face and fingers. My leg is shaking and I know it won't be much longer before it gives out. My eyes are starting to roll when he replaces his fingers with his tongue.

"You taste so damn good Elle," he growls into my pussy.

"Come, Elle. Come on my tongue."

I couldn't stop it if I tried and I wail as the first orgasm in a year that's not self-induced rages through my body. His strong hands hold onto my hips and his face stays buried in me until every last drop of pleasure is gone.

He lowers me into his lap and straddles me around his waist. He places both hands on either side of my face before slowly, lovingly attacking my mouth with a brutal kiss. I can taste myself on him and it only spurs me on even more.

He trails kisses down the side of my face and buries his head in my hair.

"Thank you, beautiful," he whispers into my locks.

"Why are you thanking me Ryder?" I frown because I don't understand. The man hasn't gotten his yet, why the hell would he thank me? He pulls back and locks his eyes with mine.

"I know it wasn't easy to give up what you just gave me Elle, and not only do I appreciate that; I'd like to do it again. So thank you."

I appreciate his kind words, but still feel the need to put some light into the seriousness of this encounter.

"You speak of me as though I'm a virgin, and I'm not. Second of all, I notice the menu tonight lacked dessert, so I figured I'd provide for you."

His head falls back on a laugh, "Vixen, you want to provide dessert every night I'll go back for seconds. I promise." He smiles wholeheartedly.

I am completely serious when I reply. "I'll hold you to that."

He lifts us both up off the floor and pulls me in for a hug. It feels warm and wonderful, yet too much to handle at this moment so I slowly pull away.

"I'll finish cleaning up. You head on home before I try to bury more than my face between your legs," he says, swatting my ass.

Old me would've objected and returned the favor he just gave me. But I can see he's not expecting it. Our moment was perfect as it was.

"Thank you, Ryder," I say in the sincerest tone I have. I truly mean it.

I turn for the door whistling for Norma to come as I go. I send a quick wave over my shoulder noticing him still watching me as I leave.

Ryder Callaghan.

He may be the fucking death of me.

Chapter Thirteen

KNOCK! KNOCK! KNOCK!

"Who the hell could be here now?"

I haul my suitcase back toward the front door of my mother's house. Almost ready to load up and head for the hotel, I spent four more hours tied up behind the broken train and as much as I don't want to get back in a vehicle; I'm ready to hit the road.

I flip on the outside light and see two dark figures standing on the other side of the frosted window.

KNOCK! KNOCK! KNOCK!

"I'm coming!" Christ, and I thought my patience was lost? I whip the door open and come face to face with two police officers.

What the hell?

"My mom get caught cheating at cards again fella's?"

Sometimes my humor comes at the worst times but the fact that Sylvia accused my mother of cheating at their weekly poker game last week, I had to get it out.

"Ms. O'Connor?" the older gentleman asks.

He's all business. Despite the slightly wrinkled suit, he has serious eyes that give me nothing, not a hint of a smile touched his pudgy face.

His partner is not hard on the eyes. Maybe pushing forty, he exudes confidence and judging by their size difference I'd say he spends a lot more time at the gym.

"Yes, I'm Ms. O'Conner. However I don't live here, Mrs. O'Conner is on her way to the airport hotel at the moment."

The officers share a look that makes me uncomfortable, I hate beating around the bush.

"Jesus, spit it out already. I'm late, seeing as I missed my ride to the airport due to the broken-down train on highway sixty-three today. You fella's don't seem big on small talk so can we get to the point so I can hit the road please?" I hate to be rude, especially to a police officer but after sitting in a car for so many hours at a standstill, I'm not looking forward to spending two more in the car, and now these guys are holding me up.

"Ms. O'Connor, I'm Detective Braumer. This is Detective Miller," the old man says with a gruffness to his voice that tells me just how unhappy he is to be here, most likely because he probably missed his dinner. Or maybe it's my attitude.

I never said I had patience.

"What can I do for you?"

I hope he can sense the exasperation to my tone because I'm in a hurry. Good looking Miller speaks up. His voice is as pleasing as I'm sure his body is underneath his clothing. "Ms. O'Connor, do your parents drive a 2013 white Lincoln Navigator?"

My heart stops beating for a moment while I concentrate on his eyes. I'm good at reading people; I'm good at telling when they are lying. Most times I consider it a gift, but at this moment it's nothing but a curse.

I can feel it.

His mouth is relaxed, but there's tension around his eyes. He doesn't like his job at the moment.

He doesn't want to tell me.

"Yes, now tell me!" I'm reaching in my bag for my phone. I'll call her, and then I'll know what the hell this is all about. Oldie pipes up before I get the chance.

"Ma'am if you could-" I cut him off. "Don't 'ma'am' me, officer. I said spit it out!"

I find my phone and I begin scrolling through my contacts to get to my mother's mobile number.

"Ms. O'Connor, your family was in a car accident." Miller tells me softly but firm enough to grab my attention. The blood is rushing in my ears. I know I have to ask it but I don't want to. I don't want to hear it. I know what he's about to say because if it were a better case scenario, they'd be rushing me to the hospital, or the hospital would be calling me to tell me to rush there.

My breathing is becoming shallow.

Fuck. Fuck. Fuck.

Dick detective Braumer cuts off my train of thought with the most un-sincere voice I've ever heard.

"I'm sorry Ms. O'Connor but no one in the vehicle survived."

He's sorry...

An accident?

I can't fucking breathe.

My phone falls to the floor.

Then I do, too.

I stare out the window as I remember when my life started turning to shit. I know my dream occurred because the day of their death is coming.

I hate it.

I want to forget why I'm here and why this all happened. I wish so damn badly I was in the car with them that day so I wouldn't have to be here but with them instead. I understand that it's twisted logic but sometimes we can't help how we feel.

I shake myself out of it for now and head for the shower. Today might call for some extra wine and comfort food. The rain began late last night and has yet to let up. I don't enjoy the simplicity of rainy days like I used to but I'll make damn good on the food and wine.

* * *

My cart is half-full of the makings for comfort food; a good Irish stew is on the menu for tonight. The other half of the cart is filled with alcohol. One might pass me and think I have a problem, but since I never really gave two shits about what other people think of me, I add one more bottle.

The grocery store is pretty quiet today; obviously people aren't very eager to venture out in a torrential downpour for food. Once again, I'm not most people; therefore shopping while the store is practically empty pleases me.

THE UGLY ROSES

It's cooler because of the rain and I get to wear my full armor today, a long black jacket with a high collar around my neck and tall black boots once again with my knife tucked inside. The rain also warrants my trendy hat so I feel well and truly protected at the moment. The only skin showing are my hands and face—no marks visible. My tights are black as well which suits my overall mood.

Despite my release with Ryder yesterday, which was heaven, my shit mood still occurred when I woke up this morning. I don't suppose that will change any day soon since I've been this way for years, especially around the day of their deaths.

Someone might wonder why I don't call it the 'anniversary' of their deaths.

The reason is that an anniversary usually signifies some sort of celebration. Whether it's a wedding anniversary, a graduation anniversary, or any other anniversary, it's a day that celebrates a past event that occurred on the same day at a different time.

So, in my opinion why the hell would someone want to celebrate an *anniversary* for death?

It's bullshit.

Celebrate their birthdays; celebrate their life randomly throughout the year. But for god's sake unless someone was suffering and death took away their pain I see absolutely no reason to consider their death any type of anniversary.

My entire family was healthy, and not for one damn second do I believe any of them were ready to die.

I begin to head towards the checkout when an irritating voice pierces my eardrum. "If it isn't Belle, I believe you owe me an apology."

I turn my head to the left to greet the plastic behind the voice. With fake tits pushed up to her neck, dressed for a day at the beach instead of a rainy day in a fishing town, Ginger gives me a look that says she thinks she is better than me. Which is funny considering she lacks the common sense to dress herself properly.

Stupid cunt.

To top it all off, her cart is filled with salad.

Go figure, they're all the same.

Being supremely thankful for my shit attitude today, I respond to her. "Apparently, you've been watching too much Beauty and the Beast, seeing as I'm not Belle, she's a Disney character, Ginger. Oh, and I don't owe you shit."

I'm not about to give her the time of day, but I sense this little argument isn't finished. I'm in the mood for a good confrontation despite Tiny's words of wisdom, so I'll let her think she has me—for a minute or two.

"You rudely ruined my date. So yes, I think you do." She says.

It's now that I notice what appears to be a friend with her. I didn't think this bitch would have the balls to confront me on her own. She may have five inches on me, especially with those ridiculous shoes but I'm certain that anyone who looks in my eyes these days gets wind pretty fast that I don't put up with anyone's shit.

I slow my cart and face her head on before speaking.
"A little lesson on dating for you Ginger; most women already know this, but since you can't clue the fuck in, allow me to enlighten you. When a man drops a woman off at home early, it means he's done with her. Simple as that. In the one percent chance he really did need to get going, you would've

gotten an apology or at least a phone call the next day. Now, judging by the look on your face I'm going to go with the first option, which is that he's just done. So don't embarrass yourself. Pick the fuck up and move the fuck on."

I turned my cart so I could continue toward the cashier.

"Oh my god you are such a bitch, and for your information it's not the first date we've been on, and it won't be the last."

I can tell she's trying to say that with confidence, but it just makes her sound petty and desperate. I look over my shoulder to see her eyes when I reply.

"I'm truly sorry Ginger; he failed to mention that last night when he had his head between my thighs. But *come* to think of it, the man has great table manners. He knows it's not polite to eat and speak at the same time."

And with that parting shot, I cash out of the Green Grocer and make way for home.

Catty bitches.

* * *

I arrive home a little after three and haul ass from the truck to the house. I dump all my shit in the entryway while I rid myself of the wet clothing on the way to my bedroom. I throw on a loose pair of lounge pants and white tank followed by my comfy rainy-day cardigan and big wool socks.

I put all the groceries away and get my stew started. I throw in lots of beef, a few cans of beer and some root vegetables. I'll let it simmer on the stove for a few hours while I curl up on the couch with some smut and wine. I crave to be like my former self sometimes, and so long as the memories and the anguish don't take over, hopefully a good book will hold my attention.

* * *

The sound of the rain is soothing as I read my book in front of the fireplace. I look at the clock and realize two hours have passed and decide to check on my stew.

Almost ready and smells divine.

I add a bit of flour to thicken the sauce then turn up the stereo. I love music when I cook. Other than the odd silence during my coffee time in the morning, the quiet often kills me so the music is always on.

I hear a quick knock at my back door and Norma starts wagging her tail. Knocking still causes my heart rate to spike, but it's getting milder as time passes.

It's stupid really, what psychopath knocks?

"Come in!" I holler from the island where I've begun cutting fresh bread to go with the stew.

"Smells good in here, Elle," Ryder says as he shuts the door behind him.

He looks damn good again today in a black long sleeve Henley and dark jeans. The sleeves are pushed up so I can see his tattoos and he has a hat on which always makes him look a little younger. His stubble is still present, ensuring to keep his rugged and manly good looks.

"Well I'll be honest, I wasn't expecting company. But as you can see I have enough in this pot to feed a family, so you might as well stay and eat."

He has a slight grin on his face that makes me wonder if he just came for the food.

"I don't want you to think I just come over here for your cooking."

The full-on smile gracing his face after that statement makes me want to invite him for dinner every day of the week. Maybe lunch too. Shit, maybe I might even start making breakfast.

"So you didn't time your arrival to when I'd be cooking dinner then?" I ask on a half-smile. I still can't seem to manage a full one.

"Actually, I just came over to make sure there were no leaks after I fixed up the eaves and gutters. But if you're offering food I won't pass it up, beautiful."

I turn my head away since the beautiful comment still irks me a bit. Not a lot, it's nice to hear a man call you beautiful. I just have trouble taking the compliment seriously after everything I've been through. I shake it off for the time being and try to keep this dinner as platonic for the moment as possible.

"Well like I said no worries I have lots. Grab a beer and a chair, it's just about ready."
I carry the bread over to the table while he grabs a beer from the fridge.

"So, no leaks I take it?" I ask to keep the conversation going. I may not enjoy speaking much, but if it gets Ryder to talk more I'll put in the effort. I also don't like to give him too much time to analyze me— but I don't want to lead him on either.

If I can keep this to friends with mild benefits without the amount of passion he began to show me last night, this may work. He takes a seat at the table and tilts his head to study me.

"No leaks," he replies in a short manner which doesn't sit well with me and tells me he's catching onto my game.

I'll have to up my acting skills.

"Well that's good news," I reply as I dish out two bowls of stew.

I carry them to the table along with the spoons and settle in, avoiding as much eye contact as possible.

"You alright, babe?"

Of course he would pick up on something. I never fully asked him what he did in the corps or what exactly he does with his security company now, but from the way he assesses people and places I'm sure he's had some form of lie detecting skills.

"Rainy days, Ryder. Mellows me out a bit I guess you could say."

It's not a total lie. Between the book, the wine and the heat from the fireplace I was quite good and mellow before he showed up. He seems to believe it because his features softened considerably.

"I hear you," he replies before shoveling a huge spoonful of stew in his mouth. "This is delicious."

I know it is—everybody loves my stew.

"It's all in the beer," I reply on a smirk before eating.

Ryder went through two and a half bowls before he declared himself full and rinsed his dish, putting it in the dishwasher.

"A man who helps in the kitchen," I say, shaking my head. "Still leaves me a little speechless."

I grab the dishcloth and head back over to wipe the table down. I'm almost finished when I feel warm hands on my hips and hot breath in my ear.

"I can think of more ways to make you speechless vixen. But it doesn't involve cleaning up the kitchen," he rasps with a long lick up my neck.

I can't help the small moan that escapes the back of my throat. His fingers dig into my hips a little and then begin to work their way up. For fear of his hands going under my tank top I decide to turn this power play around.

I turn in his arms and run my hands up his chest. His palms slide down to rest on my ass which is what I was hoping for. I take in the tanned skin and sharp cut jaw. His silky dark hair falls to his nape. I run my hands up around the back of his neck and brush my fingers through it. It's much thicker than mine and incredibly soft. I lean up on my toes and summon the inner vixen I left behind long ago, but he seems to know.

"Handsome, I'm sure there are a number of ways you can make me speechless," my raspy voice declares. Sometimes I hate it, but in times like this I know it adds to the seduction. "But I'm a fair woman who likes to keep things even."

I run my hands back down his solid chest toward his belt buckle. I slip my hands underneath his shirt and touch his bare skin. His sharp intake of breath doesn't go unnoticed. "That being said, I believe it's my turn to make you speechless this time."

I lean forward and press my lips to his neck. I sneak my tongue out as I begin to undo his belt. His hands put more pressure on my ass and he pulls me forward until my hands are squished between us.

"Fuck, you're full of surprises," He says before grinding his erection against me.

As much as I would love to feel it inside me, it's my turn to play tonight. I push back and pull his belt lose as I continue my assault up behind his ear. I pop the button on his jeans and lower the zip.

I pull my mouth off his neck and look at the tension on his face before easing my hand inside his jeans.

Commando.

Christ that makes me happy.

My hand touches his smooth velvet skin and I attempt to wrap my hand around his incredibly well-endowed self. My eyes widen, while he glances back at me with pure lust.

He's not a gherkin! I chant to myself.

"I guess you're full of surprises too," I smartly say while I stroke my hand down and back up again.

His breathing is becoming slightly labored and he squeezes his fingers into my ass. He tilts his head to the side and studies my face.

"What were you expecting, beautiful?" he chides playfully and thrusts his hips forward into my hand while leaning down to kiss my neck.

"Well I'm not sure, but to be certain I should have a better look."

I keep eye contact as I pull his jeans down below his ass. I move backwards until I feel the chair and I lower myself onto it. His gaze is challenging me to look down, and when I finally do I'm floored.

He's long, thick and perfectly smooth. I love a well-groomed man and have refused this very act for those who can't keep that shit cleaned up.

Ryder doesn't have that problem.

In fact, I'm eager to get started and my panties are soaked just thinking about it.

"Meet your expectations vixen?" his whisky rough voice cockily asks as I sit stunned on the chair.

Fucker knows just how perfect he is down here and I'm sure I won't be the first woman to tell him so.

Later.

For now I nonchalantly say, "Yes, it'll do."

He starts to respond but doesn't get the chance to finish because I lick the head of his shaft while running my hand down to the base and underneath his balls.

I sneak a peek and he's watching me intently, biting his lips. I lean forward remaining eye contact as I lay wet open mouth kisses down the length of his shaft, adding a bit of suction on the way. I lick my way back up as he hisses out in pleasure.

"Fucking Christ your mouth feels good."

He runs his fingers into my hair and rests his hand there. I open my mouth and take him in as far as I can. His smooth flesh feels good against my tongue and I hum in pleasure. His fingers tighten in my hair; I know he's enjoying this. I add one hand back in on the action as the other moves back down between his legs. I stroke in and around before gently rolling his balls between my fingers.

"Fuck! So good, Elle."

I release his cock from my mouth and keep at it with my hands while lick around his balls with my tongue before taking one into my mouth.

"Agh! Fuck Elle, I'm gonna come!"

I shove his cock back into my mouth as far as I can seconds before he shoots down my throat. I swallow every last drop and kiss the tip before looking back up at him. It's a mixture of sated pleasure and awe on his face.

I did well.

I stand slowly and begin to tuck him back in.

"That was perfect, and I'm not lying when I say I've never had my dick sucked so well beautiful." He paused on the last bit and I have a feeling he would have made good use of his dick, but I continue tucking him away and doing up his jeans.

"My pleasure, handsome. As I said, I like to keep it even."

I smirk at him before placing a chaste kiss on his chin. He won't let me stop there and pulls on my neck to claim my mouth. The passion in this man is unbelievable. I pull away with a small smile on my face to keep the mood light and not progress his passion any further. I don't want to send the wrong message and I'm half hoping he has the idea that this will be much like his trysts with Ginger. Mildly sate our needs on a casual basis, minus the hooker attire and whiny voice.

"I gotta hit the ladies room handsome. You can finish putting the dishes away."

I tap him lightly on the chest and walk back through the kitchen. I swing my arms out to grasp the counter as I slip across the floor.

"Fuck!"

The bottoms of my socks are soaked and so is the majority of the kitchen floor. I notice water running out of the cupboard underneath the sink and fall to my knees.

I fling the doors open and get a blast of freezing cold water.

"Shit!"

I reach under the sink to turn off the valve that supplies water to the faucet and the decrepit old piece of plastic shit breaks off.

"God dammit!"

Ryder storms into the kitchen and I bark at him. "Top drawer under the toaster. Pliers!"

He grabs them and turns my way to help, but I rip them out of his hands and dive back under the sink. A few more turns than necessary due to the rust and the fucker finally quits giving me a shower.

"Finally."

I sigh as I sit back on my knees and use the dish towel to wipe the water off my neck. Everything is soaked.

"Looks like a split in the line between the valve and the faucet. I can fix it for you tomorrow Elle. It's a little late to head into the hardware store now."

Ryder is now squatting down beside me looking under the sink. He still has his boots on so his socks are dry but his shirt didn't fare so well.

"Yeah, not a big deal. Just shocked the shit out of me and makes me wish it were the hot water line," I say on a shiver.

I move to stand up and he lends me a hand. The water is pouring out of my cardigan as he grasps my arm. I shake my head and move to walk around him but he's a statue. I look up at his face to find his eyes planted firmly on my chest. I don't need to look down to know he's taking in the effects of a wet white tank top with no bra on underneath. I'd like to say the no bra is a fluke, but I hate the things and usually the minute I cross the threshold of home it comes off.

The vein in his neck pulses and he clenches the fist that lies at his side. He wants to touch, I can gather that much. I grab the sides of my cardigan and begin to pull it over my chest. His head snaps up to mine and his beautiful face is a mask of lust and something else I can't put my finger on. I think about last night at his place and crave his mouth on me again but I need to keep this light and even.

"I'm going to go change before I get a cold."

I'm not shivering anymore; in fact I'm quite warm now under his gaze. His lip twitches and he says, "No, we wouldn't want you getting a cold."

I laugh a little and skirt around him on my way to the bedroom.

"Towels in the closet in the bathroom if you need one!" I holler over my shoulder on the way.

I close the door on the laundry room so I can dump my soaking wet clothes in the wash. I take off the cardigan, tank top, socks and pants. Everything is wet but my underwear. I walk through the connecting door to my closet and grab similar clothes to replace them with before moving to my bedroom. I move toward the bed so I can sit and put my socks on, but trip on something and twist my bad ankle.

"Ouch!" I hiss through clenched teeth as I fall to my knees on the hardwood floor.

I see I tripped over a pair of my boots. I'm not normally careless and messy with my shit, but my mind was elsewhere while I was getting ready this morning.

I grab the edge of the bed and pull myself up to sit down just as I hear Ryder from the connecting door to the bathroom.

Which is never shut because I don't have company.

Fuck.

I hear his sharp breathing, like someone who can't decide whether they are fuming mad or deeply pained.

My back is to the bathroom.

He went in to get a towel.

I didn't think about the open bathroom door.

Now, he's seen my nightmares.

"Get out," I hiss.

I don't turn around to look at him. I don't want to see whatever expression is on his face.

I can't see it.

If it's pity, I'll lose it.

Fuck, why is this happening?

This is one of the reasons you told yourself no friends Elle, I think to myself.

"Elle who did that to you," he says softly. I can't take it. I cut him off with more venom in my voice. "I said get the fuck out Ryder!"

I hate myself right now.

"I'll leave, I can tell your upset. But this doesn't change anything. Mark my words Elle, I'll be back." His tone is still soft but there is determination in his voice.

I don't for one second think he won't come back. It's the questions that will come with him that'll make me want to run.

Chapter Fourteen

I sit on the bed long after I hear the door close behind him. It's not until the tears have dried up that I look at the clock and see it's almost midnight. I can't stay here. I need to go. I can't face him or answer the questions that he'll have. I think back on our conversation over dinner to remind myself why I need to leave.

"So what kind of security work is it that you do?" I finally asked him. Not to get personal, but to find out more about his business since we're becoming closer, and to figure out whether his line of work will do me harm or good.

"Mostly risk assessment for gatherings of important people and a few political parties lately. I have about a dozen men working for me. We run security as well as analyze any potential threats to the people involved and how to prevent it. I've also done a lot of hostage rescues and missing person's cases over the years, but not so much anymore."

That could go either way for me.

"I'm leaving the day after tomorrow for a few weeks on a job actually. I have to say I'll miss your cooking. Road food doesn't taste as good."

If he's gone for a few weeks I'll leave tonight and come back to get the rest of my shit. Not that it's important, but I need to clear out my accounts here and I might as well empty out my closet and let Tom know I'm out. Fuck, I don't want to move again but I don't think I have a choice.

Shit, I can't stay. I don't want to see him now because the way he's always looked at me won't be the same anymore. It won't be those black heated eyes staring back at me. It will be dark eyes filled with pity aimed directly at yours truly.

It's settled.

With that revelation in mind, I finish getting dressed and grab my go bag from the closet.

Running.

Sadly, it's what I do best.

I think back to the last time I ran from the only woman who ever meant much to me in life aside from my mother. I'll never forget my last day with my best friend who is more like a sister.

God, I miss her.

"What do you mean you're leaving? No! No Jayne you are not fucking leaving. I don't care who believes you or what happens you're practically my only goddamn friend, so you're not leaving me!"

I stare at the woman who's the closest thing to a sister I'll ever have. She knows deep down I need to do this. She knows. I'm a walking target. I'll endanger everyone I'm close to if I don't get the hell out of here.

"Listen to me babe. Everyone in this town, including Detective Braumer can think I'm nuts. Hell, if you want to think I'm crazy I'm okay with that too. But I know down to my bones that there were two of them. And I can't fucking sit here awake at night waiting to be taken again! I won't do it Laura!"

She struggles for words, knowing I'm right but not yet ready to give up.

"I thought Miller was with you on this! What the hell is going on? I don't give a shit what Braumer says Jay, if Miller is working on it I know he'll fix this Jay. He'll figure it out and then you won't need to leave!"

She clasps her hands over her face before she begins to sob. Heavy breath taking sobs that would make me consider staying if I didn't think she would be in any danger. God, I love this woman more than I love myself. She's kept my feet on the ground more times in life than I can count.

"I love you Laur'. I will love you until the day I die but babe, today is not that day. You have a man who loves you and beautiful children that need you. If I stay you're going to be a pawn in a game you'll never win. So I have to go, for my family, for myself and most of all babe for you. Because if something ever happened to you and the kids because of me?" I shake my head sadly, "I will tell you right now I would never forgive myself."

I squeeze her as tight as my stitched body will allow and I let her sob into my neck. I haven't cried yet. Those tears dried up a long time ago. I fear I haven't got any left.

"I know I can't stop you Jay. I know I can't. It doesn't mean I don't love you any less for not trying harder. You're a one-track woman bitch and I know I can't change your mind."

She clings to me gently; the majority of my body is still battered. I don't feel it much anymore, but I don't tell her that. The pain takes away from my thoughts and right now that's a blessing. The thoughts hurt more than the wounds on my body.

"Promise me something you sloppy slut?" I ask with a grin in my voice which earns me a small chuckle from her.

"Anything, hooker. You name it."

"Marry that man. But before you say yes he needs to adopt your adorable children. You just make sure he knows that Aunt Jay always has the final say with them when you're suffering from Alzheimer's and I have to make crucial decisions for you."

She pulls her head off my shoulder to stare at me.

"You bitch. We were supposed to suffer through Alzheimer's together!" She complains with tears still streaking down her face, voice heavy from crying.

I pull away and give her one last kiss on the forehead before letting go and grabbing my bag. I take one last look at what's left of my world, her short curly brown mop and beautifully tanned skin. The kindest heart a person could ever hope for in a friend.

"Your right, and that's when we'll become new friends babe," I say, referencing our inside joke that we'll make new friends each day at the nursing home, since each day we would wake up suffering from Alzheimer's and not know each other anymore.

I give her a wink and head for the door.

I don't look back, and I don't say goodbye.

I hit the highway at three in the morning, just me, my dog and the road. It's become the norm for me lately so I'm not sure why I'm so upset. I don't do upset and I don't do heartache. Why I'm feeling this gaping void in my chest can only be described in one word.
Him.

I promised myself I wouldn't get attached to people in this new life of mine. That promise went to hell in a hand basket the minute Ryder Callaghan walked into my life.

My mind is going a million miles a minute, thinking of all the scenarios and different ways this could pan out since he saw my back. The part of me that once had a warm beating heart and used to dream of happy things, imagines us baring our souls to each other and living happily ever after.

But that dream is exactly that, just a dream.

My family is dead, and my body is living proof that dreams don't come true. It's a fairy tale parents tell their children to help them sleep peacefully at night.

The honest side of me with the stone-cold heart is better at assessing a complex situation such as this one. That side says my cover is potentially blown and he will most certainly be repulsed by my back. At the end of the day, I didn't plan on letting him put a ring on my finger so it shouldn't be a big deal our time together was cut short.

I program my GPS on Virginia and head toward a cabin near Richmond. I'll spend three days there to ensure Ryder is gone for work before I head back to pack my belongings. I could leave it all behind, but I'm not running like I did when I left Canada so I might as well take my stuff with me when I go.

Starting a life from scratch sucks. I would rather take my towels and salt and pepper shakers with me than have to buy everything new again.

* * *

It's early morning when I arrive in Virginia. I pull into a twenty-four-hour roadside diner on the outskirts of town and let Norma out of the truck. I know she won't go anywhere without me, so I tell her to stay and head inside the restaurant.

It's a dull, dead area of town so I'm not too worried. It's also too early for traffic, which would be mild considering I've yet to come across a stoplight or another vehicle on the road. I head to the counter to order some food to go.

"Pretty dog you have there. Where ya's headed so early in the morning?" I look up to see a mid-sixties waitress in true diner fashion. I look to her name tag, *Adele*. I know she poses no threat so I answer her.

"Just going to visit a friend outside of Washington." The lie about where I'm headed falls easy from my lips and I almost feel bad for doing it to this kind woman who wears a gold cross around her neck, a telltale sign she most likely attends church three times a week.

"Obedient too I'd say." She drawls in a typical southern accent, noting the dog who waits patiently, staying close to the restaurant. "Had a dog once, dumber than the stump he sat on that one. Kids always wanted 'em, and I couldn't say no."

She shakes her head reliving the moment before she continues. "But one thing 'bout that mutt. Didn't matter who came around, even if it was that bastard ex-husband 'a mine that he grew up with, damn dog still barked. Still tried to kill 'em too. 'Spose I can't call 'em dumb after that, cheatin' bastard my husband was and all. 'Spose it's true what they say 'bout animals: they know like *they know,* and 'ain't nobody gonna tell 'em different," she says, reminiscing while watching my girl on the lawn.

"You stayin' to eat hunny?" she asks in the sweetest voice I've heard in what feels like an eternity.

I debate for a moment and look outside. I know it'll be at least an hour before I can call the cabin owner, but I just planned on eating in the truck. I'm exhausted, running on adrenaline before the older woman breaks through my thoughts.

THE UGLY ROSES

"Ain't nobody comin' in here for another hour, sugar. Call your girl in and sit in the booth by that side door over there and I'll get ya some coffee. Looks like ya need it baby girl. No offense," she says before walking away.

I haven't been called baby girl since I was a child, but god bless this kind woman for making me feel at home.

I let Norm in and point to the floor beside the booth. She lies down.

Adele comes back and fills my coffee cup.

"Know what you want sugar?" she kindly asks, cooing to the dog. *"Ain't you a fine girl, pretty thang. Bet your mama takes good care 'a you don't she?"*

She caresses Norma's ears before standing back up.

"I'd like the special please, eggs over easy and a side of sausage to go," I say, staring at my dog who is most likely as hungry as I am. Adele eyes me knowingly before responding.

"You want something for this fine girl here sugar, all yous' got to do is ask." She winks at me.

"My girl likes her food just as much as I do. And between you and I, what the vet doesn't know won't hurt her."

She cackles at my joke before grabbing up the menu.

"Girl, I don't know how anybody says them animals can live off that dry stuff ya feed 'em. They's wolves once ya know. I'll bring her out a plate, don't you worry."

Adele is officially the happiest person I've ever met awake before seven in the morning. I've never been here before, but on highway 258 running from home (or soon to be old home) to near Richmond Virginia, I found the best roadside diner off that highway and I think one of the kindest women I'll ever meet. I'm lost in thought when she returns what could be minutes later.

"Here you go girl and let me set this plate down here for you too pretty lady."

I see she has a plate full of sausage and potatoes all cut up for the dog. Damn, there really are kind people in this world, even when your life has gone to shit.

I've spent the last year avoiding people as much as possible. Low and behold the first few people I actually begin to have a conversation with turn out to be some of the kindest people I've ever met.

My eyes start to burn. I'm so tired I could cry at this woman's kindness, but I just stay silent and watch instead. I feel a warm hand on mine and I look up into Adele's piercing eyes.

"Always gonna be some bad sugar. Can't nobody stop that. I see you got some bad hangin' 'round and I'll be the first one to tell ya. Ain't nobody in my sixty-four years gonna get me down and they won't get you neither. You eat yourself a good meal; you get yourself some nice sleep. And when you feel better, you find yourself a nice man. You do it in that order hunny. Never the man before the better 'cause he ain't gonna do it for ya. You hear me baby?"

I take in everything she said with a deep breath. I've never been transparent but this woman on a side road off the highway could be a fortune teller. She knows her shit. And I don't doubt for one fucking minute she knows what she's talking about. I look at her with misty eyes and a full heart.

"I hear you Adele. And I promise I won't forget."

Chapter Fifteen

"Do you know how long I've watched you Jayne?" He asks as he slowly runs his knife down my bare back. Not piercing the skin but enough to get his point across. I hang as still as a dead man and listen.

"Years and years, Jayne. I watched, and I waited."

The knife drags back up my spine. His voice is eerily calm. We both know this was planned. This room was ready for me when I got here.

"Yeah, I gathered that from the pretty collage of photos you have of me over there. Did you ever think I might want to be asked before I have my picture taken?"

I can't help my smart mouth. I can barely see out of my eyes anymore, but I don't give a shit. I don't want to look at his face. I'll never forget it so I don't need to see it anymore.

The knife slashes up one side and down the other on my back. {iercing the skin in a fiery inferno of pain.

"Ahhh, you bastard!"

"That's right, scream! Nobody will hear you. It's just you and me down here Jayne. Scream in pain until you learn your lesson and tell me you're sorry. Are you going to listen to me now, Jayne? Are you going to apologize?"

I dig deep with everything in me. I feel it all, I smell it all, I breathe it all in. That will to survive, or the will to kill this man before I bleed out and die.
He wants me to scream?
I won't give him the satisfaction.

I take one last deep breath and let out every feeling I've ever had.

Love.
Hate.
Pain.
Loss.

It's expelled from me in a whoosh of air until the numbness settles in. I take another deep breath and ask myself what I feel now.

Nothing.

Empty.

I open my eyes and stare the sick bastard in the face.

"I won't apologize. Not when I don't know what it's for. So no, you sick son of a bitch. I will not tell you 'I'm sorry'."

* * *

I take one last look around the cabin to make sure I haven't forgotten anything. Three days of sleeping and I still feel like a bag of shit. The bags are still heavy under my eyes and I haven't bothered to do my hair or any makeup in that time. No point really. The nightmares have been endless, even while I'm awake—the most predominant one being when I first woke up in the basement. Face beaten and hung from the ceiling, it's on a constant loop that won't shut off. I need to get out of here.

Time to leave this fucking place, time to hit the road. First stop, North Carolina.

Second, unknown.

* * *

I walk into the little home I've been able to call mine, even if for a short little while. The first thing I notice is that the empty bottles from mine and Ryder's dinner the other night are missing.

The towels that were still on the kitchen floor are gone, and I'm sure if I check under the sink the water line will be fixed. I want to let it warm my heart because he did those things for me, but I need to keep the numbness for now so I'll be able move forward. When I get settled somewhere again, I'll process it all.

I head toward my bedroom to begin packing. I could sleep more but I'd rather just be ready to move. I'll pack up and then search the internet for my next temporary abode. Hopefully it'll be somewhere like here, by the water, with the silence. It calms me more than anything has in a long time. I'm going to need that in the next place I rest my head. I dump my bag on the end of the bed and spot a note on the pillow.

Ryder.

I leap for the note and take in his slanted scrawl on the front of the note.

'Elle'

Fuck, my curiosity takes over and I open the white page. As much as I would love to have a bottle of wine to go with this, or maybe whiskey, I can't move my feet from where they're rooted to the floor. I tear it open and begin to read.

Elle,

I didn't get enough time with you, beautiful.
You're a runner. I sensed it when we met.
I'm asking you not to run from me, please.

*I wish I could have waited longer than two days to
see if you came back, but I have to personally finish
up this job in Chicago.
Please wait for me.
Elle, what happened in your past is exactly that—
it's the past. I don't think of you any differently and
I don't want you to treat this differently because of
what I saw. To be honest babe, it only makes me
want to be near you more now that I have an
overwhelming need to hold and protect you.
I'm not sure how you feel about me, but I would
really like to see where this goes between us. I don't
ask for much Elle, but I'm asking for you to please
be here when I get back in a few weeks. If you're
not ready to talk when I get back, I'll wait. As long
as it takes, I'll wait until you're ready.
 But I need to be near you beautiful, and I need to
know that you're okay.
If you won't see me, call me.
Please, Elle.*

Ryder

His number is scrawled on the bottom of the page, not that I
plan on using it but I don't plan to get rid of it.

This letter confirms more than the beauty on the outside of
this man. For the first time in a long while I feel a familiar
ache in my chest. My head says run but my heart wants to stay,
even just for a little while.

I curl up on my bed with the letter clenched in my hand. I
stare across the room into my closet at the safe that's bolted to
the floor. The box from my old life resides there. I haven't
opened it since I picked it up in Denver. Originally that was
the plan; lay it all out and process it all. Put the pieces together
to try and prove my case wrong. I know the case was still open
when I left, but that was many months ago now.

THE UGLY ROSES

My claim that there were two people torturing me was unheard of to Detective Braumer's ears. The old prick was so close to retirement I'm sure he just wanted to close the case and get his fat ass out the door.

"There was only the DNA of two people at the residence of Mr. Andrew Roberts, Ms. O'Connor. His and yours. I don't know how many times we have to go over this. Mr. Roberts had no known living relatives and was the only person listed to that address. Without further evidence, aside from your claim there's nothing more I can do."

It took all I had in me not to pummel the bastard. My shoulders were still messed up from hanging in the basement and I had one hundred and sixty-two stitches in my back that prevented me from doing so.

While lying on my bed I come to the conclusion that I need to call Detective Miller. He was a good cop, he went behind Braumer's back a lot to help me out. Sadly, in the end, most of it was still out of his hands.

Calling home is dangerous; I haven't had contact with anyone since I left Canada and popped back up with a new name. I decide I'll drive out of town, somewhere much further away from here and make the call. I can't risk him finding my location or tracking my call in any way. I'll see if anything new has opened up with my case before I dig back into the box and try to figure it out for myself.

On that last thought, I fall asleep.

* * *

Carte Blanche.

That's what I think to myself as I sit here on my back deck drinking my morning brew.

A lot of people would be thrilled with a carte blanche. Ask them what they would do if they had money in the bank; a car full of gas and no responsibilities. No family.

What would they do?

Where would they go?

Of course we'll leave out the fact they have to change their name and assume the possibility that someone out there wants them dead. But aside from those little tidbits, most people would be thrilled.

Start over. New people. New place. New identity to make as you wish.

I'm not thrilled right now.

I take in the beauty this little abode gives me. Not on the outside, but the *peace* it gives me. I run over a million scenarios in my head if I were to go or stay. Ryder will most definitely have questions, and as much as I don't want to put him up on this pedestal of hope for me to stay, I can't help but remember how he makes me feel when I'm around him.

It's not that ridiculous high school crush. It's not the butterflies you get when you lose your virginity to your high school sweetheart. It's not that ridiculous notion in the movies when they try to make you believe in love at first sight. It's none of those things.

It's serene? Is that the right word for it? I don't know. Maybe it's not able to be explained. It's a feeling on a deep level that both calms and excites me. It's that comfortable silence when he could sense I did not want to talk and it's the energy that hums through my body when he touches me.

I have no doubt in my mind every word in his letter was true. I'm positive if there were ever to be a man able to protect me, Ryder would fit the bill. But then I have to think about his lifestyle, his trysts with the Gingers. I don't judge him for that. I too have had my share of sluts only for a certain benefit. They were of the male variety of course. But what if deep down that's his norm. One nighters, or friends with benefits to keep it regular before he ships off to god knows where for however long for work.

I once asked myself why he never had a family and five kids. Maybe that's why. Maybe he doesn't want something full-time and he likes to keep things light and open. If that's the case, then sticking around here for a man would make me just as clueless and dumb as Ginger.

What if 'seeing where this goes' turns into a disaster and by that point he's already figured me out? He's a man of the law so to speak. Military background and his security work for influential people? How will that work for me?

If shit with my case doesn't get sorted out and he finds out my real name, there's nothing stopping him from shipping me back to Canada. Deep down I don't think he would do that, but I have to remember that anything is possible.

Time to make a phone call.

* * *

I drive for three hours until I hit a little rundown town that only has cell phone service in the center of it. The town consists of one gas station, a small market and a beer store.

All the essentials.

I pull into the side lot of the gas station; it's not the kind that has cameras watching the pumps. In fact I'm surprised I still have cell service. I'd be floored if they get internet in this town.

I pull my phone out of my bag and dial one of the few phone numbers I have memorized into my prepaid. The area code will be from Denver and if they track it the signal will come up to this little shanty town. It will look like I move around a lot and I plan to dump the phone when I'm done anyway. I'll pick up a new burner later.

"Miller," he snaps into the phone on the fifth ring. I was almost ready to hang up, nerves getting the best of me.

"Am I still wanted for more questioning, or have you found the second attacker and proved my ordeal self-defense?"

I cut to the chase. No small talk, no beating around the bush. I need answers. He's silent. Shocked to hear from me I'm sure.

"Jayne?"

I hear the surprise in his voice. No time for that.

"Answer the question please."

"Jesus fuck, forgive me, I thought you were in a ditch somewhere! Give me a minute."

I hear his long exhale into the phone. He's most likely running his hands through his hair, a telltale sign when he was frustrated.

"I don't have a minute. Please answer the question Miller," I say as sincerely as I can and hope that I get my point across.

"Shit! Alright; you're a missing person Jayne. However nobody is avidly searching, considering you said goodbye to Laura so we know you were alive and well when you dropped off the grid. Shit here has been on hold. No charges laid yet but no second attacker has been found. Braumer never dropped the warrant that says you still need to be brought in for more questioning regarding the death of your attacker. He's retired, but still sticks his nose in on the case from time to time."

This isn't news to me, that old prick will nail me to the wall for anything he can. I don't know why he hates me so much, and I don't really care. However, I would like to know the real reason as to why he just won't fucking drop it.

"So all the police in the surrounding area have my photograph and know I'm wanted until questioned further? Is that what you're telling me?"

Fucking Braumer, I figured the lazy bastard would've given up by now.

"That's what I'm telling you. Not like you'd be arrested if you came in willingly, and I'm sure it will all blow over. I'll be honest, the only one pushing for this is Braumer, the rest of us consider it finished. I'm sorry Jayne."

He's been kind to me, and I know he means well but I can't stand when someone says they're sorry.

"Gotta run Miller, thanks for the update."

Wanted? That old prick still thinks I could've done things differently when I escaped hell. I can't go back to Canada, still wanted for questioning. I know it's some twisted tactic Braumer would use to try and nail something on me. I have no clue what I did to piss that man off other than my attitude when we first met, but Christ give me a break.

Chapter Sixteen

I've spent a little bit of time each day this week packing. Not that there's much. I just can't seem to get it all in one go. The fight to stay versus leaving is a constant battle for me. I know deep down I'll leave, but I crave to see him one last time before I go.

The feel of his hands on my skin and his mouth on mine is enough to make me hold out a little while longer. I've never felt the passion he gave me from anyone else in my life, and it's become a drug I crave. I wish to experience it once more and then pull a runner in the night.

I'm skilled at that.

I grab my new prepaid and order a pizza since I've been too lazy to cook lately. I've also been too busy searching for a new place to live. I've found a few places online in Indianapolis that look promising. I don't feel the same about them as I do this cozy place, but it will have to do.

I'm torn between a little bungalow near the river and a shabby house that needs quite a bit of fixing up more secluded near a lake. My options are slim; wanting to still be near the water but far enough away from neighbors.

I'm weighing the pros and cons of the two when I hear a knock at the door. I didn't hear a car pull up and the dog is barking, frantically.

No tail wag.

Too early for pizza.
Not Ryder.

I grab my gun and edge along the wall toward the door, close enough they can hear me.

"Who is it?" I holler out while taking shelter in the hallway.

"It's Anna."

I don't know a fucking Anna, but she doesn't sound threatening. I make my way to the door and peer out the window to see a beautiful woman with a blonde bob. She's tall and slender dressed in well-fitted beige slacks with a frilly red blouse. Her pale skin is glowing under the porch light. I unlock the door.

"What can I do for you?" I ask as she looks me up and down. My jogging pants and faded out tank top are not up to par with this woman's wardrobe.

"I can't get into the house or get a hold of my fiancé. I assume he must be working late. I've been away so I'm not sure what time he's been coming home. Have you seen him today?" She asks in a haughty voice that grated on my nerves the minute she opened her mouth. I assumed an Anna would have a sweet, kind voice.

"Who did you say you were?"

I've never met any of the other neighbors, and I'm still disappointed she's on my porch and not the pizza I'm waiting for.

"Anna," She says with some bite in her tone, as if I see her every damn day.

"I don't know any 'Anna's', and I have no idea who your fiancé is so I can't help you."

I begin to close the door but her words force my back to go straight and my head to whip around to face her again.

"Ryder Callaghan," she half hisses, like she's sick of talking to me.

No.

It can't be.

"As I said, I've been away. Could you please tell me what time he's been coming home? I've lost my key," she quips, and I know in that moment the bitch doesn't have a key.

Like I said, I'm good at reading people. I would consider all her words to be a lie until I look down and notice the small, but pretty little rock on her finger.

Why the hell does bad shit seem to find me?

If it can happen, it will happen right? Well it certainly does in my world. *That fucking asshole*. The letter he wrote me? His mouth between my legs. The connection I felt with him?

I suppose it's true. At the end of the day we all want what we can't have. Ryder seemed like a great catch, probably because the entire time he was unavailable.

Engaged to another woman.

This feeling of being a home wrecker gives me that last push to get the hell out of Dodge and not look back.

"I'm not certain what time he gets home, mind you, we don't talk much and I haven't seen him lately as I too have been away."

Not a total lie, we really don't. And I was away.

She humph's a little before shaking her head.

"He's probably off playing G.I Joe somewhere at the moment. I'll leave him a note since his phone must not be working properly. However, if you see him let him know I'll be at the Hilton."

Her prissy attitude is more than I can handle so I simply nod and shut the door.

The man my heart had softened for.

Engaged.

To be married.

What the fuck?

* * *

It's early morning and the last of my stuff I want to bring with me is loaded in my truck.

I haven't called Tom to let him know I'm leaving. This place is paid for the next three months and I know Ryder will be back to look after it. He'll let Tom know when I don't return. I have no doubt it'll be in good hands until then. I packed up my cooler with the remnants from the fridge and took the garbage to the curb.

I lean against the truck with my phone in hand.
'It will be goodbye,' I tell myself.

Enough for closure.

I've rolled the conversation over in my head of all the ways I can tell him what a lying sack of shit he is. I saw Anna's little red car parked in his driveway this morning.

Bitch must've found a key.

I dial the number I memorized from his letter and wait for it to connect. I half hope to hear voice mail before his whiskey voice rasps down the line.

"Callaghan," he grunts into the phone sounding out of breath. Probably fucking some other whore on the job, while his muse packs to hit the road and his soon to be wife waits for him at home.

"I thought about staying Ryder, until you got back to give you a proper goodbye."

I hate that my voice cracks a little on the 'bye' and I hope he doesn't notice. I take a deep breath and center myself before speaking again.

"But that's changed," I say with the firm tone I was originally going for.

"What—what's changed Elle? Stay and talk to me. *Please.*" He begs. "Three more days. Four max and I'll be back so we can sit down and talk about why you're refusing to stay. Give me that much Elle, don't make me come back to find nothing but an empty house."

There's a desperate tone in his voice, and at this moment it makes me hate him more for seeming to be so interested in me and my life, all the while lying like the bastard he is.

I go in for the kill.

"Don't worry handsome, someone will be here for you when you get home."

The venom in my voice won't be mistaken.

"What are you talking about Elle?"

I clear up his confusion in three simple words before hanging up.

"Anna, your fiancé."

Click.

Chapter Seventeen

Two and a half months later

"Get your head in the game Elle! One two, punch! He's not gonna wait for you to get your shit together babe, and neither am I!"

My back slams down against the mat and the air whooshes out of my lungs. I run my arm across the sweat running down my forehead.

Brock is kicking my ass today. I only managed three hours of sleep last night due to the nightmares and my body is exhausted after the past hour on the mat with my trainer.

He stands above me and reaches a hand out to help me up. He knows not to go soft on me. I need the release of someone kicking my ass and giving everything I've got in return to get myself out of the situation.

It's cleansing, paying to get your ass kicked. It's my new form of therapy.

I don't often win, and I've never taken him down. Brock is huge. From afar he seemed a bit intimidating when I first met him. He's over six feet tall, covered in colorful ink and has shaved light blond hair. He's built like a mastiff, but I know deep down he loves like a kitten.

In another life I might be attracted to him, but the love he has for his wife Sam along with the strictly business attitude he gives me makes it easy to stay in the teacher-student zone.

"You need sleep Elle, go home. We need your head here, and it's not today, girl. Go home and sort that shit out okay?"

Brock pulls me up and gives me a pat on the shoulder. I give him a head shake but I don't deny his claim. I know I'm a useless sack of shit today. If someone were to come at me right now, much like with Brock I'd be put flat on my ass.

"Yes, sleep. I think after today's ass kicking it should be a good one," I joke. My way to lighten the situation.

Brock heads to the boxing ring and I make my way toward the showers. I've been coming here for two months now. What started out as a self-defense class turned into one on one lessons with a personal trainer named Brock.

I'd like to say I took the lessons that were offered because I had a genuine interest in going home bruised three times a week, which would give me another excuse to soak in the tub.

The real reason is because during the self-defense class I enrolled myself in, I blacked out and lost my shit when Brock wrapped his hands around my throat.

 It took me straight back to the basement and I knew nothing in that moment other than true survival. Of course he was only teaching our first demonstration before he would implement how to take down an attacker.

Instead of a friendly demonstration where he would've come out unharmed, Brock walked away with a broken nose, black eye and most likely a reduced ability to make children should he hope to do so in the future.

While the blood poured out of his nose and he lay in the fetal position on the floor protecting his man parts, he opened his mouth to speak what I assumed would be something along the lines of you *crazy bitch, get the fuck out.*

He said no such thing.

"That was badass Elle, but we definitely have more work to do. Be here Monday at six and we'll work on some alternative maneuvers. No group class, just you and me."

I walked out that day with lingering stares from PTA looking moms who probably thought I belonged in a mental institution. I still don't give a shit what other people think of me, so I gave them the finger and showed up on a Monday two months ago to start my personal training with Brock.

He gets me.

Never has he asked personal questions or made comments about the marks on my body which are impossible to hide in a gym setting. Long sleeve shirts and scarves are null and void when you're sweating your ass off with boxing gloves on.

We've been training many times a week together and I couldn't have asked for a better sparring partner. My muscle mass is through the roof and I'm pleased that on those nights I don't need alcohol to ensure myself a few hours of sleep.

I leave here exhausted.

I wave at a few of the guys as I make my way toward the exit. It's dark out. I prefer to train late specifically for the sleep benefit, usually arriving here around seven and getting home around nine.

As usual, Brock watches me leave through the window on the side of the building and stays there until I'm in my SUV. He's very protective when it comes to my safety.

We've bonded these past few months, and although I turned down his wife's invitation for drinks a few times, he seems to understand and still holds a candle for me. If I were ever in trouble, I know he'd help me out. He's a good person.

I climb in my truck and head for the highway. The gym is only ten minutes from home which is convenient for me. I drive through the small town outside Indianapolis that's much like the old one in North Carolina, only a little bigger.

Instead of one grocery store there are three, and also many small chain stores that provide anything I need. I haven't left town much since I moved here simply because I don't need to. There's a small mall on the south side of town that curbs my retail therapy when in need. And instead of having only one liquor store, this town actually boasts one dedicated entirely to wine.

It's an all-around win, minus the man I once thought highly of who gave quite possibly the best orgasm of my life.

I pull onto the little lane I live on; thinking about the man that still makes me feel warm at times.

Ryder.

I can't say I hate him, he just deeply disappointed me. I didn't know him long and I've been gone for just over two months, but I learned I can put that 'attraction by proximity theory' right out the window. At least once a day he crosses my mind, and it's not for lack of eye candy around here, especially at the gym. But shit happens, we learn to move on, end of story.

I've had more than my fair share of offers for companionship. Brock eventually stepped in and put his foot down. I appreciate his protectiveness, even though I can take care of myself in that department. However, it was getting a bit relentless and we both wanted to focus on my training, not worrying which man was going to ask me for drinks next.

Not many women venture into *Fist*. It's mostly a man's gym, aside from the self-defense classes they offer. The few fake-titted bitches that came to 'work out' here quickly moved on.

It's not spin class and Zumba at *Fist*. Its sweat, blood and tears. Sadly that would ruin their makeup, so they didn't stay long.

I reach my house and take in my surroundings as usual. My little bungalow is nondescript. It doesn't attract the eye, but it's not cluttered either. A little grey-sided abode on just under an acre of land.

There is a scattering of trees throughout the property and it's about a hundred and fifty feet to the river's edge. There's privacy fencing on both sides of the property and a garage to park my truck in. It's not my old little cottage style home, but it works for us.

The neighbors on both sides of me are old enough to enter nursing homes. I've learned most of the lane seems the same. These houses were built in the fifties and I think the original residents still live in most of them.

It's quiet, and they don't get out much.

My first week here I had a few knocks on the door and a muffin basket delivered. I learned I don't need to answer the door with a gun in my hand. Not in this neighborhood, but I still keep it close by.

I pull in the paved drive and press the garage door opener. I scan the surroundings once more before pulling in.

I've felt extremely off the past two days. The lack of sleep from the nightmares, and my random feelings of being watched certainly doesn't help. The hairs on the back of my neck aren't standing up so I try my best to shrug it off.

THE UGLY ROSES

I go through this from time to time; nightmares inflicting my paranoia. I do feel more comfortable now that I've been training with Brock. I know my skills have improved immensely and should someone try to attack me they are in for a surprise. I may still be small, but even Brock comments on the strength I've gained.

Most people would get excited at something like winning a trip to Vegas; I get a thrill out of knowing I can lay someone on their ass if they try to touch me.

As per usual, I'll always be different.

I get out of the truck to a happy tail wagging dog, more excitedly than usual. The garage is heated and when I'm gone for more than a few hours I leave her out here. I installed a dog door on the wall and a good sized fenced-in portion outside for her to use when I'm gone.

"Why so happy pretty girl, huh?" I reach down and nuzzle her fur.

She smells different. Perhaps old Mr. Clemens from next door brought over his wife's famous pot roast for her again. He does this once a week when his wife cooks said pot roast because it's more like beef jerky—his dentures can't handle it.

I don't blame him for not wanting to eat it, and Norma appreciates it. Usually he brings it over Sunday night when his wife catches up on her knitting. I don't recall seeing him yesterday, but that's not uncommon since I don't sit staring out the window like most of the old folk who live around here do. Still, it could mean that he brought it over tonight instead while I was at the gym.

I open the connecting door to the house and Norma runs in first. This is our routine. If someone is in there, she'll let me know.

I watch her make the rounds through the hallway to the two bedrooms, and then back toward me. She heads towards the couch and sits down.

All clear.

When I first moved in there was a wall separating the kitchen from the living room. I hired a contractor to clean it up after I took a sledge hammer to the drywall keeping them apart. I couldn't stand the closed off space. He then cut out the two-by-fours and made what's basically a large opening above the counter to the ceiling. It's not an island with kickass barstools, but now I have a clear view to all exits from the kitchen and living room.

I paid him cash and he quickly went on his way.

I haven't done any decorating here, just demolition. Most walls are all still white and the linoleum floors are clean enough that I didn't replace them. I bought a giant area rug, cheap furniture for the living room and a bedroom set.

That's it. This place is rented through an agency and I had no urge to make it feel like home. I just needed it to be livable.

There's one small hallway that has two doors off the living room. On one side is the master bedroom, which holds my small double bed, nightstand and a dresser. The closet is useless but wide enough to hang a few items.

The other bedroom is my makeshift closet. No furniture, just a few clothing racks and my safe bolted through the old dingy carpet inside the closet there.

Off the kitchen is a small bathroom with a tub-shower combo, pedestal sink and a toilet. It has the essentials but holds none of the flare my old home did. I know deep down I haven't made this place my home because it's not that—a home. I have no intention of living here forever. It's merely middle ground to get my shit together and have somewhere to sleep at night.

It's plain and it's ugly. It will also be a whole lot easier to leave behind.

I head into the kitchen for a glass of wine and some cheese. I never replaced anything in here either. The older yellow appliances still remain; that and the melamine countertops pulling it all together. I grab what I need from the fridge and head toward the bedroom.

I have a small flat screen on the dresser. I fire it up as I change into my sleepwear. A hefty glass of wine and some mindless television should put me to sleep.

Chapter Eighteen

I'm in the middle of flipping eggs when there's a light knock at the door. Norma barks and heads in that direction before plopping her hefty ass on the floor.

Neighbors.

I've gotten a lot better with this; a few old birds out for a walk once a week or so want to talk about their lovely grandsons who would be pleased to meet me. I've softened to their tactics but firmly state I'm not interested at the moment.

Bad divorce and all, is my story.

I peek out the curtained window and see Greta on my front stoop. She's pushing seventy and doesn't leave the house much, other than for her bridge club on Wednesday and church on Sunday. She's invited me a few times but I think she took the hint I too don't like to leave the house much. I also don't play bridge, nor am I religious.

"Hi Greta, what can I do for you?" I ask the old bird. It's nine in the morning and she's dressed in her usual attire of a silk blouse with shoulder pads, which are always lopsided, and a long skirt with nude stockings and open toed shoes. It's the old bird getup around here.

I don't judge.

"Hello, Miss Elle. Hope I didn't disturb you?" she asks. Unwanted knocking without a calling card would make Greta say a few extra Hail Mary's at church if she thought she inconvenienced me.

"No worries Greta, just making breakfast. Everything okay?"

I'm not usually so attentive with people, but this little lane filled with senior citizens makes me feel responsible for them somehow.

Last month I called an ambulance for old Mrs. Butler's husband who had fallen from his walker and busted up his hip getting the mail. These people are not threatening, and I do what I can to help them.

"Oh yes dear, we're all okay. I was just wondering if you had a friend in town. I saw a man here yesterday, but he seemed to be right at home. If you're dating again Miss Elle, I was hoping you could maybe see my grandson this weekend?"

I blank out at that point.

A man.

At my house.

I need details.

"Greta, I'm sorry; your grandson is a fine young man. But could you please tell me who it was you saw yesterday? What did he look like? Did he have a car?"

She's taken aback for a moment before she seems to gather herself to respond.

"Oh Miss Elle, I don't want to cause any trouble. This not being the marital home yet and all, but he seemed to know the place and your puppy, so I assumed he was someone special like, you know?" the kind old bird replies.

No, I don't know. But I can't startle her any more than I have.

"It's okay Greta, I just haven't had many visitors yet and I was out late last night. Can you tell me anything else?" I ask, kindly trying to coax the details out of her.

"Well dear, he was a big man. That puppy of yours was sure happy to see him. But I don't know what kind of man he is dear; he had those tattoos all over his arms that everyone seems to get now. I hear most people get those in the prisons so I hope he's not a bad man."

She's shaking her head at the disbelief that people mar their bodies with art, but I know the minute she mentioned them who she's talking about.

There's only one man that Norma loves who's covered in tattoos on his arms. Well, two men. She's met Brock and loved him from the get-go; another sign to me that he's a good man. Any other man and she would have ripped the fence apart.

It can only be him though.

Ryder's found me.

It's the only option since I was with Brock last night. However, I went to dinner and did some shopping before the gym, so it could've been him. His wife has made him stop by a few times with her baked goods from the café she owns. Brock has also been around, or close enough to wave when he's out jogging sometimes.

"I don't think it's a bad man Greta, it's most likely the trainer from my gym. Did you see what he was driving?" I ask.

Brock and his wife live two miles away and there's a running trail on the other side of the lane I live on. He definitely could've been jogging through.

"No dear, I didn't see a car. I just wanted to check in and make sure you were okay. You don't get many visitors, after all," she says in distaste.

A woman my age should be married with four children by now in her books.

"It's okay Greta. Thanks for stopping by."

I can smell my eggs burning on the stove. Now I just want to call Brock to verify it was him.

"No problem dear. I'll head to town now; need some more flour so I can finish making my biscuits. You take care."

She ambles down the steps.

"You too Greta, have a good day."

I all but slam the door and dash for my prepaid.

"Hello?" Brock's groggy voice greets me from the other end of the line.

"Brock, its Elle." I say out of breath into the phone. His voice perks up at the mention of my name.

"What's up girl?'

I cut straight to the chase. "Were you at my place yesterday?"

"No, haven't been there since last week when your dog chased me down on my run. Talk to me Elle."

This man is so awesome I could cry. I know if I tell him someone was here, he'll be over before I hang up the phone. But I can't do that to him, or me. I need to keep my cool and play it down or he'll be camped out on my front step for the next three days with a gun tucked in his waistband and his gloves on.

He's that protective.

"Nothing to talk about Brock, neighbor thought she saw someone here, but her Alzheimer's gets the best of her sometimes, so I thought I'd ask," I play off with an amusement in my tone, hoping he buys it.

"You need me girl, I'm there. Just say the word."

It's moments like this when I take a deep breath and thank the universe for sometimes putting such awesome people in my life.

"I know Brock thank you, she's probably talking about your visit last week. Like I said, Alzheimer's." I play it off again.

"Alright Elle. I'll swing by tomorrow morning on my run. You need anything before then you call me or Sam at the bakeshop."

"Will do Brock, thanks."

I need to settle my mind after that fiasco this morning, so I make a tea and take it to the large dining room table. I've turned the table and the wall adjacent to it into my work station.

One week after moving in I decided to dig out 'the box'. Well, most of it. I've spread all accounts and statements of my attack across the table and pasted the photos on the wall, photos from the parking lot where I was taken, photos from the basement, and photos of the man responsible. I drank for three days straight when I brought this all into the light. It made the nightmares worse and the three-day bender did little to help.

I spent that bender and a few days after embracing the numb feeling I found in the basement that horrid day. I've slowly learned with passing time that if I distance myself from the situation and look at the evidence as an outsider it's much easier to handle.

I purposely put all photos that include me back into the safe. I know what I looked like, I don't need to see it again. It won't help me solve anything.

I study everything, the witness account from the parking lot, my statements I barely remember giving in the hospital while I was doped up on morphine. I look over the basement photos with a magnifying glass making sure I haven't missed anything.

I'm relentless.

I could recite every detail from memory; I've spent that much time looking at it. *I can't stop.* It's as if this is my life purpose, to catch a potential killer. Not get a job at the local beauty salon, not cure cancer and save the whales. Not get married and start up a family in the 'burbs.

No.

My purpose is to catch the man that helped that evil bastard Andrew. I know he's out there. I can *feel* it, regardless of the DNA, or lack thereof. He's out there and I will find him.

It's late evening when I call it quits. I stretch the aches out of my back from sitting so long and head into the kitchen. It'll be soup and a sandwich tonight since I lack the drive to cook a hearty meal.

I curl up on the couch with a tray of vegetable soup and a ham sandwich and tune into the Food Network. It's enough to keep my mind occupied while I slowly eat my dinner.

My body still aches from last night's training with Brock, so once I'm finished I grab a half-empty bottle of wine and head for the tub. I have a small docking station for my iPod on the shelf in the bathroom so I plug it in while I soak.

I think back as I stare at the peach colored wall. I think about the people I've lost; those who've died and those I've ran away from. I think of Jimmy and Laura and her beautiful kids.

I wonder how much their looks have changed since I've been gone? I think of the locals from my old watering hole and old acquaintances from work. Then I think about the people I've met on this journey—Tiny, Doc and kind old Greta across the street. Some of these people have drastically changed my life more than others. Some I never would've met if it were not for my past.

As much as I still feel the guilt weighing on me for how things have happened in my life, I try to focus on the small positive things like calling the ambulance for Mr. Butlers that day, and providing Tom with enough money in prepaid rent to continue living life on his fishing boat. Maybe one day the small things will add up to bigger things and the guilt will ease away.

***

"I wish it didn't have to go that way Jayne. But you left me no choice. You waited too long and I had to make a decision."

The psycho sits on a chair to the side of the room with his hands pulling at his hair. I'm guessing I've been here for about three days.

I've been given water and a few granola bars since I've been here. Much of my time is spent trying to read this man, to understand what makes him tick and what makes him cool down. I barely spoken since the first day I've been here other than to say 'bathroom'. I refuse to piss myself even though I've been wearing the same underwear since I got here and haven't showered. I know I smell bad.

I'm absolutely certain he planned on killing me sooner. I haven't spent much more time being hung and stabbed with the knife. He seems to be slowing down. He needs sleep, I can tell. I've gotten a few hours randomly each day on the floor in the corner. He's still afraid to take his eyes off me to get any shuteye himself.

If I was not tied to the floor I would consider some heroic escape plan where I take him out as I flee. Sadly, there's nothing in this corner I'm lying in to use as a weapon, and the five feet of slack on the rope I'm given only allows me to go over to a bucket to piss in.

"If you had just paid attention, better attention Jayne, more attention, I wouldn't have had to do it! I didn't want to see you hurt, and then you wouldn't leave the house so I couldn't see you as much anymore. I needed to see you, so I had to take you. You were supposed to come to me after they died, that was the plan. Then you would need me."

The accident.

But it wasn't an accident if what he's saying is true.

The lazy detective's words ring though my head. "The brake line was torn, Ms. O'Connor. Most likely something caught it and pulled it loose from the wheel. These things happen ma'am. Could've been a tree branch for all we know and it slowly leaked out over a short time. Not something you realize until it's too late."

It clicks, and instantly the fog is cleared from my brain.

I settle my eyes on the sick bastard across the room. If I had no fight in me before, I have it now. I will scream, I will fight, and I won't stop until this heartless fuck takes his last breath. I feel the angry tears building in my eyes and the increased beating of my heart.

He killed my family.

I buried my little girl.

Lilly.

Now...

I'm going to bury him.

* * *

I'm hefting the garbage out to the end of the driveway when Norma takes off across the street barking and tail wagging.

Brock.

"Jesus Elle, I think your dog's blind." He's chuckling at the fact she still barks like a rabid animal whenever he comes running toward the house.
"Nah, she's just protective."

I set the bag of trash down and face him.

Brock is looking around the property and surveying the street. He's perceptive, and not so subtle about it. He knows I have demons, and he makes a habit to check the surroundings whenever he's close by.

"All good around here, Elle?" I know what he's asking, and I'm still going to play it off. Even if Ryder has found me I know he poses no immediate threat. He hasn't approached me, so either Greta's Alzheimer's really is in full effect or he's just checking in. It's been two days; surely if he was going to make a move he would've done so by now?

"Yes, all good. Just getting ready to head into town. Maybe stop by Sam's for some sugar," I say with a small smile.

He's studying me intently and I know I'm not going to like what comes out of his mouth.

"Your mind has been elsewhere for almost a week. You've got bags under your eyes and you *never* call me, for anything. So what's up with the phone call yesterday? Bullshit somebody else babe, but not me."

The genuine look of concern on his face is enough to make me crack, a little. He'll lose sleep over something like this, worrying about me. His wife is one lucky woman and I'm thankful to have someone like him in my life.

"Got a little freaked out Brock, that's all. I have good neighbors who spend all day looking out their windows at what's going on. Unfortunately they get their days mixed up sometimes. If something is wrong, I'll let you know."

Brock shakes his head and puts his hands on my shoulders. He rarely touches me, and I'm thankful for that. The way he's looking into my eyes softens my heart a little.

"Babe, you're not stupid. I know that. But you're stubborn as hell, so I give you space. If you're in any kind of trouble Elle, I will get in your space quicker than you can fucking say *help*. I know your hiding from something and you don't want to talk about it. But I need you to take me seriously when I say if you need help, in any way, you call me."

I'm at a loss for words and my throat is dry, so all I manage is a jerky nod. Before I can blink, he pulls me into a hug. It's the first one I've had since my days with Ryder and I feel the tears starting to build. I give him a quick squeeze on his sides before pulling back.

"Gotta run Brock, I'll see you tonight."

I don't look back as I walk toward the house. So I don't see him wait until I'm safely tucked inside before continuing on his jog.

Chapter Nineteen

"Fuck ya girl, hit me! Get those elbows in!"

I'm full of fire tonight. After my little chat with Brock this morning, I went back to bed and woke up centered and fueled with the desire to hurt someone.

Last night's nightmare did a number on me, so I got the anguish out this morning, letting the anger settle in deep before I came to the gym tonight. It's a good kind of anger, and its keeping me on my toes.

I see Brock's leg swing out in his attempt to knock me on my ass. I jump backward, swinging around with my own leg out, nailing him behind the knee. He starts to go down so I throw an elbow into his ribs and a right hook to his jaw.

"Enough! Ya got me. Fuck, babe!" He wipes the side of his mouth. I notice there's a little bit of blood there.

It makes me smile, a full-on genuine teeth baring smile. He stares at me like I've grown two heads, before I lend him a hand to get up.

"Guess I should be thankful I brought a smile to your face, even if it cost me my balls getting whipped by a woman."

Still smiling, I shake my head at him. "I won't lie dude, if feels fuckin' good."

I throw my hand out for a fist bump which he reciprocates before throwing his arm around my shoulders.

"I guess I'll look on the bright side, seeing as Sam likes to play nurse when I'm banged up."

He imitates a limp and I chuckle before moving out of his grasp. "Ha! Well you better get home to your nurse then."

I grab my bag from the side of the mats and throw my gloves in. Tonight warrants a bath at home instead of a shower here, and maybe some takeout from my favorite Italian place.

Feeling like I could walk on water, I wave as I make my way outside. Brock has a grin on his face and watches through the window like usual as I go. I spare a quick glance up at the sky and thank my family for bringing such a great person into my life, even if only for a short little while.

I hit the key fob to unlock my truck and stop dead in my tracks when I see the lone figure leaning up against it.

His face is in the shadows and his silhouette is illuminated by the interior lights that have come on inside the vehicle. His hands are in his pockets and his posture is tight.

Ryder.

I ignore the mild flutter in my stomach at the sight of him.

"You happy with him Elle?" he asks. I understand exactly what he's referring to, or whom I should say. I don't bother correcting him because I'm more interested in how he came to be here.

"How did you find me Ryder?"

This is the only thing I need to know right now. I don't like the idea of someone being able to track me down. Not that I'm totally unhappy to see him, just a little unsettled about how he's standing in front of me right now.

In Indianapolis. Not North Carolina.

I hear the gym door open and quick footsteps headed my way. Ryder looks over my shoulder and soon Brock is standing beside me. I feel his hand touch my arm before he speaks to me.

"You alright, babe?"

He's speaking to me, but he's looking at Ryder. Ryder doesn't move from his position leaning on my truck, attracting Brock's attention. He turns his head toward me and talks a little quieter, but loud enough that Ryder can hear. "Elle, you know I don't get in your business but is there something I'm missing here, or you want me to take you home?"

Ryder gives him a hard look but Brock finishes before he can say anything.

"No disrespect yet man, but I've known her for two months; I don't know you at all. Don't doubt you could be a good guy but forgive me if I need to hear that from her mouth before I believe it, seeing as she doesn't seem too happy to see you."

I love him even more in this moment. After I kicked his ass today I didn't think that was possible.
"Brock, meet Ryder Callaghan of Callaghan Securities. Ryder, Brock West, my trainer and the owner of this gym."

Ryder still stands firm, but the hold Brock has on my arm relaxes.

"You work out of the East Coast?" Brock asks. Ryder nods his head and seems to calm, slightly. "That's me," Ryder says with the little bit of pride in his tone he always has when speaking of his work.

Brock nods, a confused look on his face when he asks, "Denny Black. He used to work with me here at the gym before he left for the East Coast, taking a job with Callaghan Security. Haven't heard from him. Did it work out?"

I'm stumped with where this conversation is headed before Ryder breaks through my confusion.

"It worked out. I hired the big bastard on the spot and posted him up near Virginia."

Brock rubs his hands over his face and nods his head. "Fuck man, small world. But good, I'm glad to hear that. He was going through some shit here and I hoped he came out alright on the other side. Needed change, I'm glad he found it. He doing okay?"

Brock's concern for his friend is unmistakable, and I'm happy Ryder puts him at ease.

"He works hard at his job through the week and spends his weekends chasing with my other guys. Not the friendliest fucker, but he does his job well and so far has no complaints. Can't tell you much more than that."

Ryder's assessment of Denny seems to satisfy Brock. The look of relief on his face doesn't go unnoticed.

"Thanks for the info, you see him again tell the prick to call me, would you?"

"I will."

Ryder turns his head to look at me and the tension in his posture returns.

What the fuck is he tense with me for?

"We need to talk Elle." Those black eyes bore into mine. My happy mood from kicking Brock's ass earlier has long since vanished and my stubborn pride sets in.

"Nothing left to talk about Ryder. Now, if you'll excuse me I have a hot bath and a bottle of vino waiting at home for me."

I give Brock's shoulder a squeeze before I go, silently thanking him for his concern tonight.

"Go let Sam play nurse. I'll see you Friday."

I notice Ryder's posture, the way he studies me when I touch Brock. Not that it's any of his business but I was not about to let my new friend go home without a thank you, even if it was a silent one.

"So, you're into sharing your men now Elle? Didn't peg you as the type," the smug bastard declares.

It's enough to set me off and put a hand to Brock's chest to stop any altercation between these two. Ryder has moved away from my truck and is now standing a few feet in front me. I speak to him in the sweetest, most condescending voice I have.
"No baby, I don't share. And Brock, being the good man that he is, doesn't stray from his beautiful wife."

I look him up and down and register the shock on his face before taking a step around him and speaking over my shoulder. "Can't say the same about you, can we Ryder?"

I don't wait for his reply as I climb in my truck and close the door. He spins around and runs his hand through his hair, boring holes into the side of my head.

I don't wait for him; I don't roll the window down to hear what he has to say. And I don't give a flying fuck in this moment if Brock pummels his ass into the pavement.

Why did I get that damn flutter in my stomach like a horny teenager? And why these past few months did he still invade my thoughts? Even knowing that he was engaged, I still couldn't get my mind off him. Perhaps it's a case of 'we all want what we can't have'. He became the unobtainable, so I could not rid him from my thoughts.

I don't look at either of them as I make my way out of the parking lot.

* * *

I've drank almost a full bottle of wine. I'm too disappointed for it to fully hit me. I wish I could be angrier, but I'm just fed up.

Such a good night turned to shit in an instant. My bath is finished, and I dress in a tank and panties, my usual sleep attire plus my robe. I'm trying to decide whether I just want to curl up in bed and sleep or get drunk, so I sleep peacefully when my head finally does hit the feathers.

I'm pulling the towel out of my damp hair when I hear a knock at the door. I'll bet its Ryder. But looking at the time it could be Brock after he closed up the gym.

I'm hoping on the latter.

Norma is at the door wagging her tail and sniffing around it. The storm door is locked, as well as the main door. I unlock the main and face a defeated looking Ryder.

"Please let me talk Elle," is the first thing he says before his eyes travel up and down my body.

"I said what I needed to say on the phone to you almost three months ago. Then I finished it in the parking lot tonight. I'm done Ryder. The only thing I want to hear from you is how you found me. After that you can leave."

My voice is firm, and I keep eye contact with him regardless that his are wandering.

"I'll tell you."

"Now Ryder, I want to know *now*."

I cross my arms over my chest, willing him to hurry the fuck up with the story.

"It took a while, and it will take some time to tell it. Let me in and we can talk about it. Please."

He's genuine in wanting to speak with me, I'll give him that. But the moment sweet nothings come out of his mouth is the moment his ass will be kicked out the door. The fact that his black long sleeve shirt is hugging his beautiful body and his jeans hang perfectly on his hips isn't helping this situation.

I need to put some clothes on.

"I want to go to bed. You'll be quick, and then you'll get the fuck out."

I unlock the storm door and make my way back in the house. "Wait on the couch. I'll be back in a minute."

I head to my room and throw on a pair of sweat pants. I need more armor around him and being half dressed is not going to help. I grab my wine bottle from the kitchen and make my way back to the living room. I settle in the comfy chair beside the sofa, not wanting to share it with him and wave a hand for him to commence talking.

"This place isn't you Elle." He muses looking around.

"You don't know me Ryder, and I don't know *you*. Now cut the small talk and tell me how you found me. I'll give you ten minutes to explain and then you can go."

He looks visibly hurt at the way I've just spoke to him but I really don't give a shit anymore. The lying engaged bastard deserves that and then some. Thankfully he cuts to the chase.

"When I got home and saw that you really were gone, I started looking for you Elle. I got a lot of dead ends. The first bit sent me up to some cabins in Virginia where you used your driver's license as identification and debit card to book a stay there. But I later learned that was before I spoke to you last. You used cash obviously for your trip out here and closed you bank accounts back home before you left.

"You were gone for almost a month before you opened up a bank account here, next town over from this one. I spent a little over a week in that town, waiting for a hit to come up on your bank card after I hacked into your accounts."

What the fuck? I'm not naive enough to think that couldn't happen but shit, the fact that anyone can know where I spend my money if they try hard enough is a little unsettling. I'm about to tell him so but he cuts me off before I get the chance.

"You didn't use it for two more weeks until it popped up being used at a specialty wine store in this town. Unfortunately, when I got the hit on that I was back in Virginia setting up a job for my team. I came here last week and drove every side road within ten miles of this town that had water near it. Even drove up and down this street but didn't know you lived here. I still kept making the laps, hoping your obvious love for being near the water stayed true when you moved here.

"I came back through this street a few days ago, and who do I see outside? A dog that looks just like Norma. I parked my truck and walked toward her. She was some fucking happy to see me." He reminisces with a gentle smile on his face. I may not like him much right now, but that doesn't mean Norma shares my feelings.

Black eyes bore into mine as he says, "So I watched, and I waited Elle. To see if you were alive and well, to see if whatever it is you ran from last time finally caught up with you. Then I saw you with Brock, here at your house, and then at the gym. I understand I jumped the gun on that one and I apologize. He seemed friendly with you, and I wanted to beat the fucking piss out of him because I was jealous of the smile he put on your face."

He shakes his head and runs his hands through his hair. "I would have *killed* to make you smile like that, Elle." Sounding defeated he continues, "Not fucking happy I wasn't the man to do it, but I'm happy someone did."

His elbows are on his knees and he's still staring directly at me.

His time is almost up.

"Not that it's your business Ryder, but I've been training with that man for a little over two months now. The smile was because my hard work finally paid off and I took him down tonight. That smile wasn't for anyone but myself, and I fucking *deserve* that."

He moves his hands up in surrender and agrees with me. "Yes, you absolutely do Elle. I just hope I get to see it again."

"Times up, Ryder." I move to stand but he stays with his ass planted on the couch.

"I told you how I found you. I've spent weeks on the road and now that I'm finally here, I'm not leaving until you fucking listen to what I have to say." I'm shocked at his outburst. It's not yelling, but it's loud and firm enough that he gets my attention.

"I gave you the info you wanted first, now you can give me mine. Because woman, if there's one thing I fucking hate in this world it's when people jump to conclusions without asking questions first. So you can sit down and listen, because I'm not fucking leaving until you do."

He's pointing toward the chair, and as much as I would like to show him exactly how fucking stubborn I can be, I know he's right. I didn't listen to him or ask any questions.

I packed up, and I left.

I grab my phone out of the pocket on my robe, ready to call Brock if he pushes this conversation any longer than I like.

"Brock ain't coming to help you beautiful. He'll tell you to sit and fuckin' listen too, so get comfortable."

I top up my wine glass and sit back down in the chair. "Five more minutes, and yes, he *will* come and help me."

The frustration is rolling off of him in waves. He looks tired, like he's been on the road for a while. If I was a nicer person I'd offer him some food and a bed to sleep in. But as I said, *if* I was a nicer person.

"I was engaged for four years. Been single for about eight."His black eyes on mine show nothing but the truth. His gaze doesn't waver and his posture stays firm, faced toward me.

"I met Anna in my twenties. She was fun, she was friendly and wanted nothing more than to make me happy in the beginning. We moved in together in Jacksonville after a while and started talking marriage. I was away a lot with the Corps and she didn't like that, she also doubted my commitment being gone six months at a time. I bought her a ring to keep her happy and started working on the cottage, making it into a home so one day we could move out of the apartment and start a family. She didn't want a shotgun wedding; she wanted a big one where the flowers cost more than my truck. I didn't have that kind of money back then and her rich parents cut her off when she flunked everything in University.

"I spent more time overseas and working extra jobs at home to give her what she wanted, but it was never enough. I was young and stupid, and unfortunately it took me too long to realize she was more interested in the vanity of things than the meaning of them."

He's staring at the wall now, lost in the history of his life with this evil woman. I spotted that bitch a mile away; I don't understand how he couldn't. Men are blind sometimes, and women can be conniving catty bitches.

"We opened up a joint bank account, so I could send money to help pay the bills while I was away. She still had a small inheritance from her family but I wasn't making my future wife pay for everything when I was gone.

"A month after that, I got a call from my bank saying a Ms. Anna Walters was trying to access my savings fund but her name wasn't authorized on that account. I quickly learnt what a money hungry bitch she was but put that in the back of my mind a lot because when a man comes home from a war to a warm bed with a woman in it, there's not much else that matters.

"When I got home, not only did I find out she'd missed the rent and hydro bill because she spent it on a trip with her friends to the Bahamas, I also found out she'd been sleeping with the mayor's son."

Shit I want to pummel the bitch, and wish I did when I had the chance.

Resolute he continues, "I didn't care about the mayor's son. Still don't. After the call from the bank I knew I would be leaving her. Unfortunately I had to wait three months before I got home to speak with her about it face to face. Long story short Elle, I packed my shit and moved to the cottage. Gave my notice to the landlord and left her to the wolves. Not my fucking problem she can't manage her money. She soon moved in with the mayor's son and then anyone else with money who would take her in.

"My guess, her showing up at the house this time means she's out of money and her recent sugar daddy kicked her out. Once again though beautiful, not my problem. This isn't the first time she's showed up, and it probably won't be the last. I've never taken her back and I don't intend to."

Wow.

That's a lot to take in.

"Greedy bitch," I say, hating when someone kind is taken advantage of.

"That about sums it up. I have money now Elle, *a lot*. My security business does well and I'm sure she's learned about that too, which is why she still comes around."

"I don't care about your money Ryder," I say honestly, because I don't. I certainly don't need it.

"I know you don't Elle, but I'm sure it gave Anna the push to come back. I'm just sorry I wasn't there to keep her away from you. Not sure what all she said, but I imagine it wasn't good."

"I told you before Ryder, I don't do the catty bitch routine."

We sit in silence for a few moments. Both processing I'm sure. Him able to breathe a little easier because he found me, and me going over everything he just said. I'm not sure how much time passes before he's in front of me with his ass on the coffee table. Elbows back on his knees, head leaning closer to mine.

THE UGLY ROSES

"I miss you Elle. I miss seeing you on your back deck for your morning coffee and I miss your smart mouth. I also miss your cooking, but that's not why I'm here."

I stare into those beautiful eyes and breathe in the scent of him. Fresh laundry and man. No cologne for the road but it still lingers on his clothing.

"Why are you here then Ryder?" I solemnly ask.

I'm mentally exhausted, on top of my two hour workout with Brock I can't take much more.

"I'm here because I want you with me Elle. I want you home where I can see you, and not just because I'm a selfish bastard but because I know this is not where you belong. This place is temporary beautiful, it's not your home."

If anyone would figure something like that out it would be Ryder. We may not have known each other long but sometimes you just *know* someone. Sometimes better than you know yourself.

I wish I had of gave him the benefit of the doubt when it came to Anna, but I have to remind myself that I was leaving anyway after he saw my scars.

"This is a lot to take in Ryder, and to be honest with you I can't process it all right now. I'm exhausted. I'm sure you are too. I need to sleep on this and deal with it tomorrow."

He leans over and runs his hand down my face and curls it around the back of my neck. He leans in close so his forehead is against mine.

"You can take the time beautiful, I told you I would never push you and I won't. But I'm not leaving here without an answer. Whether that takes you until tomorrow or a few days from now, I'm going to be right here, waiting."

He leans forward and places his lips on mine. He's firm enough that I know he means every word he said but he doesn't try to take it further.

"I'm staying the night Elle, I've been in every shitty motel from here to the East Coast and I want to share a bed with you."

I take in a deep breath, prepared to reject him but his words stop me. "Just to sleep, I just want to sleep next to you Elle."

He sounds so defeated so I just nod. At this point I can't say no.

I grab his hand and lead us down the hallway. My room is not pretty but I never cheap out on a mattress. I let go of his hand and move to my side of the bed. I reach under my pillow and move my gun into the drawer of my night table.

"Good call beautiful."

He too removes a gun from an ankle holster and does the same thing on his side of the bed.

"Mind if I borrow your shower?" He asks as he takes off his boots.

"That's fine. Towels are in the closet beside the bathroom. Lock the front door please when you're out there," I ask as I pull the blankets back.

Ryder moves around the bed and places a kiss in my hair. "Be back in a few."

He leaves the room and I hear the front door open. Most likely he's gone to grab a bag. I don't wait up for him. I shut off the overhead light and leave the small one on that sits on the nightstand. I rid myself of my robe and sweat pants and climb into bed.

A while later I hear him come back in the room. I'm faced away from him and I don't turn around. I feel the bed dip and the covers move as he settles in and turns off the light.

A warm arm comes around my stomach and he spoons me into his front. It feels good, and warm. Like coming home. He inhales my hair before placing a kiss there.

"I missed the way you smell." A kiss is then placed on my bare shoulder before he settles down into the bed. "Thank you."

I'm not sure if he's thanking me for the cuddle, or the killer mattress. I don't ask.

"Goodnight Ryder."

"Night, beautiful."

His whiskey voice is the last sweet thing I hear before I fall asleep.

Chapter Twenty

I wake up to warmth. Deep to my soul warmth. I also feel a hand running up and down my arm, and my legs entwined with another's.

Ryder.

I'm not sure when we moved in the night, but my arm is thrown over his stomach and my head is on his shoulder. I slowly open my eyes and hear the smooth whiskey morning voice above me.

"Mornin' beautiful."

I crane my neck up and take stock of his face. His scruff is a few days overgrown and his long dark lashes lay heavy on his cheekbones. Those dark eyes are greyer around the outside in the morning. I think it makes him look even more handsome. He's shirtless and I relish in the feel of his mild scattering of chest hair under my hand.

"Morning," I yawn. I'm comfortable and quite rested. I quickly register that I spent an entire night without nightmares. I lift my head and glance across his torso and notice it's ten in the morning.

Eight hours of sleep. I can't remember when I last slept solid for that length of time.

He rolls toward me. His thigh hits me in exactly the right place between my legs. I took off my sweats because I can't stand to sleep in them if it's not winter.

The feel of his warm skin against mine is enough to make my heart rate speed up a little. His hand begins making a beautiful soothing journey up and down my back. I close my eyes and let out a little hum.

He places slow random kisses along my hairline while I move my hand up to lay above his heart.

"Feels good to wake up with you, haven't slept that good in a while." He repeats the earlier thoughts going through my head as his hands continue their wonderful journey up to my shoulders, and down around my hips.

I groan when his hand meets my thigh, still feeling a bruise from Monday's session with Brock when he took me down on the mats.

Ryder reaches up and moves the blanket down past my ass. The movement causes his thigh to push harder into my core and I moan a little at the contact.

"Jesus, its blue. This from training with Brock?" His hand moves lightly over the bruised area.

"Couldn't get my head on straight the other day. I learned from it and went back last night to kick ass." Which I totally fucking did and hope I can pull it off again.

"I wish he didn't leave you like this afterward, but I get it. If it makes you feel good and teaches you something, then I'm happy you're doing it Elle."

His hand glides down towards my knee and he leans the upper half of his body over mine. I mewl at the loss of his thigh between my legs but when I feel his lips touch my hip I sigh out in relief.

It's still quite dark in my room, the blackout shades are drawn but light seeps in from the hallway. His hands work their way down my leg and when he gets to my ankle, he stops with the kisses to speak.

"How's the ankle been?" It's kind of him to ask and I respond truthfully. "Tender a few times after landing wrong in a kick at the gym, but it's okay," I reply in my still sleep filled raspy voice.

His hands nudge me onto my back and within moments he's looming above me. His dark hair hangs around his face and his eyes roam my features. The majority of his weight is held on his forearms, but the lower half of his body has settled into mine.

His eyes continue to search my face as his hands move into my hair. He's studying me, for what I don't know.

"I'm gonna kiss you now beautiful. Because if today, tomorrow or the next day you tell me to leave, I want to make damn sure I gave it everything while I was given the chance."

I don't get the chance to respond before his mouth is on mine. It's deep, but slow and *oh so passionate*. He nips my bottom lip lightly to gain access into my mouth. His tongue twirls with mine in a sensual dance that further relaxes my body.

Wet lips work their way across my face and down my neck. He licks a trail from ear to collarbone and slides his hand down my side. I moan in pleasure when his thumb moves over my breast and he takes it further by moving his mouth in that direction.

His mouth surrounds my nipple through the threadbare tank top while I push my fingers into his silky hair. His hands continue their journey south until they reach my panties and he moves his large body further down the bed.

He places open mouth kisses across my hip and then my still covered center. "Ahhhhh," I moan at the contact. Strong hands grab onto the sides of the only piece of clothing separating my aching center from his mouth and he slowly lowers them down my legs.

He lifts my ankles, one at a time and bends them at the knee before planting them back on the bed. His eyes stay glued to my waxed core before they meet mine.

"Beautiful everywhere, babe. I'm going to taste you now. Don't stop me please." I couldn't if I wanted to, but I also lack the ability of speech. I spread my legs wider in invitation and it's all the answer he needs before he dives in.

"Gahhhhh, fuck!" I scream in pleasure. He lays one long lick from bottom to top before attacking my clit and bringing his fingers into the folds. Last time was quick and fast. This time he's prolonging it, but it makes the act that much sweeter.

One finger then two enters me and I can feel it start to build. "Shit, don't stop!" I rasp bringing my feet up and placing them on his shoulders.

"Not a fucking chance." He growls against my clit and it's enough to send goose bumps over my entire body. He's relentless and I'm close. His skill is perfect and I can't hold out much longer.

"Shit Ry, I'm gonna come!" I pull on his hair with my fingers. He grabs my wrists to remove my hands, the loss of his fingers inside me slowing down my orgasm.

"No," I start to whine, but Ryder's already sitting up and moves to lay back on the bed grabbing me by the hips on the way.

"Not like that beautiful, you'll sit on my face when you come. "I'm stunned a little and slow in my movements due to my semi-sated state. I'm taking too long, and he grabs one of my legs and pulls it over his body before hoisting me by the hips up to his face.

"Grab the fucking headboard Elle and sit down, *now.*"

I don't need to be told twice. I do as he says and he trusts his tongue up inside me and pinches my clit between his fingers.

That's it, I'm off.

"Ahhhhhh, shit! Fuck, fuck!" I grind onto his face as he seals his mouth over me. My legs are shaking and I feel like I'm smothering him but he holds me tight, unable to move.

"I missed the way you taste. So fucking sweet." He places one last open mouth kiss to my core before moving me down his body. I fall forward onto his chest, my breathing heavy.

His hands resume running up and down my back and I register his bulge between my legs, separated by his boxers. I grind myself against him and moan at the contact.

"Sorry, beautiful. Can't help it after my mouth was on your sweet pussy and now it's smothering my dick. Why don't you go clean up and I'll go start the coffee."

He lays a playful smack on my ass which causes me to grind further against him.

"Ughh, I don't want to move yet Ry," I say in a soft sleepy voice.

Regardless of how well I slept last night I feel like I could use another hour after the delicious orgasm he gave me.

He slowly rolls up, careful of my bruised hip until he's on top. "Open your eyes beautiful." His hand gently caresses the side of my face as I open my eyes and take in the beautiful man above me. His fingers trail from the top of my hairline down to my cheek and around the other side. He lays kisses on my eyelids and nose before resting on my mouth.

"Love your green eyes babe, and a lot of other shit about you. I would also love nothing more than to bury my dick deep inside you." He lays a few more sweet kisses across my face before he continues in a soft but serious voice. "But beautiful, when I take you, I want all of you. I don't mean everything about your past because I can sense you're not ready to talk about it and that's okay. I said it before and I'll remind you again, I will never push you. What I mean is I want nothing between us. I want my hands on every bit of your body and I don't want your clothing in the way."

I try to look away but his hand at the side of my face holds firm. I can feel the moisture start to build in my eyes because I'm angry at what he'll have to look at when he sees all of me.

I worry that mid-fuck he'll turn me over to go at it from behind, one of my favorite positions, and he'll lose his erection due to the ugly sight that is my back. I don't see it much. I feel it, and I know what it looks like. But it's not something I physically have to see every day. It pains me to think about it and embarrasses me to have him look at it. He holds my face steady, his kind eyes stare into mine.

"I've seen you Elle, everything but your bare tits. Unless you count the wet t-shirt night at your place."

I can't help but let out a small laugh.

"Nothing left to hide from me, I want it all Elle. And until you're ready to share that with me, it's my fingers and mouth from here on out."

He leans down and places a promising kiss on my lips before getting up. "When you're ready babe. Until then, I'll make the coffee."

I lie in bed for a while resting in post orgasmic bliss, hashing out everything Ryder said between last night and this morning.

The man is relentless, I've gathered that much. He knows what he wants and he goes after it. I can appreciate that in a person. I'm much the same way. What gets me is the *why*?

I completely understand that we *know* each other, deeply like chemistry. It's one of those things I realized before that just happens. You can't slow it down, you can't really speed it up. All you can do is strap in and trust where the ride is going to take you. It may have bumps, it will certainly have a few forks in the road, but you know the ride is going to be so good that regardless of the dips and dives you hang on for dear life, and pray that you'll come out intact on the other side.

That's what Ryder is, a ride. A damn good one judging by his hands and face but he's still completely unpredictable and I think that's what intrigues me the most.

Growing up in a small town, you learn to create your own unpredictable situations and fun times, because if it weren't for yourself nobody else is going to do it for you. You take more chances and heighten the risks because without them life would be bloody boring.

I didn't go sky diving with Ryder or any outing for that matter, but the man still blew me away by showing up at *Fist* the other night and pulling a fast one on me by refusing to leave.

I've always worn the pants in a relationship. Not that any lasted very long. I had a few throughout high school and university, and a short-term fling that resulted in the most beautiful child I could ever ask for, but unfortunately not with the right person. Most of us always parted on good terms. Minus a creep or two in my early twenties, I just have yet to feel that deeper connection with someone.

What bothers me about this whole thing is that as much as I want to embrace it, there's still a question that won't stop nagging at my mind.

Is it a case of pity? Pity for the woman who lives alone with her dog that's extremely recluse and never answers personal questions? Does he want me because I come off as the so-called damsel in distress that needs saving? It's what he does for a living, right? Essentially solves problems and puzzles and protects people.

Will the thrill of me wear off eventually when my case has been solved? Will he choose to move on to something, or someone else?

Am I a job to him? He told me he worked missing persons and rescue missions. Will he rescue me, and then send me a metaphorical bill for services rendered in the mail? The metaphorical bill in this case being *'thanks, but this isn't working out'*.

I shut off my mind and throw on my robe. I need coffee. I look at the clock and see that it's now almost noon which means I've been laying in here locked in my mind instead of getting answers for almost an hour.

I'm a straight shooter, always have been. I tell it like it is and I don't care what you think of me. Minus the personal details of course. Time to drink up some java and search for some answers.

I stop in the bathroom and take care of business and then brush my teeth. I don't hear him in the house and figure he must have gone outside.

I head to the coffee pot and make a cup of the wonderful brew. I see no sign of Ryder out back and quickly realize why when I hear the chair in the dining room.

No.

No, no, no!

I'm stiff as a statue as I turn my eyes to peer into the dining room. Ryder's angry eyes stare back at me, a handful of paperwork in front of him. My case files. What happened to me, and the mess I'm trying to figure out is all laid out before him.

He could've been staring at me from the time I went to the bathroom but I didn't notice. My mind was set on coffee, and the conscious effort to avoid that room like the plague unless I'm going in there to work on things. Otherwise, I steer clear, especially before coffee and usually not until I have something containing alcohol in my hand.

He lowers the papers down in front of him and settles his elbows on the table. His head rests in his hands and he loses eye contact. Judging by the mess in front of him he noticed my load of casework not long after he started the coffee, which was almost an hour ago.

"I wish you would have told me babe. Fuck!" His voice carries an amount of agony I wasn't expecting to hear. I don't know how to handle this situation. I don't know what to say to him or what I should do. I know at this point I can't deny it, but I don't think I can handle the questions either.

I'm sure he's noticed the wall with all of my sticky notes trying to piece it all together. Then I wonder if he too after reading the case files thinks I'm a nutcase for arguing there were two people in on my abduction.

I know I won't be able to handle the rejection if he does believe that. I also know I'll need to change my name if he does try to ship me back to Canada to solve this mess. Hopefully that doesn't happen, but I question what he holds in higher regard- having my back or obeying the law.

I grab my coffee and smokes and head out back. I don't have a porch, but whoever lived here before me made a small area of pavers which holds a picnic table. I sit down and light up.

Today I need it.

* * *

A short while later Ryder comes and straddles the bench beside me. He doesn't look at my face though; he stares out toward the river. I'm not stupid, I understand he needs a moment and I don't interrupt him.

Long after my coffee is finished and I'm on my third smoke he finally speaks but doesn't look at me.

"I'd like to say this doesn't change anything beautiful, but it does." My disappointment couldn't be greater, but I don't dare show it on my face.

I'm tough.

I've been through enough of this shit for the past year, and before then when my family was taken from me. You learn to live with the fact that when people learn shit things about your life, they tend to treat you differently.

I can understand that. I don't think less of them for it, but for some ungodly reason I least expected it from Ryder. The man has dealt with this kind of shit. So instead of speaking, I harden my features and nod my head like the cold-hearted bitch I learned to be and roll with the punches.

I'm good at that.

"I can't be with you like this now Elle. I can't do this after seeing what I saw on that table. Fuck, Elle I *can't*."

He still isn't looking at me. I'd like to call him a coward and tell him to say it to my face, but I don't. I butt out my smoke and face the man regardless if he'll look at me or not.

The numbness is back—or should I say I'm back to Numb. That place I inhabit where the population is one.

"No worries handsome. I didn't figure anyone could, which is why I keep the fact that I'm a wanted regarding a murder to myself. So you just let me know if you're going to keep your mouth shut when you leave, otherwise I'll be moving again."

His head snaps back to mine so fast I'm surprised his neck doesn't pop.

"What the fuck do you mean, *leave*? I told you yesterday I'm not going anywhere Elle and I fucking meant it!" He's vehement with his words, I don't believe his eyes have ever been so angry.

I scoff, "Well color me fucking surprised handsome, you just told me you couldn't *'do this'*, so forgive me if I don't understand!"

Firm hands grab onto my shoulders and he roughly pulls me toward him. His face inches from mine, his breathing harsh through his teeth.

"I can't do the fucking lies Elle! That's what I can't do! You think I don't want to be with you now? You're fucking wrong! I want to know everything! The where, what, when, who and fucking why! I don't want to do this if you can't open up to me!

I need it Elle, and if you don't give it to me I will make it my business to find out on my own. With or without your fucking help!"

He smashes his lips down onto mine in the most brutal kiss he's given me yet.

I don't know whether I want to hit him or cry. I do know I won't kiss him back right now. This man is practically all I have at the moment, but it's all going to come down to one crucial answer.

I tear my mouth away from his before questioning him.

"How much did you read Ryder?" I ask with my hands pushed against his chest and my eyes firmly on his.

He leans his face closer to mine before he replies. "All of it, Elle. All your notes, most of the case file and also noticed everything that was missing about you. Your detail of injuries, as well as most of your statement. It's cut off where a Detective accuses you of having an imaginative mind in your 'state' about there being two attackers. Pages eight through thirty-two are missing as well as pictures forty-seven through ninety-six of your personal case files. Talk to me Elle, because if you don't, no fucking joke woman I will find everything out on my own and I'll fly to Canada to do it if I have to." I feel the tears leak out of my eyes and he softens his voice when he continues, "I'm guessing you don't want that babe, so my suggestion would be to let me in. Fill in the blanks and let me help you figure this out. Together, Elle," he pleads.

Flashbacks of those days in the hospital and a few times at the station being questioned filter back into my mind. I can't go there right now, I can't explain anything, yet I still need to know.

"Tell me Ryder; from your years in the service to your time spent in security and hostage rescue, what exactly is your experienced opinion regarding what you *did* see on that table? And don't fucking lie to me, you give it to me straight."

My voice is firm and so is my gaze into his.
He doesn't waver, doesn't blink. "No bullshit, no sugarcoating and no fucking lying Ryder."

I know he's assessed and gathered what he needed to before he came out here, he knows his answer and he shouldn't have to think about it. Ryder is a smart man, not just because of what I've seen but because of what he does for a living.

He rests one arm on the picnic table and the other on my thigh before speaking while looking directly into my eyes.

"I think someone sick and twisted was obsessed with you for a long time. I believe he spent as long as he said he did planning your abduction and subsequent attack. He was calculated, and he took a few risks. The biggest one being the death of your family which I don't doubt for one second was his doing in a way to get closer to you by preying on a victim with not much left to live for."

I close my eyes at the pain piercing though my chest. It's one thing to look at the files as I've been these past few months and remove myself to think of it happening to someone else. Not that I would wish that upon anybody else, but it's easier dealing with it as an outsider looking in.

To hear it coming from his mouth is enough to make tears form in my eyes, tears I haven't had for a very long time. I wipe the snot from my face and the angry tears off my cheeks. My breath is stuttering, and he wraps an arm around my shoulders before continuing.

"What someone is not factoring in though Elle, is that he held a full-time job with a software development company where he worked long hours making code and spent his extra time at the gym. He didn't have much of a social life and no apparent living family which makes me wonder how he was able to take so many photos of you during the daytime at your own work, and out for lunch with your friends."

I know there aren't any photos of the old me whatsoever on that table, but I know the written document of evidence gathered from the basement lists in detail the photos collected from his shrine, as well as what each photo contained.

"A man who worked ten to fourteen hours a day and spent six hours a week at the gym doesn't have that much time unless someone at his work was covering for him, or he had help, seeing as it's physically impossible to be in two places at once."

I heave a sob since he's first person other than Laura to state the same conclusion suggesting my attacker probably wasn't alone. Strong arms wrap around my body as he pulls me into his lap. I straddle him and shove my face into his neck and cry like I haven't cried in a really long time. His hands alternate between squeezing and running up and down my back in a soothing gesture.

He believes me.

Chapter Twenty-two

I sit on the couch with a glass of wine and music in the background. The blues. Not because I had a bath, but because today has been one of those days where you sit back and reflect on where your life is at. It's a mellow moment with a lot of brain activity and the music helps calm my nerves.

After the conversation with Ryder at the picnic table where he held my sobbing sorry self for a while, I took a long shower to rid the dry tear tracks from my face, while he went to make lunch.

It's been a quiet day, mostly with Ryder hovering around or out in the yard with Norma. I know he's giving me space, time to think about how this is going to play out, and I appreciate that. It's not always in life that when we have a bad or shitty moment we need someone to talk to.

No, sometimes we need the silence. The stillness and calm of not having to carry on a conversation you didn't wish to have in the first place.

Sometimes you just need yourself, some wine and cigarettes.

I managed to put lasagna together for dinner, not because I felt like cooking but because it kept me busy enough that my mind wouldn't wander too far. Ryder decided to mow the lawn for me while he was outside. Now he's in the shower while the lasagna bakes in the oven and I take time to reflect on my life with a glass of wine on the couch.

So much has changed for me. Not just in the last year but since I've met him. It seems like yesterday he was jogging down the street being drooled at by an old woman, but then sometimes it feels like it was a lifetime ago.

My new life here with people like Brock and Sam, although we are not close, has made a huge impact on my life in a positive way. I've put most of the past on the back burner unless I want it to be up front and center, in which case I head to the dining room and work on the case.

When Ryder is around, everything feels front and center. He makes me remember all that I had, all that I lost and what potentially could be found with an amazing man such as himself.

Things change, as do people. I can't help but wonder what life would contain with him in it and whether that would lead me to the better, or further into destruction if what we were to have comes crumbling to the ground.

That's the thing about loss, isn't it? When we've lost most of what's dear to us, we don't sit around and wax poetic quotes pertaining to what our life will be now that we're still living, about all the glorious things we'll do to embrace life and pretend that even though we've lost, we're going to hold on to life's horns and ride that bitch into the sunset with a smile on our face, thankful we're still breathing.

No.

We regular folk sit around and think about the shit hand life has dealt us, and how we'll do whatever fucking possible not to experience that pain again.

We keep people at a distance and do our best to wake up and shower each morning.

I'm sure a therapist would have a field day with someone like me. I can hear the words coming out of said therapist's mouth now.

Denial.
Depression.

Anger.
PTSD.

The list goes on.

When I think about not giving a shit whether I lived or died, I can completely understand why I'd need mental help. The kicker is I would never intentionally kill myself; I just went through a point in my life where I didn't give two fucks if someone did it for me. Hopefully it would happen in some heroic moment where at least it meant something, like sacrificing myself for someone worthier. But at most points in my life I truly believe that as long as I die, and not some innocent person with something left to live for, at least my death would serve a purpose.

Would living life now with a man like Ryder give me more purpose? Should I care whether I lived or died more because of the man or the people in my life?

Would I be able to feel comfortable living, knowing it wasn't for me, but for someone else?

Is that a life worth living?

Did I live for my family? Did I live for my daughter Lilly? Or was I living the whole time just with the added benefits of some pretty amazing people in my life?

No, I understand now.

They were not my *purpose* for living—they were my *life*.

We complimented each other in ways only a close-knit family can. I lost my family, therefore I lost part of my life, and part of my purpose.

What is my purpose now?

What I had was wonderful. My family was fantastic, and ultimately at the end of the day losing a man like Ryder should not compare to losing the family I had. If I can live through the mess that's been the last few years of my life, I can live through anything, right?

Can I survive the life and times with Ryder Callaghan and come out alive on the other side.

Can I handle more loss?

Yes.

But do I want to?

* * *

I hear the shower shut off and know it's time to make a decision. He's been wonderful today seeming to know exactly what I needed, when I needed it. Not many women can say that about the men they keep company with, and I need to decide just how much of myself I'm willing to put out there.

I just finish topping up my wine glass when Ryder strolls to the fridge in the kitchen. He grabs a beer and slowly makes his way to the couch. His hair is extremely dark, due to the fact that it's still wet, and he's wearing a dark t-shirt and loose worn out jeans.

Barefoot.

When he reaches me he bends down and plants a kiss on my forehead before settling on the couch with about a foot of space between us. He turns toward me and puts his arm across the back of the couch and takes a long swig of his beer. I lean back into the armrest with my feet tucked under me half facing him. I know this is the time to talk; I just don't want to be the one to break the ice.

I study his handsome face for a while as he studies me from top to toe. Being home warrants the usual attire, I didn't change because he's here; loose drawstring pants, tank, and light cardigan with my hair in a messy knot on top of my head.

Ryder's whiskey voice calmly breaks the silence. "Gave you space today beautiful. I know that's a lot of shit for you to go over in your head since from what I understand, you've been alone for a while and haven't talked about it. But I'd appreciate it if you could give me a little more."

He reaches down and gives my thigh a reassuring squeeze before continuing.

"If you can't right now, I'll understand. But it's like ripping off a band aid, babe. Today, tomorrow, eventually it's going to come to us sitting in this place about to go over what we should be going over. I'm saying it's better now to get it over with, not just for me, for you Elle. It's time to get this shit out there and over with, and I need your help to do that."

Those eyes don't leave my face and I know I have his undivided attention. Once again, remaining eye contact, something I have always respected. It says something about a person when they keep their eyes locked on yours. They're confident, they have nothing to hide and they're actually interested in what you have to say.

There are also the cases where it's an intimidation tactic, but this isn't one of those cases. This is him, respecting me, and genuinely interested in not just what may come out of my mouth, but me as a person. Or at least I hope. Time to rectify that.

"Do you need my help, or do you *want* to help, Ryder? Because I need to know that you're here because you want to be, not because this is a job to you. You're curious by nature, top that with what you do for a living I can't help but wonder if you're still here simply because I'm another puzzle for you to solve.

"I'm not asking you to feel the emotions I do, or be as emotionally invested as I am. But clearly this is personal for me and the last person I shared my shit with that had no emotional or personal connection to me royally fucked my case. Hence why I'm not only living in a different town, but a different Country."

He's about to speak but I put my hand up to stop him before he gets the chance.

"I don't take this lightly Ryder, and I will not share what was once my life with someone, if they simply view it as a job. It's not a job. *I* am not a job. This about *my* family, and this is *my* life."

I'm proud I didn't raise my voice throughout my rant, remaining relatively calm. If this conversation happened a few months ago it would not have.

As much as I want to push him away sometimes, I know he's incredibly intelligent and level-headed and that it's best I stay the same to get through this. It also helps that I've been pouring over all the details since I've been in Indy, so this isn't too big of a blow to the head.

Ryder sets his beer on the table and returns to grab my hand that isn't currently keeping a death grip on my wine. His eyes aren't exactly hard, but determined. This is one thing dare I say I love about him. His eyes are so expressive when he's with me, or maybe they just connect with mine in a way that we *see* each other.

His warm hand envelops mine, firm but not too hard. He brings it to his lap and turns further to face me directly before he responds.

"Not one day Elle, not one where I was driving across the country trying to find you, did I ever once consider that this was a job. I didn't set out knowing there's wrong in someone's life and knowing it's my civic duty to right it.

"I set out knowing that the woman I enjoyed spending time with, the one I miss seeing on her porch in the morning, was no longer there for me to see drinking coffee." He reaches out and brushes a lock of hair from my face. His fingers trail down the side of my cheek before continuing, leaving his hands connected to me and his eyes glued to mine.

"I went through more than one tank of fuel in a day driving up and down the streets of this town, knowing that regardless of the lack of sleep I had and the shit places I slept in, that if I got to see you alive and well, it would be worth it. I pushed off jobs, Elle; I got one of my men to take over the daily work shit so I could devote one hundred percent of my time to making sure you were okay."

He leans in so his face is just inches from mine and curls his hand around the back of my neck. I can feel the warmth of his body in close proximity to mine and the energy that connects us. It's euphoric, the emotions and feelings this man brings out in me I've never felt before.

We've all felt love, we've all felt lust. Put those two and every other emotion together and you get this incredibly deep connection that could never be described, only felt from top to toe and deep into your bones.

It's everything.

"I will never, not once Elle, consider you a job. You're the first woman who's ever called me on my shit. You're also the first woman who's ever refused my help with something like cleaning gutters and a water line blowing when most women would run the other fuckin' way.

"I told you once you were different Elle, and I meant that in a good way. You're my kind of different, beautiful, and you didn't have a hope in hell if you thought you could run without ever letting me see you again. I didn't lie when I said I want to see where this goes, and babe, this is me seeing where this will go. The only difference now is I'm that much more invested because of the puzzle that's become your life.

"I won't lie babe, it's shit, and I hate that that happened to you and I wasn't there to help you through it. But I'm here now beautiful, and if you'll have me I'm not going anywhere. Before, or after we figure this shit out. You're not my *job* Elle, your becoming my life."

His black eyes penetrate mine and I'm stunned.

Speechless.

It's the only thing I can think of after the spiel Ryder just fed me. It's not because the man has a way with words. It's because he too tells it like it is. He didn't bullshit. He didn't sugarcoat. He laid it out for me.

Respect.

I reach up and bring my hand to his face. Once again he's not shaved in a few days and his stubble does little to deter me. When my hand connects and runs down his jaw, his eyes soften even further than when he told me I was becoming his life. I run my thumb along his chin and move it to his bottom lip.

I've never been this connected with him. Never this hands on in a way that shows such intimacy. So far I've avoided this type of contact with him because of exactly that, it's too intimate.

After the things he's done, and the things he's said, I don't feel like I owe this to him. I feel like I can finally give him this part of me that I've been holding back because I understand now he won't take it for granted.

His lush lips kiss my thumb before his hand still holding onto my neck begins to pull me closer. It's slow, but steady in pace and he tilts his head to press his lips to mine. There's no tongue, it's simply the steady pressure of his beautiful mouth to mine letting me know he understands what I just said through my touch.

It's amazing what actions can do. And he completely understands that I just gave him the small part of myself I've been holding back. The part that might give you a kiss before you leave to get a carton of milk. The part that might put your dinner in the oven to keep it warm when you're running late at work. And lastly, the part that gives them a little off your load when it's been breaking your back to carry all by yourself.

He'll help me carry it.

And if I give up, he'll take it all.

That's what just passed between us without words.

That's our connection.

Chapter Twenty-three

We held each other for I don't know how long before Ryder places a sweet kiss under my ear and leans back into the couch. He reaches his arm out under my legs and pulls them onto his lap.

He settles himself back against the couch and I lean back into the armrest. His hands gently rub from thigh to calf, not in a sexual way, yet, but in a soothing way that calms me and allows the words to flow from my lips.

I take a sip of my wine and stare toward the front window facing the street.

"When I was in my early twenties, I thought I had it all; a few years out of university, many life experiences under my belt and a new fling to fill the gaps between the long hours I put in at work. I didn't always plan on working for my family, but it wasn't just something I knew, it was something I enjoyed and was good at.

"My Dad's company wasn't huge, but big enough that any architectural development taking place in the surrounding bigger cities was always completed by his company. He believed in restoring the old before demolishing to build something new and I appreciated that. I grew up with a love of architecture and the sentimentality that came with it.

"Who lived there? Who worked there? What happened behind those doors? He started out small, eventually turning his work into recreating and blending the old with the new.

"So in between years of learning how to properly restore floors in an old centurion home, to building a state of the art modern library, it didn't leave me much time for anything else.

Other than making time for my best friend Laura, I was a workaholic. I was okay with that."

I pause to top off my vino and earn a squeeze on the thigh from Ryder to continue when I'm ready.

"Laura was my best friend—is my best friend. She's been with me through it all. She's the only other person I've met in life that's enough like me that we don't clash. She tells it like it is, and calls me on my shit. She's consistently late and incredibly forgetful unless it's important. All those things are redeemed for what she's done for me in life, and vice versa. She's my sister and I'll never consider her anything less.

"One night while we were at a local waterhole drinking tequila, I met Cory. He looked good; he was easy enough to talk to and so I started my next fling. I knew with him and many others before him that it would never be something serious. He knew the score, as did I. I was always up front with the people I connected with. Not to say there were a lot, just a handful, and never at the same time, but there when a woman needed a release without the complications of a relationship. Friends with benefits.

"We didn't set dates; we didn't introduce each other to our families. It was two consenting adults that were single and wanted to have some fun.

"Cory and I kept each other's company for about two months, a few times a week. Low and behold at the end of month two, I'm late and carrying."

Ryder moves his hand from the back of the couch to my shoulder and up to the side of my face. He wouldn't know that Lil' was my daughter because those are some of the pages missing from my case. I left the part in that three family members died in a crash, but left out the detailed pieces mentioning who they were, aside from two adults and a child. His thumb caresses my cheek softly as he speaks.

"Jesus Elle. I think I'm putting it togeth- " The gates have opened and there's no stopping them now. I feel the wet gather in my eyes but I still press on and cut him off with a choked up voice.

"She was beautiful. A lot of people say that about their children but this one—there wasn't a nurse that didn't maul her at birth, she was that damn beautiful. The brightest eyes that soon turned the greenest you've ever seen. She had brown hair like her Dad."

I close my eyes and feel the wet run down my cheeks. There's no stopping it, I know. I don't bother to wipe them because this is only the beginning and I know there will be a whole lot more.

"Her Dad and I knew we were never meant to be together but became close enough friends. I respected him, and he respected me, and we made that work for Lil. She was loved, whether she had two parents under the same roof or not. He moved a street over from mine, both of us still pretty rural in the town we lived, and we could walk her back and forth in between visits. It worked."

I can picture her Dad walking her home, coming up the road with an ice cream in her hand and her stuffed cow in the other.

"I had a doctor's appointment, one that I didn't need to go to but after I had Lil I had some trouble with my uterus so it was my yearly routine check. I didn't need to go, all was fine. But rescheduling would mean waiting another six months to get back in, so I went. We were scheduled to leave for the airport that afternoon with my parents on a trip to Disneyland.

"Lil was four, she loved fish, cows, and wanted desperately to meet Cinderella. I will forever regret not cancelling my Doctors appointment. I got stuck in traffic due to a derailed train and after hours of waiting for it to get cleaned up I told

235

my Mom and Dad to take Lil and go ahead without me. I would meet them at the hotel."

I stop because my nose and throat are thick with emotion and it's hard enough to breathe, let alone continue to speak. Ryder pulls the wine glass out of my hand and quickly wraps his arms around me and squeezes me tight.

I'm not sobbing, more like a constant heave to get my breathing back under control. I've never told the story; everyone at home knew what happened. I didn't need or want to repeat it again.

"Breathe babe," Ryder whispers while rubbing up and down my back.

I take air in through my nose and out through my mouth.

"Wh-whe-hen I -" I'm cut off by Ryder's lips to my neck before he speaks.

"Babe, a bit at a time. If you don't want to continue that's okay," he says in a soft voice filling my ears.

I need to do this.

"When I got to my mom's, I changed and grabbed my suitcase to leave. That's when the cops came to the house."

I press my face into Ryder's chest and clutch at his shirt. "My sweet baby girl on her way to meet Cinderella was killed in a car accident after the brakes f-f-failed and the SUV crashed into a tr-tra-transport truck."

I sob now, heavily. I can't hold it back. Ryder's arms hold me closer, if even that's possible.

This is the only reason I'm still here. It feels like it's the only reason I'm still alive, not because I fear the man left out there might do to another woman what he did to me. I would be devastated by that but it's not my reason.

I'm here because in a sick and demented way I live for the fact that if I could get my hands on the person that ended my little girl's life I will take pride and pleasure in slowly and painfully taking theirs.

This isn't just about revenge, this is about justice.

This is about fate.

The fate he earned when he ended the lives of innocent people that were loved beyond measure.

I've lived since the attack knowing their deaths were intentional, knowing that my life's new mission was to inflict pain and death on the people responsible for it.

I've had nothing left aside from Norma. Laura will go on and would one day understand if I were to lose my own life in the process.

I could live with that.

I've had no second thoughts.

Before Ryder.

I can't let him cloud my judgment, my plan. I've spent a long-time healing to prepare myself for this. I was too weak right out of the hospital, and I changed my appearance, so I couldn't be found or recognized, giving me more time to figure my own shit out before proceeding.

Should I make it out alive, all the better. I would've gone back to my home in North Carolina and slept well at night after taking someone's life. There are no second thoughts, or never were. I'm completely okay and don't lose sleep over the thought of killing someone like that.

Why now is Ryder making me rethink my plan? Not the plan to kill, but the part to make certain I come out alive on the other side of it. Before, it was a moot point.

I live, I die, don't matter.

So long as *he* dies, I'll rest in peace.

Now I want to be here.

"They killed my family Ryder," I release on a breath so low I don't think he could hear it.

His hands claim my face and pulls me out of his chest. His determined eyes zero in on my teary ones, touching his forehead to mine.

"Fuck babe." He presses his lips to mine in a sweet kiss. "We'll find him babe, or I will alone if you're not ready. This will end, Elle. I don't make promises I can't keep, but I promise you one day, as soon as I'm able I'll make sure this shit is dealt with. I promise, beautiful."

Chapter Twenty-four

I managed a bit of lasagna, and after the carb overload, albeit small, I knew I needed a bath.

My go-to for calm.

I lay in the hot water with my soft tunes playing thinking about how it felt to get that off my chest to Ryder. I assumed it could've been worse. Telling the story and reliving the emotions was as painful as ever. But Ryder's reaction to it is what I reflect on.

He's an amazing man to handle me the way he did, allowing me to speak when I needed. He knew when to put a word in and when to be quiet.

A woman would seldom ever describe a man as perfect. I think it's ludicrous to even think it. People fuck up, people make mistakes and people take shit for granted.

It's a part of life and one can't go through it without these things and making many mistakes along the way.

Mistakes are simply that, a mistake. So long as you learn from it. When you make the same mistake twice, it's no longer a mistake—it's a choice. If you take it as such, you're excepting it as a bad habit.

Ryder is not a man who would make the same mistake twice. He's learned and lived enough that he knew exactly when and what I needed. Right down to rubbing my back, giving me gentle kisses and even returning the wine glass to my hand.

I don't drink to forget. I don't drink because I'm a drunk. I won't lie, I have been. I once drank for five days straight along with the odd pain med. Laura finally took the pills away because she knew I hated them. She added some soda to my next wine and told me I needed to tone it down before I died of liver failure or possibly became an alcoholic.

That's her.

She knows me.

Have I used cigarettes and alcohol in time of need?

Absofuckinlutely.

Would I cry if you took my drink away and poured it down the sink?

No.

But sitting in the bath reflecting on my life while gazing at the water, having an extreme come to Jesus with a man I could love, and while having a glass of wine, does not once make me question myself.

Some people like to knit; some people like tea, some people like to fuck their problems away.

I like wine, cigarettes, good music and currently a good rub down by a tasty man named Ryder Callaghan, who knows how to make a woman think about nothing but the act he's performing.

It's time.

I get out of the bath and proceed with my usual rub down of coconut oil. Getting everything on my back is a chore but I always continue with a Cirque du Soleil act, arms bending in ways which they shouldn't to try and tame the mess that is my back, in hopes that one day it'll fade. The ridges have lessened and the color has gone from bright red to a deep purple.

I lather from top to bottom on my front and put on my robe. I exit the bathroom to a quiet and dark house, minus the bedroom.

Ryder is sitting on my bed, shirtless, leaning against the headboard, concentrating on his iPad. He notices me the minute I cross the threshold of the bedroom and sets it on the nightstand.

He climbs out of bed and pulls the covers down. He's wearing nothing but his boxers. It takes everything in me not to jump him right now.

I need to feel him out first.

I make my way around to the end of the bed. He walks slowly to meet me there.

I look up at his beautiful face, hoping I'm not making a mistake. I hope he doesn't think less of me, and in a sick way I hope he still sticks around because at the end of the day, I do need his help.

I reach into the pocket of my robe and pull out the container of oil. I reach for his hand while maintaining eye contact and set it in his palm.

"I can't promise you yet that I'll be here next week, or next month. That's not to say I don't want to be, it's because honestly, I don't know. I've been doing everything on my own Ryder for a long time, and that's what I'm used to. Me, on my own. I can't promise you anything, other than the fact I'll try."

I close his hand around the oil and try to read his eyes. He doesn't give me much chance before he speaks. "I know that Elle, you just have to know I don't want you to have to do it on your own. And I'd like to be here to help you to do that. As much as you'll let me babe. If the best you can do is promise that you'll try, then I'll take that. I'll take whatever you want to give me."

He opens his hand and looks down at the product and back up to me, confused. I need to clarify it for him. And I look into his eyes to do so. This isn't a moment to be had while staring at the floor.

"The only other person in this world that has looked at me, at my back, was the doctor and the nurse that helped him put it back together. I do my best to keep oil on it so it doesn't look so terrifying, but it's not always easy, especially in the beginning with fractured bones and a dislocated shoulder. I don't like asking for help. I don't like to look at it, much less have anybody else do so."

I take a deep breath and move my hands to the belt of my robe. "If you do this, it's not because I asked you for help. It's because you want to. It's because you don't feel pity toward me, but instead the need to take care of the woman you miss watching drink coffee on her back porch in the morning.

"It's because you want what's best for the woman who's cooking for you and who calls you out on your shit. It's because you want to, never because you need to."

I loosen the tie on my kimono and let it go. It slips down my shoulders and onto the floor. I remain eye contact the entire time and, props to him, he doesn't lose it either, despite the fact I'm only wearing what I was born with.

Ryder sets the oil down on the bed and reaches his hands up to my neck. His thumbs caress slowly as he moves them up into my hair.

His lips descend on mine and he kisses me deeply. I open my mouth in invitation. He takes it without hesitation.

No holds barred, nothing held back.

One hand moves down along my torso. He curves it around my ass before pulling me close to him.

It's hard, but not rushed.

Gentle, but firm.

He pulls my face into his chest and moves his hand down the back of my neck. It slowly makes its way past my shoulder blades and begins to touch the awful markings reaching deep into my soul.

"Your beauty reaches deeper than these marks do, remember that beautiful. If you don't, let me know and I'll remind you." I nod my head and he presses a sweet kiss to my temple. I can feel him against my stomach and I'm impressed with how well he can hold himself back.

"Lie on the bed babe, on your back," he whispers into my ear.

I'm confused, seeing as I brought the oil in for him to do just that, my back; an offering that means more than my virginity as far as I'm concerned. He halts that train of thought.

"Trust me babe, we start slow." He gives me a gentle nudge and I sit on the bed. As elegantly as I can, I crab crawl backward toward the pillows.

I settle down and lean back while he still stays planted at the foot of the bed.

Ryder leans down and grabs the oil while his eyes roam my body. I'm more toned than I used to be, with all the training I've done with Brock. To be honest, it's hard work well earned. It's paid off in more ways than one and if the way Ryder is looking at me is any indication, then I'm pleased.

I just hope he remains pleased when I turn over.

He puts a knee on the bed and climbs on, making his way toward me. My legs are stretched out, slightly bent at the knee. After a moment, he straddles me.

"Gonna start at the top babe and make my way to the bottom. Then, you're going to turn over and I'll repeat the process."

I have nothing to say so I simply nod and watch him remove the cap and gather the oil in his hands.

Rubbing firmly, his eyes come back to mine while his hands move toward my shoulders.

His firm hands touch my skin. Regardless of them being in a non-erogenous zone for me, I break out in goose bumps.

He notices. "Glad you respond to me that much, beautiful. It's the same for me with you," he says sincerely, remaining eye contact. I know what he means as I see the bulge in the front of his boxers. His hands move down my arms.

Every finger is given the same attention before he moves downward to my thighs and calves, completely ignoring my bare chest and center. Many mewls and moans are softly let loose from my mouth. When he reaches my feet, I'm gone.

Any woman that has ever been pregnant and lost sight of them will forever appreciate a good foot rub, and he doesn't disappoint. No toe is left untouched and when he lowers his mouth to begin kissing the arch of my foot, with his eyes on mine, I'm lost.

His fingers work deep in between my toes. He moves his hands up my calves, under my knees and eventually they come to a rest on my bottom. He leans down and places a kiss above my belly button, one to my chest and then settles at my lips.

"Time to turn over, beautiful," he softly says.

THE UGLY ROSES

Judgment Day.

I hold his eyes and reach my hands up to cup his beautiful face. The scruff is still there, the dark eyes stare back at me, and his thick dark hair falls around his face.

"If it's too much, or you can't handle the sight of it. You talk to me or you stop, Ry."

I won't be disappointed in him if it's too much to handle up close. I'll be upset, but that's a natural feeling when someone you care about sees a part of you that you keep hidden.

His strong hands hold me tight while those dark eyes implore mine. "You'll never be too much, if anything its not enough. I told you I'll take it all, now turn over babe."

He kisses my forehead and releases his firm hold, letting me know it's up to me. He's still straddling my body and I take a deep breath and release with my eyes on his. I nod before turning over.

I may have imagined the low growl that came from his chest, or it may have been real. However, the only thing I can currently feel are his lips at my neck and the continuation of them slowly making their way across my back.

His hands frame my ribs and his forehead soon rests at the center of my back, his breath is warm against it.

His hands don't move, his grip gets tighter and for I moment I fear that maybe, regardless of what he's seen and been through, it's too much.

"Ry? You don't have to handsome," I whisper softly. I knew it might be too much for him. Maybe this was a bad idea.

His lips press firm, making their way back up along my spine. Not sexually—just reassuringly. "I knew there was no turning back before you made me lunch the day I cleaned your gutters. This doesn't change things," he says as his hand runs down my back. "Just makes me upset and makes me want to inflict some serious pain on the man who did this."

His hands continue their journey around the road map that has become my back. He knows enemy number one is eliminated; he's seen that in the files on the kitchen table, but he doesn't know how. Unless curiousness prompted him to search on his iPad.

I feel the warmth of the oil connect with my back. Ryder wastes no time making me forget the previous comment. Strong hands work my body like none other before. Shoulders, hips, thighs, calves and back to the top again. He reaches my hips on round three and if it wasn't for the mess in my head, I would've fallen asleep by now.

I feel the warmth of his lips above my ass at the bottom of the longest scar. It starts above the right buttock and crosses up to below my left shoulder blade. His lips travel the length of it and when he gets to the top, he starts at the next one and works his way back down.

I don't know how much time has passed, a few minutes, an hour? But when I feel his hands turning my hips to roll me over onto my back, I open my eyes.

Ryder moves so his weight is settled above me and his face inches from mine. His hands cradle my head while his fingers sift into my hair.

"Met a lot of women in my life, babe. Some good, some shit, and some extremely messed up. Not one person in life you meet is perfect, but Elle, I'll tell you right now, regardless of what you may think of yourself, you're the closest to perfect I've ever met."

"Ryd—"

"You're beautiful babe, and not just because of what's on the outside, but because you recognize things in people that others don't. Because you know how to look after yourself without others having to do things for you. You're beautiful babe because regardless of what happened to you, regardless of the marks on your skin, you stick up for yourself and tell people, including me, how it is.

"You're beautiful because you help old people like Mr. Clemens when he fell. And before you freak out, I got a hit on your name through the 911 call you made."

I chuckle a little. He leans down and presses his lips to my jaw, working his way to my ear before he continues.

"I'm not here just because of those beautiful green eyes and your wonderful body babe, I'm here because I know you're *you*. And regardless of what other people may think, or regardless of the way people may want you to act, men included, you still remain the same person.

"That's what's beautiful about you Elle, and I'm going to hang onto it as long as you'll let me."

He pulls his face out of my neck. I can't hide the tears that have formed in my eyes. One sneaks out and rolls down my face but before it has its chance to reach the pillows, his lips catch it and the other two that follow.

It's time.

I reach my hands up and push them into his long dark hair. I pull his face away from mine and settle my eyes on his.

"Show me how well you'll hang onto me Ryder." I whisper before bringing his mouth down to mine.

What started off as a slow kiss quickly turned heated when I press his mouth harder to mine. I want him now, more than ever. This is not just lust; this is wanting to feel something deep within another human being you have an intense connection with.

One of his arms snakes under my back while the other fists in my hair. I move my hands between us, down his firm hard chest and over the ripples of his abdomen before I reach his boxers.

No holding back, I hook my hands underneath and over his firm rear pushing them down as far as I can before letting my feet take over, pushing them the rest of the way.

He cooperates, of course, and kicks them off the end of the bed. I allow my hands to wander over his firm backside as his hands move toward my breasts. When his fingers meet my nipples and my hands pull his groin to mine, we both moan out in unison.

"More," I moan as his hands tease and pull my nipples.

He moves his mouth to latch on as my hand moves round to his front. I grab him and move my thumb over the tip. His hissing breath doesn't go unnoticed. I move my hand further down and back up again as his teeth trap my nipple. He then runs his tongue across it.

"Ahhhhh, Ry!" I exclaim and grind my core up into his.

"Say it again," he growls against my chest, but I'm lost.

"What?" I rasp, not knowing what he means.

"Ry, baby. You rarely ever call me Ry. It's handsome, or Ryder. But Ry and handsome are yours beautiful. Say it again," he says as he latches on to girl number two.

His hands are everywhere and finally one sneaks down between my legs. He cups me while settling his finger in between my folds.

He doesn't move it, just leaves it there and moves his mouth up to mine and growls. "Again Elle."

"Jesus! Yes Ry. Ryder. Handsome, whatever, just touch me, *please*!" I wail before his fingers dive into me and then quicker than I could say please he leaps down the bed to put his mouth on me where I need it most.

"Aahhhhh!!! Don't stop." His mouth attacks me like a man starved, and I pull the hair on his head to push him closer, harder.

"Not a fucking chance beautiful," he growls against my pussy, bringing back memories.

He doesn't stay long as I pull him roughly by the hair to yank him back up my body.

"I gave you it all handsome; I need you inside me, now." I rasp before his mouth settles on mine.

It's a duel of tongues. I can feel him start to slow down the pace we have going, though I'm completely content with it. It's been a year, and dammit I need him now.

Ryder's mouth slowly pulls away from mine and I open my eyes.

"Want you bare babe." He must sense my hesitation when my body locks still because he quickly reassures me.

"Haven't had bare since my twenties babe, and only a few times. I'm clean and if you're prepared, I'd rather not have anything between us."

His tone is gentle, and I know he's not lying. Ryder Callaghan is not a man to go out and knock up random and familiar women, just for the fuck of it. He's also not a man who would put himself at risk of contracting a disease.

He's too calculated for that. I move my hand to the back of his neck. "I can't get pregnant Ryder, but I can catch diseases. Oddly enough I know that's not something you would gamble with. So, if you're okay with me handsome, I'm okay with you."

I thought he'd dive right in but he wants to talk more.

"I'm tested regularly and I'm clean. So, you can't get pregnant, or you're on the pill babe? Not asking 'cause I don't trust you. I'm asking because I'd like to know what we're protected with right now."

He has every right to ask that question and it makes me respect him more, considering the amount of men in my life who've tried to have me without protection.

"Tubes were tied a long time ago Ryder."

It's the truth, and I don't need to explain any more than that.

His mouth lowers to mine and this time it's just passion. Slow, loving passion. His hand continues its work between my legs.

"So wet babe. I need to be inside you." His words wash over me. I don't give him time to contemplate taking longer before I grab hold of the wonderful part of him between his legs and aim it toward my center. He takes the hint and removes his hand from between my legs before taking over, pushing my hand out of the way.

"You ready beautiful?" he asks, looking directly into my eyes.

I do nothing but nod and bring my legs up around his back. He reaches underneath my back and holds onto my shoulder while his other hand moves to grasp my hip. He slowly pushes inside.

We both moan at the same time as he enters me. It's a tight fit. "Jesus babe you're tight," he says through clenched teeth.

"It's been over a year," I softly say with my arms around his back. His eyes shoot to mine before his lips claim my own. He growls into my mouth before taking my tightening thighs as invitation to start pushing a little deeper.

"Jesus Elle, a year? I can feel it babe, I don't want to stop. Hang on beautiful, and if it's too much you let me know."

This is the last thing he says before slowly but steadily pushing the rest of the way in. I wrap my legs tighter around his body in preparation for the fucking of my life.

I don't get it.

He moves his arm down and under my hips, cradling my face with the other before pulling out and pushing back in. "Gonna savor you as best I can right now beautiful. I don't know how much I can hold back because you're so fuckin' tight but I promise I will never come before you do."

He seals his mouth to my nipple. I wonder if there ever was such a man that waited until his woman came before he did.

He'll prove me correct.

No part of my body is left untouched.

His body is like a well-oiled machine, pumping relentlessly slow but steady in thrust, hell bent on making me come. I know it won't take long with the steady pace he has going.

"I'm close Ry," I whisper. I can't do much else, he has me there and soon I know I won't be able to speak at all.

"Give it to me beautiful, give me everything you have," he says before his mouth crashes down against mine. His thumb works its way between us to circle my clit.

All it takes is a few small circles around my nub, combined with a few more deep thrusts to bring it home.

"Don't stop Ryder! I'm coming!" I wail as Ryder continues his relentless rhythm driving into my core like he too hasn't felt the warmth of another human being for a long time.

He doesn't slow down, and he doesn't lose any stamina. He's literally driving his shaft home while keeping his eyes glued to my face, studying me to make sure I'm enjoying this as much as he is.

"Look at me Elle," he growls as my head rolls back on the pillow.

I do my best to connect my eyes with his, but it's incredibly hard to keep them open when I'm shaking from head to toe. My orgasm is still going, and once my greens finally connect with his black's, he finally let's go.

"Jesus, fuck babe!" His voice vibrates through my body before I feel his release inside me. Our chests are heaving. Sweat coats our bodies but doesn't deter either of us to let go yet. He rests his forehead on my own before he speaks. "When you come babe you keep your eyes on mine, every goddamn time. You get me babe? I need that."

I nod my head, speech difficult.

"Get you Ry."

Rigor has set in and my body stays locked onto his, not willing to let go.

It was beautiful.

It left me breathless.

I'm home.

* * *

Strong arms come around me and roll me onto my side. His warmth surrounds me, and we still remain joined as one; body, soul, and a little of my mind.

I'd love so badly to remain in this moment completely and utterly with him but the thing about the mind, especially mine, is it never, or rarely, shuts off.

"Stop thinking babe."

His hand wraps around the side of my face and tips it up to face his. My head rests on his arm and the warmth of his breath rushes across my face as he continues to speak.

"Shut that shit down Elle. You just felt me, now look at me."

His deep dark eyes look into mine. The sincerity in them is enough to steal the breath from my lungs. This man is like no other, the compassion is rolling off of him in waves.

His fingers move into my hair as he settles his lips to mine. It's not open mouthed, it's not forceful.

It's just a promise.

"I'm going to be honest beautiful, you'll always get honesty from me. I can't remember the last time I blew so hard, or had sex feel so good. That's the truth babe, and if that's what this is going to feel like from here on out I never want to feel it with anyone else, ever again."

He takes my mouth more forcefully this time and I don't hold back. I know what we just shared was mind blowing.

I was there, I felt it too.

I won't for one second think it was lack of sex for so long, or the first thing other than a vibrator to touch me in over a year.

The connection we share played a major part in what was the most mind-blowing orgasm of my life. I went all in, as did he.

And it paid off. *Big time.*

His lips move against mine as he speaks. "Sleep, Elle. Don't think, just sleep." he softly says.

I press my lips to his once more before settling my head under his chin. His lips touch my forehead and his arm tightens around my shoulders as he rests the other on my hip.

We're still joined. That's the last thing I think before I fall into a deep and blissful sleep.

Chapter Twenty-five

"Do you know how many times I watched you Jayne? How many times I made sure you made it back to your apartment on campus okay? That nobody tried to harm you? I watched you, and took care of you, and you've done nothing to thank me! You've been nothing but a selfish fucking bitch!"

His hand reaches out and hits the side of my face with an impact like a sledgehammer.

I'd like to say it doesn't hurt anymore. Once the numb took over I could handle anything he gave me.

Perhaps it's the loss of blood, sleep and lack of food. Maybe all three combined. Either way I'm exhausted. I don't know how long I've been holding on, but I don't know how much more I can take.

I guess it's been at least three days now. I could be wrong; maybe it's been one long, drawn out day. But judging by the few times he's slept hunched over in a chair while I lie against the cold concrete wall, I assume it's been a few days.

I won't ask him.

I have too much pride for that.

And at the end of the day, what does it fucking matter. I'm down here, tied up in nothing but my underwear, silently thanking the universe I haven't been raped. It wouldn't make me a lesser person, and I wouldn't think less of myself if that had or does happen to me. I'm just not sure if I'm strong enough to survive something like that.

I remind myself that even through my injuries this body of mine is a machine. Much like a car, or the strongest animal in the jungle, it has the ability to both rejuvenate and heal, or have parts replaced to be fixed.

Whether at the end of my hell here I need bondo to fix my dents, an organ transplant to replace a damaged one, or coma induced sleep to heal my wounds, I can survive.

It's a body, it can be fixed.

My soul is what I need to hang onto.

He told me his name today. Andrew.

Who is Andrew? I still don't know. The reference to campus and the University I went to still ring no bells.

Think Jayne. Think!

I hear the door open, its steel hinges squeak. The only sign that someone is entering since I can barely see out of my swollen eyes. I hear Andrew's footsteps and murmured voices. I have yet to see anyone else in here and I don't ask.

What's the point?

"Open your eyes you dirty bitch. You want to avoid me, maybe now you'll learn to pay attention."

Thump!

I crack open my right eye which is less swollen than the other and stare down at the floor. Not because I want to, but because my neck and back are so fucking stiff I can barely lift my head.

"Noooooooo!!!" A heaving sob leaves my body as I stare at the lifeless body sprawled across the floor.

"That's what you get Jayne!" He points to the slumped man on the concrete, "This is what you get for not paying attention!"

He hauls his foot back and slams it into the back of the body on the floor.

The body doesn't move, no grunt, no whimper.

Nothing.

He's gone.

"W-wh-why? I-I dddooon't unnddeerstand?"

I shake my head, why why why?

What the fuck did I do to deserve this? What did he do to deserve this?

Nothing!

"Love is a sacred thing Jayne. I loved you, and you threw it away. You threw it so fucking far that I had to do this, I had to do everything! Now you'll know. Now you'll learn! You're just as fucking selfish as that bitch you warned me off in school."

He leaves the body and comes to stand directly in front of me. His evil eyes focus on mine, his chest heaves, and his hands roll into fists at his side.

His sweaty face is inches from mine before he gives the final blow. "He cared too much about you. Nobody should care about you. So he deserved to die."

I look down at Cory's lifeless body, the father of my child and the man that literally gave one hundred and ten percent of his love to his child without once expecting anything in return.

He didn't need to be told he was a good Dad, he knew it. So did our little girl.

He knew we weren't compatible, but we both held a deep amount of respect for one another and gave our best as separated parents. We focused on what was important, who was most important.

Lilly.

My sweet little Lilly who's no longer with us has now gained a parent in heaven.

That's where Cory went—heaven. He's a good man.

Was a good man.

Fuck!

I swing my head forward as fast and hard as my body will let me and slam my forehead into his.

Fuck him!

Andrew stumbles back and trips over Cory's lifeless body before falling onto his ass.

I gather every last bit of strength I have left in me.

For Mom.

For Dad.

For Lilly.

For Cory.

I wrap my fingers around the frayed rope and pull my legs up as far as I can. The gashes on my back re-open; I can feel the sting of the wounds and the fresh blood pouring down my back.

I don't care, this is it.

I'm done.

Andrew jumps to his feet, holding his right hip that took most of the impact from the fall. I don't give him a chance to get close. I'm done letting him near me.

If I die, so be it.

I don't fucking care.

This is it.

This is the end.

I use my arms to lift the majority of my weight while swinging my right leg out in front of me when he gets close. He quickly moves his hips back thinking I'm going to kick him between the legs.

Wrong move for you asshole, perfect move for me.

Moving his hips back moved his head forward. I continue with my right leg and swing it up onto his right shoulder while my left foot hits him in the back of the left shoulder, forcing him closer to me.

He's taller, and at this point it works to my advantage. He turns his body away from the hit of my foot which gives me enough room to bring my leg completely around his neck to swing it back toward me.

He's not expecting my maneuver and before I know it the tall man has my weight suspended, which has loosened up the slack on the ropes.

I reach my arms above my head to grab onto the beam while simultaneously pushing my left knee into his back which tightens the hold my right leg has around his neck.

"You fucking biiitccchh!" Andrew manages to choke out of his rotten mouth, while I continue to hopefully crush his windpipe with my legs.

His filthy hands grasp for purchase and his fingernails dig into my thighs. Not long enough to do serious damage but enough to make scratches that will take a few weeks to heal.

I want to let up on the pressure enough to move my leg higher, more toward his jaw. If I could do that then I could push my knee hard and quick into his back and pull hard right with my other, hopefully hard enough to snap his neck.

I can sense what that would feel like, the quick pop, and right now in this moment I would kill to hear that sound.

Pun intended.

Pop!

It would be music to my ears. The following silence.

But I'm afraid to let up, I'm so weak and the new blood rushing down my back isn't slowing. It's a steady and constant reminder that I don't have a lot of time before I pass out again.

His hands pull strong and I know for a fact that if I let up and attempt to kill him by snapping his neck, he will get the upper hand.

I can't let him beat me.

Now it's all about avenging my family and getting some justice for the lifeless and innocent man lying on the floor in front of us.

THE UGLY ROSES

I don't look at Andrew.

I look at Cory.

I squeeze my leg as tight as I can. After what feels like hours, but is at most like a minute or two, I feel his body start to go slack.

The dead weight is slowly overtaking mine to the point that my arms holding onto the beam are now carrying both our bodies. But I don't let go until long after his hands have fell to his sides, and my arms can't bear the brunt of our combined weight any longer. I loosen my legs from their hold on his neck and haul myself upward at the same time.

I watch his body drop to the floor, his head smashes against the hard concrete. I've no idea if I killed him, but I know I need to move fast.

I use what little strength I have left and swing my legs up a few times, unsuccessfully, trying to get them around the beam so I can swing myself over.

After the third try, I'm almost ready to give up. The blood dripping down my legs has made the beam slippery. I give it one last go while clutching the prickly rope and manage to get one leg over.

I pull with everything I have and don't stop for one second as I allow myself to freefall ungracefully over the other side.

I wail in pain when my back comes into contact, half with the floor, and half with Cory's body.

I don't have much time!
I reach out to push myself up and encounter longer, shaggy hair.

Cory's hair is short, so is Andrew's.

I turn my head to the side and study what should be Cory's body. Only it's not my daughter's wonderful father. Those dark now dead eyes stare back at me. His dark longer hair falls over his face and blood runs out from under his chest.

No, No, No!

Ryder!

* * *

"Elle, wake up!"

My eyes shoot open and I take in the beautiful man hovering above me. His hands are pushing my shoulders into the bed and I can feel sweat coating my body.

He's alive.

I don't care what I look like, I don't care what I smell like or how slippery my skin is from the terrible dream I just had.

I reach my hands out and throw myself into his body, burying my face in his neck. I kiss him under his ear and hold on for dear life since it feels like I might never see him again.

Dreams are funny like that, and in this moment, I'm going to hold onto him as tightly as I can while I have him.

He wraps his arms equally tight around my small frame and holds onto the back of my head. His warm voice washes over me.

"Just a dream, beautiful." He rolls us to our sides and holds me close to him. I haven't let go of my death grip on his body and I'm not ready to yet when he loosens his hold on my head and puts his face close to mine. "Tell me Elle; tell me what that was about," he says softly into my hair as his hands begin stroking my back.

I shake my head into his chest. I don't want to talk about it; I don't want to relive it. I just want to feel him, right here, right now and not let go.

"Tell me, I'm not going anywhere beautiful." I take a few deep breaths and speak just above a whisper. "He killed you."

I shudder, and he squeezes me closer, if that's even possible.

"Not going anywhere babe. I've survived the jungle, many tours in Iraq and numerous missions breaking up some of the world's worst cartels in Mexico. If I can survive that shit, I can survive one man hell-bent on making your life miserable. I promise you Elle, I'm not going anywhere you don't. And I'll make damn fucking sure we both make it out alive on the other side."

His declaration has relaxed my arms enough that he's able to pull back and claim my mouth. He doesn't stop there, and neither do I.

This is one of those do or die moments.

Take the opportunity before it leaves you.

Take what's in front of you, before you never have the chance to experience it again.

So here, in the middle of the night, we take it.

Twice.

Chapter Twenty-six

I wake to the smell of coffee and warmth surrounding me. I don't open my eyes yet, since I'm not much of a morning person regardless of whether I get up early or not.

I'm too blessed in the cocoon warming my body and the smell of coffee waiting to want to move. I'd say it's a tossup, being as I usually like my coffee more than anything or anybody in the morning. But the feel of Ryder's arms surrounding me right now is the most humble and warming thing I've felt in longer than I can remember.

Warm lips touch the back of my neck and I feel his scruff along with it before his deep morning voice vibrates through my ears.

"You awake, beautiful?"

His lips begin a pleasure filled journey down the back of my neck and across my shoulder blade.

"Umhmm," Is all I manage to get out.

His arm moves around in front of me and holds my back tight to his front. I feel the evidence of his morning arousal and can't help but press my body into it, regardless of how tender I am from overusing a body part that hasn't had a good pounding in a long time.

"Babe, as much as I would love to ravish you right now, I'm pretty damn certain you need a break. And if your life back in the Carolina's was any indication, you're going to go into shock if you don't hit the coffee pot in the next five minutes," I whine in protest which earns me a chuckle.

"Tell you what, we get up, do coffee and eat. Then we'll take our time in the shower. I have something I want to talk to you about, and I'd rather get it done sooner than later. I'll wait until you're caffeinated before I start though."

My body goes stiff at his declaration. I know he notices because his lips seal back onto my neck and his arms go tighter around my body.

"Not what you think beautiful, but I have something I want to run by you about your case. I think it's a good lead."

I swing my head around to look at his disheveled, but beautiful morning appearance.

"A lead?" I ask.

I haven't had one of those in a long time and frankly, anything or any idea coming out of Ryder Callaghan is not something to take lightly. I know he wouldn't bring this up without being completely serious about what he found.

Does it suck that it's the morning after? Absolutely. He gives me one last squeeze on the hip before placing a quick kiss to my lips.

"I'm going to let Norma out. Meet you in the kitchen babe," is all I get before he leaps out of bed, jeans already on, and heads out the door.

I get through my bathroom routine quickly before throwing on my robe and making my way toward the kitchen. I would love a shower after my nightmare last night, however the smell of Ryder left on me is enough to calm my nerves on the subject and wait until later.

Ryder isn't in the kitchen, but my coffee waits for me on the counter, as do my smokes.

I grab my java and head out the back door. As always Norm greets me, eager for her lovin' in the morning. She follows me over to the picnic table where I find Ryder with a stack of papers spread out before him.

My casework.

I noticed it was nine in the morning when I came out here, so I wonder how long he's been at this since I smelled the coffee when he woke me up.

˅"How long have you been awake Ryder?" I ask as I settle next to him at the picnic table.

Upon closer inspection I notice the papers in front of him are mostly witness accounts and the description of the life and times of one Andrew Roberts.

He looks at me and settles a hand on my thigh. It seems to be a comforting gesture, not only for me, but for him. "A few hours babe. I don't usually sleep late, especially if something's on my mind."

He leans in and places a kiss to my forehead.

"Have you had enough coffee yet for me to dig into this, or do you need more before I start?"

Shit he's kind.

How many women in this world could say the man next to them asked if they are ready to talk and if they've had enough coffee yet?
This is one of those moments I know I need to hold onto, and as much as I want to dive deep into this pile of shit, I want to enjoy this moment a little bit longer.

Old me would say *'I am betraying the memory of my loved ones by taking more time procrastinating and not doing'*. But at this very moment in time, I feel sane. I feel half normal and I have someone next to me that's going to hold onto the load while I get my head straight with caffeine in my veins before bombarding me with the bad.

That's the kind of man Ryder is, and I'm going to hold onto him in this moment until my first cup of coffee is finished.

I set my cup down and reach up to cradle his handsome face with both my hands. I feel his scruff on my palms and watch his long lashes over his dark eyes before I slowly and lightly touch my mouth to his.

"If you can wait until I finish my coffee that would be great. Because I want nothing more right now than to sit here, with you, at my picnic table and pretend for just five minutes that my life isn't as fucked up as it is, and that the wonderful person sitting next to me is willing to give me just a little bit more time to feel normal before analyzing the bomb that is my past."

Ryder brings his arms up around my back and pulls me into his chest. It's a familiar position now and I revel in it. It's warm, it's inviting, and regardless of the fact he hasn't showered yet this morning he still smells like home.

I feel his lips in my hair before he settles me back and grabs his own cup of java.

"I told you babe, all the time you need. I'll still be here." With one last chaste kiss, on the mouth this time, we both settle in and finish our morning brew.

* * *

After many moments of silence and Ryder transferring his attention between his iPad and my case files, I can't take it any longer.

I've drunk my coffee and smoked my cigarettes and now it's time. I know it is. I also know whatever he tells me is going to blow me out of the fucking water.

A man with the intelligence and expertise such as Ryder Callaghan does not just call a pow wow to talk about the weather. He also wouldn't call it to talk about or ask something as simple as the *'why did Andrew do this'* or 'how did you feel about that?'

Ryder doesn't need my answers; he doesn't need to ask questions at this point in time because whatever he's about to throw at me is something he figured out all on his own with the information that was available to him.

I know the questions will come, but much like last night on the couch, when we had our come to Jesus about why I'm so messed up with those I lost, or more importantly, who it was I lost. I know Ryder wouldn't be so careless with a moment of questioning, case in point the way he approached me this morning.

He approached me in bed with a revelation, I felt it. If he had personal questions we would be huddled together right now on the couch, and I would have his undivided attention. He would not be staring at papers and an iPad if it were something so personal and perhaps upsetting.

I take a deep breath and rest my hand on his arm that's currently shuffling through papers.

Now or never.

"Lay it on me and rip the band aid off. *Fast.*"

He lets go of everything in front of him and stands up to straddle the bench before sitting back down again, this time closer to me. He reaches his hands out to my hips and pulls me closer to him. Enough distance to have a conversation, but not enough that we're breathing on each other.

Those intriguing dark eyes of his stare back into mine and his hands flex on my hips. He's almost nervous, or maybe on an adrenaline high from whatever revelation he's come to. Either way I'm intrigued, and I need to know.

I place my hands on his arms and squeeze lightly, letting him know I'm ready.

"The detectives weren't wrong in their assessment, neither was the forensic team."

I jolt backwards ready to bolt from the picnic table.

How fucking dare he!

He quick to placate me, "No Elle- you're not wrong either babe. You. Are. Not. Wrong."

I don't understand where he's going with this. I don't get it. My mind is already going a million miles an hour and I need to know what the hell he's talking about.

"Listen babe. Listen to me." His hands come up and trap the sides of my face, forcefully but not painfully, making sure my eyes are on his and he has my attention.

"There were only two sets of DNA found in the basement. One was yours; the other belonged to Andrew Roberts."

I scoff at him. "Want to tell me something I don't know Ryder, because I'm pretty fucking sure I told you to rip the band aid off. This, right here, is not ripping it off seeing as I've heard this stupid spiel before!"

I'm angry, I can't stop it. He needs to get to the point.

"Monozygotic, that's me, ripping it off. And it's not the first time I've dealt with the term. Are you familiar with it, Elle?"

"No, I'm not familiar with it *Mr. Security specialist and former fuckin' Rambo*! Just spit it out! In English Ryder, dammit!" I slam my hand on the picnic table.

He grabs it before I can lose my shit and do damage, nobody ever said I had patience.

His strong hands take my wrist and he jerks me to him much like he did the last time we sat here, only this time he's not angry with me. He's not as upset. His features are hard, determined.

He hauls me further into him so that our faces are inches apart. His eyes hold promise and I steady mine on to his. Warm hands work their way up to hold onto the sides of my face again as his thumbs gently caress my cheeks.

This is it.

"Monozygotic means 'identical' babe. It means twins, fertilized from the same egg; therefore, they share the same DNA."

What?

No, no fucking way.

I remember the report, I remember his background.

Only child, raised by his grandmother since birth when his mother abandoned him. Lived a normal life, mid class. Scholarship to the University of Toronto, same as me. Lived alone for the past ten years since graduating and worked at the same office for the past eight.

Fuck.

The basement.

His mood swings, the few times I opened my eyes to a bottle of water being given to me.

But he wasn't angry when he handed me the water? He wanted me to die and yet he sustained my life? It couldn't have been Andrew, it had to have been the other brother.

I remember the murmured voices when Cory's body was dumped like a sack of grain onto the floor, but I wouldn't open my eyes because I was too exhausted. Had I of opened my eyes to investigate the men behind the voices, maybe I would have seen there were two of them.

Monozygotic.

Identical twins.

Same DNA.

It all leads to the same conclusion; it's all coming to light.

Andrew Roberts has a brother.

And he wants to kill me.

Author Notes

Thank you so much for reading the first installment in The Ugly Roses Trilogy. If you enjoyed it, please take the time to leave a review on Amazon or Goodreads.

The second book, *Concealed Affliction,* and the final book, *Blinded by Fate*, are available now in both eBook and print on Amazon.

Want to chat about books?
Connect with Harlow:

www.facebook.com/harlow.stone.author

harlow.stone.books@gmail.com

Instagram.com/harlowstone

www.harlowstone.com

Acknowledgments

First and foremost, a big thank you to the growers of Pinot Gris. Without your grapes, I would still be stuck writing chapter two.
(That totally deserved bold letters)

Erin T, my first book reader and awesome friend. Thank you for all the help and for reading so fast!

A special thank you to my momma for being so judgmental.

My editor Greg for joining me on this adventure.

Thank you Barbi for our random chats to keep me sane.

And to my readers,
You are everything! Thank so much for reading my books, and to those that review I can't express how grateful I am.
You guys truly rock!

Keep it classy,

Harlow
xx

Made in the USA
Middletown, DE
17 December 2020